CHRISTMAS MOURNING

MARGARET MARON

THORNDIKE
CHIVERS

This Large Print edition is published by Thorndike Press, Waterville, Maine USA and by AudioGO Ltd, Bath, England.
Copyright © 2010 by Margaret Maron.
A Deborah Knott Mystery.
The moral right of the author has been asserted.
Thorndike Press, a part of Gale, Cengage Learning.

Thorndike Press® Large Print Mystery.
The text of this Large Print edition is unabridged.
Other aspects of the book may vary from the original edition.
Set in 16 pt. Plantin.

LIBRARY OF CONGRESS CATALOGING-IN-PUBLICATION DATA

Maron, Margaret.
   Christmas mourning / by Margaret Maron.
     p. cm. — (Thorndike Press large print mystery)
   "A Deborah Knott mystery."
   ISBN-13: 978-1-4104-3001-4
   ISBN-10: 1-4104-3001-4
   1. Christmas stories. 2. Domestic fiction. 3. Large type books.
   I. Title.
   PS3563.A679C47 2010b
   813'.54—dc22   2010041589

BRITISH LIBRARY CATALOGUING-IN-PUBLICATION DATA AVAILABLE
Published in the U.S. in 2010 by arrangement with Grand Central Publishing, a division of Hachette Book Group.
Published in the U.K. in 2011 by arrangement with the author.
U.K. Hardcover: 978 1 408 49413 4 (Chivers Large Print)
U.K. Softcover: 978 1 408 49414 1 (Camden Large Print)

Printed in the United States of America
1 2 3 4 5 6 7 15 14 13 12 11

To
Nancy and Jim Olson,
for thirty years of
friendship and support

DEBORAH KNOTT'S FAMILY TREE

Annie Ruth Langdon (1)   m.

(stillborn son)

(1) Robert   m.   1) Ina Faye
                  2) Doris > Betsy, Robert, Jr. (Bobby) > grandchildren

(2) Franklin   m.   Mae > children > grandchildren

(3) Andrew   m.   1) Carol > Olivia > Braz, Val
                  2) Lois
                  3) April > A.K., Ruth

(4) Herman*   m.   Nadine > *Reese, *Denise, Edward, Annie Sue

(5) Haywood*   m.   Isabel > Valerie, Steven, Jane Ann > grandchildren

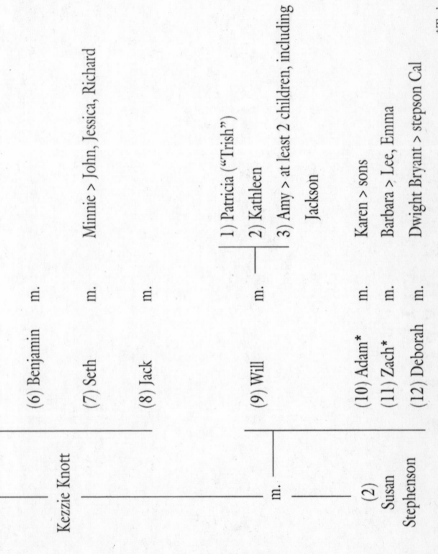

Kezzie Knott m. (2) Susan Stephenson

(6) Benjamin m. Minnie > John, Jessica, Richard

(7) Seth m.

(8) Jack m.

(9) Will m. 1) Patricia ("Trish")
2) Kathleen
3) Amy > at least 2 children, including
Jackson

(10) Adam* m. Karen > sons

(11) Zach* m. Barbara > Lee, Emma

(12) Deborah m. Dwight Bryant > stepson Cal

*Twins

CHAPTER 1

Marley was dead to begin with.
— *A Christmas Carol,* Charles Dickens

"— which means I can usually adjourn around five o'clock. After that, I may have to sign some judgments or search warrants or other documents, but most days I'm done by five or five-thirty." I made a show of looking at my watch. Although I had ninety seconds left of the five minutes I'd been allotted, it was chilly here in the gym and my toes felt frozen. I smiled at the high school freshmen, who sat on tiered benches beneath secular swags of fake evergreens tied with red plastic ribbons, and gestured to the tables over by the far wall. "So I'll adjourn for now and be back there if you have any questions."

There was polite applause as I yielded the microphone to a nurse-practitioner from the new walk-in clinic that had recently opened up in a shopping center that sprawled around one of I-40's exits here in the county.

It was Thursday afternoon, the day before the beginning of their Christmas — oops! *Winter* — break.

(Political correctness has finally, begrudgingly, arrived in Colleton County. Forty percent of our population call themselves Christian, and at least sixty percent of *those* write alarmist letters to the editor every year claiming that Christ is being dissed by the ten percent who check off "other" when polled about religious beliefs.)

Today was Career Day at West Colleton High, and I was the sixth of seven speakers that the principal, who's also my mother-in-law, hoped would inspire these way-too-cool-to-look-interested students. My name card — *District Court Judge Deborah Knott* — was on one of the long tables that lined the end wall, and I sat down beside my husband, whose own name card read *Major Dwight Bryant, Chief Deputy, Colleton County Sheriff's Department.*

He can't say no to his mother either.

My only props were a brass-bound wooden gavel, a thick law book, some gavel-headed personalized pencils left over from my last campaign, a summary of the education needed to become an attorney before running for the bench, and a list of the more common infractions of the law that a district court judge might rule on.

Dwight's array was much more impressive: a pair of handcuffs, a nightstick, a gold badge, a Kevlar vest, and an empty pistol with a locked trigger guard just to be on the safe side. He also had a stack of flyers that outlined requirements for joining the sheriff's department.

"The way the county's growing, we keep needing new recruits," he said when Miss Emily asked us to do this shortly after Thanksgiving.

That sneaky lady had invited us over for Sunday dinner and then softened us up with fried chicken, tender flaky biscuits, and a melt-in-your-mouth coconut cream pie. I don't know what she had to do to get the chief of the West Colleton Volunteer Fire Department to come, but it's a good thing that my handouts take up a minimal amount of space. Between his hazmat suit and fire axe and Dwight's show-and-tell, there was no room for anything else.

I felt a hand on my shoulder and looked up to see one of my eleven older brothers. Zach is next to me in age, the second-born of the "little twins" and five down from the "big twins" produced in Daddy's first marriage. Zach is also an assistant principal here at West Colleton.

"Good job," he said, handing me a welcome cup of steaming hot coffee. "Thanks for coming."

"No problem," I said.

Dwight had already emptied his own coffee cup, but he took a swallow of mine when offered. Sometimes I think he should just open a vein and mainline his caffeine. "I sure hope some of these kids will fill out an application form for us in three or four years," he told Zach.

"I got dibs on the Turner boy," said the fire chief. His big hand almost hid a clear plastic bottle of water and he drained it in two gulps. "His brother Donny's unit left for Iraq last week, but little Jeb there's already turning out with us on weekends."

I remembered Donny Turner from the church burnings summer before last and said a silent prayer for all the kids who have gone to the Middle East these past few years. One glance at Dwight's face and I knew he was thinking of the young deputy who'd signed on for a tour with one of the private security companies there. To lighten the moment, I said, "I guess I'll get nothing but bad jokes if I say that some of them

12

could wind up going to law school."

Zach grinned. "Adam e'd me a good one this morning."

Adam's his twin out in California and I was sure he'd emailed me the same joke. I sighed and rolled my eyes, but there was no stopping Zach.

"A lawyer telephones the governor's mansion just after midnight and says he's got to talk to the governor right away. So the aide wakes up the governor, who says, 'What's so damn urgent it can't wait till morning?'

" 'Judge Smith just died,' says the attorney, 'and I'd like to take his place.'

"The governor yawns and says —"

"Yeah, yeah," I said, stomping on his punch line. " 'If it's okay with the undertaker, it's okay with me.' "

Zach's grin widened; Dwight and the chief tried to keep their laughs down in deference to the last speaker at the front of the gym, but it was a struggle for both of them.

Rednecks, lawyers, and blondes. The only safe butts left. My hair is more light brown than dandelion gold (thank you, Jesus!), so I don't have to wince at all the dumb-blonde lawyer jokes. You'd be surprised how many there are.

"Did I tell you, Dwight?" said the fire chief. "That warm spell last week? We got a call from one of them new houses out your way about hazardous fumes."

Hazardous fumes in our neighborhood? My head came up on that one.

"Yeah," said the chief. "We suited up and went rolling out. Thing is, that's the first time the wind had blown from that particular direction since them new folks moved in."

"Jeeter Langdon's hog farm?" Dwight asked.

The chief chuckled. "You got it."

Back at the podium, the nurse-practitioner finished her spiel and headed for her spot at the next table. The school's guidance counselor took the mike and instructed the students to use the rest of the period to learn more about our varied professions.

The kids streamed off the bleachers. All were on the right side of the dress code, but just barely. The boys' jeans were loose and baggy; the girls' had not an extra millimeter of denim, although today's icy December chill had put them all in hoodies and fleecy sweatshirts or sweaters.

My brother Andrew's daughter Ruth and her cousin Richard, Seth and Minnie's youngest child, were both in the stands and both had given me a thumbs-up when our eyes met earlier in the period, but neither of them would be over to our tables for career suggestions. Last year when the family met to discuss the future of the land we owned, Richard had announced that he for one was going to stay right there and farm, while Ruth planned to open a stable with Richard's sister Jessica. Both girls have been crazy about horses since they were lifted into a saddle as toddlers.

The first to reach us was a white boy with spiked hair and clear plastic retainers where his forbidden eyebrow and nose rings would normally ride. "Were you ever on *Court TV?*"

I shook my head and started to explain the difference between reality shows and reality, but he had already moved on to Dwight.

Picking up the handgun and hefting it with more familiarity than you like to see in a boy that age, he said, "So like how many guys have you shot?"

A tattooed green viper circled his wrist and stretched its triangular head across the back of his hand. Judging by his stubbly chin, he was probably closer to sixteen than the average freshman and had probably been left back a time or two. With a better haircut and no facial piercings, he would have been a good-looking kid — clear green eyes and smooth, acne-free skin most teen-

15

age girls would kill for.

"What's your name, son?" Dwight asked mildly as he reached out to reclaim the weapon.

The boy clearly wanted to wise off, but with Zach looking on, he released his hold on the gun and muttered, "Matt Wentworth."

Dwight lifted an eyebrow at that name. "Any kin to Tig Wentworth?"

"My uncle," he admitted, realizing that we must know Tig Wentworth was currently over in Central Prison, serving a life sentence for the first-degree murder of his stepfather-in-law.

By their fruits ye shall know them.

Here in Colleton County, apples still don't roll very far from the tree, and among Cotton Grove natives the Wentworths were well known as a violent family, root and stock, for several generations back. Hux Wentworth, this boy's oldest brother, had been killed in a home invasion, and now that I was reminded, I was pretty sure that another brother — Jack? Jay? No, Jason. That was his name.

Our little weekly, the *Cotton Grove Clarion,* had used his arrest and conviction as a lead-in to an article on violations of hunting regulations. Jason Wentworth had been

16

brought up before me back around Halloween for jacklighting deer, i.e., illegally hunting them at night with a powerful spotlight that would temporarily blind them and keep them immobile long enough to get off a shot. I had fined him and, as the law requires, made him forfeit both his rifle and his hunting license. The odds were three to one that I'd be seeing this kid in court before he graduated.

If he graduated.

Just before the bell rang to end the period, Miss Emily came bustling through the gym doors and paused to answer her pager. I'm always amazed that this small wiry woman who barely tops five feet is the mother of Dwight and his sister Nancy Faye, who are both built like their tall, big-boned daddy, a farmer who was killed in a tractor accident when they were children. Dwight's brother Rob and their other sister Beth got Miss Emily's slender build along with her red hair and green eyes. Normally, Miss Emily's a force of nature, and there was no hesitation on the part of the school board to make her principal of West Colleton and its two thousand-plus students when this shiny new complex replaced rickety old Zachary Taylor High, where Dwight and I had gone to school.

But as she clipped the pager back in its case, she looked suddenly tired and drained and, for the first time, almost old. Her eyes were bright with unshed tears by the time she reached our table and looked at Dwight with anguish.

"They just called," she told him. "The Johnson girl died."

CHAPTER 2

. . . he was still incredulous and fought
against his senses.
— *A Christmas Carol,* Charles Dickens

The double doors of the gym had been
propped open, and from the hallway the
normal end-of-the-school-day chatter
abruptly changed to murmurs of disbelief.
With new cell phone applications being
invented every other month, relevant news
spreads through the ether at warp speed.
Several kids burst into the gym, teetering
between grief and drama, eyes wide. Some
of the girls were already sobbing as they
reached Zach.

"Is it true, Mr. Knott?" they cried. "Is
Mallory dead?"

Zach's daughter Emma was among them.
"Daddy?" she moaned, sounding like a little
girl again instead of a high school sopho-
more who normally tries to pretend that the

19

school's assistant principal is no kin. She was dressed in her red-and-gold cheerleader's outfit for tonight's away game over in Dobbs. "What's happening to us?"

I looked at Dwight, who had put out a comforting arm to his mother. Mallory Johnson would be the county's eighth teenage traffic death since summer; the third in this school alone.

"I swear to God I wish they'd pass a law that kids couldn't drive till they're thirty-five," I heard him mutter.

All around us, girls were openly crying, and even some of the boys had eyes that were suspiciously moist.

"Do you want me to make the announcement?" Zach asked Miss Emily.

She took a deep, shuddering breath as she pulled herself free of Dwight's arm, and I watched the steel flow back into her spine.

"Thank you, Mr. Knott," she said formally, "but I'll do it."

A few minutes later, her calm voice came over the intercom to report the death of yet another classmate. "Tonight's game is cancelled and grief counselors will be in the gym all afternoon for anyone who wants to speak to them." She closed by saying, "If you drove to school today, *please* drive carefully on your way home. Pay attention to

20

the road, turn off your cell phones, and no drinking. West Colleton can not bear to lose any more of you."

Useless to pretend that none of the kids listening to her words would leave this afternoon and go straight to whatever convenience store would sell them beer or fortified wine, texting or talking on their phones as they went. This latest death would give them all the excuse they needed.

The state of North Carolina prohibits speeding. It prohibits driving with a blood alcohol level above .08, and it prohibits all alcoholic beverages for kids under the age of twenty-one. Unless you are eighteen and have driven without any violations for at least six months, you are also banned from using cell phones while behind the wheel and from having more than one other unrelated person under the age of twenty-one in the car with you, although that last is seldom enforced or adhered to, especially where there are several siblings or, as with my nieces and nephews, several cousins who carpool.

Unfortunately, the state can't prohibit teenagers from thinking they're ten feet tall and bulletproof.

I didn't know any details about Tuesday night's accident, but when Stacy Loring, another West Colleton senior, crashed his car into a tree shortly before Halloween, he would have blown a .12. There were six kids in that car. Stacy and another boy were killed instantly. Two walked away from the wreck with only superficial scratches, one remains in a coma with brain damage, and one — Stacy's girlfriend Joy Medlin — is still on crutches. According to my nieces, her surgeon says she will probably walk with a limp the rest of her life.

Because Joy could no longer do the moves, Emma had been moved up to the varsity cheerleading squad. Mallory Johnson had been the varsity head cheerleader, and now the newly depleted squad, all dressed in their red-and-gold uniforms, were helplessly weeping on each other's shoulders, Joy and Emma among them.

I knew that three of my nieces carpooled, as did their brothers, but the girls would be in no shape to drive after this emotional outpouring. I had ridden over from the courthouse this afternoon with Dwight, and now I told him to go on without me. "I'll drive the girls home."

"Thanks, Deborah," Zach said. "It's going to be a while before I can leave."

The gym emptied out slowly. Some students lingered because they wanted to talk to the two grief counselors who had arrived almost instantly; others stayed because they were simply reluctant to leave their friends until they had wrung every bit of news and comments from each other. Eventually though, my nieces and nephews zipped or buttoned their jackets and trailed me out to the parking lot. This close to the winter solstice, the sun was low in the west and I could feel the temperature dropping as Jessica handed me the keys to her candy apple red car. The boy cousins piled into the pickup that my eighteen-year-old nephew A.K. drives and the girls got in with me.

I knew who Mallory Johnson was, of course. Her mom had graduated from high school a few years ahead of me and her dad even earlier. We were never close; but enough of the old community remains that we all have a loose idea of each other's lives. They had contributed to my last campaign and Malcolm Johnson, now a partner in his father's insurance company, occasionally shows up in my courtroom as a character witness for some of his clients or their wayward children. I knew that Mallory was a senior in high school, the younger of two children, and that her older brother was enrolled at our local community college.

On the drive back to the farm, though, I

gained an even clearer picture of her from the things my nieces said. Even taking it all with a grain of salt and allowing for the shock of her sudden death, I heard that Mallory Johnson had evidently been one of the golden ones — enormously popular, a bubbly personality, bright, pretty, and musically talented. No ego and genuinely nice, despite her dad's attempts to spoil the hell out of her.

Although a junior, Seth's daughter Jessica had taken an occasional class with her. "We sit next to each other in Spanish class," she said, choking back her tears. "We were collecting Spanish-language children's books for the homeless shelter in Dobbs."

"I might have been one of the last ones she texted before the crash," Emma sniffled. "She reminded us to wear our uniforms today for a yearbook picture."

I bit down hard on my tongue for that one. No way was I going to suggest that Mallory might still be alive if she had cut off her phone and concentrated on the road.

"Poor Joy," said Emma, who still felt guilty for how she had moved up to the varsity squad. "First Stacy and now Mallory. They've been best friends since first grade, and even though she can't do the moves, she still comes to all the practices and she's really good at choreographing. Mallory kept pushing her to come up with new routines. She thought it was helping Joy get past Stacy's death."

As a lowly freshman, Ruth had barely known the dead girl, but that didn't stop her from remembering that Mallory had come to her brother's eighteenth birthday party back in the fall and how pretty she was. "I think A.K. thought she was hot."

"Tell me a single guy in this school who *didn't* think that," Jess said tartly.

Even as the girls talked, their thumbs were busy on the keypads of their phones, the ubiquitous clickety-click that forms the soundtrack of a teenager's life like never-silent crickets or cicadas.

"Did you get a message from Kaitlyn?" asked Emma. "Everybody's going to bring red or gold flowers to where Mallory crashed. They're making a cross with her name on it."

"When?"

"Tomorrow morning at seven-thirty."

As I approached a sharp curve, they suddenly went mute. There on the ditchbank, amid a tangle of dead weeds and dried leaves, were three small dilapidated wooden crosses embellished with plastic flowers. The roses had been bright red when placed there almost two years ago. Now they had faded to a pale grayish pink. The once-yellow daisies were discolored and dirty-looking. The white ribbons had almost rotted way, the lettering on the cross was illegible, and the toy football at the base had lost its air and faded almost beyond recognition.

"We need to do new crosses for Rosie and Ben and Doug," Jess said, her voice breaking.

She wiped fresh tears from her eyes, and from the backseat I heard Ruth and Emma softly crying.

And then the clickety-click-click of their keypads.

CHAPTER 3

They said it was a shame to quarrel upon
  Christmas Day.
And so it was! God love it, so it was!
  — *A Christmas Carol,* Charles Dickens

Instead of cutting through one of the farm
lanes directly to my house, I turned onto
our hardtop and swung past Zach's house
to drop Emma off first. A.K. was right
behind me in his truck and he stopped at
the edge of the road to let Lee out before
driving on to Seth's house to take Richard
home. My sister-in-law Barbara had just
pulled into the yard when we got there.
Zach must have called her from school, for
she immediately got out of her car without
putting on her coat and held out her arms
to Emma, who had begun to cry again as
she scrambled out of the backseat and hurried to her mother.

"I could have come for my children," Barbara said tightly when I lowered the window to speak to her. Her tone was as frosty as the air that flowed in over the glass.

"I know," I said. "But I was right there and —"

The front of her black cardigan was embroidered with clusters of red-berried holly. White snowflakes were scattered across the back. I found myself talking to the snowflakes as she abruptly turned and led Emma into the house. Lee gave an awkward wave and trailed them inside.

I put the car into reverse and headed back onto the road. I did not jerk it into drive. I did not dig off. All the same, Ruth asked, "How come you and Aunt Barbara don't get along?"

"I get along with your Aunt Barbara just fine," I told her.

I could almost hear her eyeballs rolling, but nothing more was said until I drove up to her house. A.K. was waiting for her in the carport and he put a protective arm around his younger sister before holding the side door open for her. There was no sign of April, their mother, who teaches sixth grade at the local middle school, and Andrew's own pickup was not under the shelter.

I continued on through the yard, past the

shelters and barns, and down the rutted lane that led to my own house.

"No you don't," Jessica said quietly from the seat beside me.

"No I don't what?" I asked.

"Get along with Aunt Barbara. I mean, you don't snarl at each other or talk ugly, but it's like y'all's hackles rise every time you get around each other."

She was right. Not that I had ever sat down and given it serious thought.

"You two are like oil and water."

"Nothing wrong with oil or water," I said.

"No, but you sure don't mix."

"Objection," I said, trying to keep it light.

"Sustained," she said agreeably. "Actually, Aunt Barbara's the one that doesn't do much mixing, does she? Why?"

When I was silent, she said, "I'm not still a child, you know."

I reached over to pat her leg and said, "I know," even though it seemed like only yesterday that she was a kid more interested in horses and dogs than intrafamily relationships. Now she was seventeen, not a full-grown adult, but certainly cresting the hill. Like her mother, Minnie, she was growing into a steady, sensible woman. She would never be conventionally beautiful, not with Seth's square face and Minnie's sturdy build, but she had the Knott family's clear blue eyes, open smile, and sandy blond hair, and she had her share of interested boys even though her heart still belonged to Dollar, her old white horse.

"Maybe it's because she was raised in town," Jess mused aloud.

"Your Aunt Amy was raised in town," I pointed out.

"Yeah, but she and Uncle Will live in Dobbs. Maybe that's the difference. Maybe Aunt Barbara doesn't really like living on the farm."

"Can you see Uncle Zach anywhere else?" I asked.

She smiled, but then her tone turned thoughtful. "Actually, I could. He might mess around with his bees, but he'd rather read a book than sit on a tractor, and he doesn't raise any animals. Yeah, he likes to hunt and fish like Dad and the others, but he doesn't have to live out here to do that. He could keep bees in town and drive out like Uncle Will does or like Uncle Herman."

"True," I said as I turned into my own yard and coasted to a stop by the back porch, "but Aunt Barbara knew when she married him that she'd never get him to live anywhere else. He loves being part of the family's daily life too much to leave it."

I shifted into park and opened the door. The icy wind slashed at my face and made my eyes water.

Jessica came around the car with my robe in one hand and her phone in the other, then held the door for me while I fished my purse out from beneath the seat.

"You okay to drive home?" I asked, giving her a big hug. A wisp of her hair blew in my face. It smelled like baby shampoo, sweet and innocent.

"Yeah." She sighed. "You'd think we'd be used to it by now. I feel so sorry for Mallory's mom and dad. Mr. Johnson thought she hung the moon. He was so proud that she got into Carolina that he was going to throw this huge graduation party for her, then they were going to go to Spain for a week. Mallory said he already bought their plane tickets and made reservations. This is going to kill him. Christmas is never going to be the same for them, is it?"

"Probably not," I said.

She sighed again as she slid under the wheel of her car. "Well, at least Mrs. Johnson still has Charlie, but poor Mr. Johnson. He's so upset, I heard he was out yesterday morning walking up and down the road where Mallory crashed, trying to understand how it could have happened." She gave me a watery smile and said, "See you Saturday," before closing the door and putting the car in gear.

She was halfway down the lane, her phone clamped to her ear, and I was inside my warm kitchen stuffing my gloves in my coat pocket and still thinking about Zach and Barbara, before Jessica's words fully registered. I had almost forgotten that Sarah Johnson had eloped before she finished high school and that she was pregnant when she graduated. Six months later, her young husband had died in some sort of bad fall — while pruning some tree limbs? Roofing the house? Malcolm Johnson had been his best friend and everyone thought it was wonderful that he was there for Sarah.

Although . . .

I tried to remember the gossip. I'm pretty sure there was some. But that was around the time Mother was first diagnosed with cancer and everyone else's troubles seemed insignificant compared to mine.

I vaguely remembered that he had adopted the boy and given him his name, yet his daughter had been headed to Chapel Hill? While his adopted stepson made do with Colleton Community College?

"Poor Mr. Johnson," but "at least Mrs. Johnson still has Charlie." Now what was that about?

Curiosity is an itch I have to scratch right away. I tried Jess, but her phone was busy, of course, so I ran a mental finger down the list of people who might remember.

Isabel's name jumped right to the top of the list. Haywood's wife is a gregarious, opinionated gossip. Whatever talk was going around back when Sarah and Malcolm married, Isabel would surely have heard it, and what's even better, she's always ready to repeat every detail, both the real and the speculative.

"Oh, hey, Deborah," Isabel said cheerfully when she answered the phone on the first ring. "I was just about to call you. Haywood stopped by Miss Zell's this morning to take her some of Mr. Kezzie's peach brandy, and she sent you a fruitcake."

Momentarily diverted, I said, "Tell me the truth, Isabel. Is Daddy still running moonshine these days?"

"Now, honey, you know I don't know a thing about where his good stuff comes from. All I can say is that he sends your Aunt Zell about a gallon every winter, but he was a little short this year, so he had to poke around and find her another quart to finish off her cakes. And don't you know that brother of yours had to go and cut hisself off a slice of ours before he could get it here? I've had to hide it under the bed in the guest room or there won't be a crumb left for Stevie and Jane Ann when they get home tomorrow."

Mother's sister makes the best fruitcakes in Colleton County — easy on the citron and candied cherries and heavy on the fat meaty pecans. Early in November, she bakes about twenty, then wraps them in cheesecloth, gives them a periodic drenching with some of Daddy's homebrew to keep them moist, and ages them till Christmas.

Daddy swears that the brandy is left over from the time he used to finance a few stills around this part of the state. He also swears that he quit doing that forty years ago. Swears it with a straight face, too. Yet every year, for over forty years, he's sent Aunt Zell a gallon for her fruitcakes.

In half-gallon Mason jars with shiny new lids.

I've stopped telling him how embarrassing and politically damaging it would be for me if he's arrested for moonshining, and Dwight keeps threatening to run him in if he catches him in possession of untaxed liquor. (Happily for me, Dwight turns a blind eye to the pint jar in our own pantry.

I mean, I can't let the fruitcake Aunt Zell always sends me dry out before Christmas, now can I?)

"You hear that Malcolm and Sarah Johnson's daughter died?" Isabel asked. "That's just going to tear their hearts out, ain't it? And right here at Christmas, too. Not that it don't ever *not* hurt to lose a child, but to have to think about it fresh every Christmas? That's double hard. Poor Sarah. Jeff died at Christmas, too, you know."

"Jeff?"

"Jeff Barefoot. Her first husband. You remember him, don't you?"

"Not really," I admitted. "They were both a little older than me. I remember that he died, but I don't remember how. Didn't he fall or something?"

"They were renting that little yellow house there on the left as you go into Cotton Grove. Right behind the Burger Barn? Cute little house but it has a real steep roof. He was stringing up Christmas lights in the dark, trying to put a Santa Claus on the ridgepole when his feet got tangled in the light cords and down he went. Banged his head on a rock and the ladder fell on top of him. Sarah was putting the baby to bed and by the time she missed him and went out to look, he was flat dead. Broke her heart.

Malcolm's, too. Or so we heard."

"Oh?"

"Yeah, him and Jeff? They were best friends all through school even after Sarah chose Jeff over him."

"Oh?"

"Yeah, they both courted her hot and heavy, but Malcolm went off to Carolina and Jeff stayed here and went to work in his daddy's roofing business, so he got the inside track with her. Got her pregnant and that was that till he died."

"I sort of remember people talking about how fast Sarah married Malcolm after that," I said.

"Less than a year," Isabel agreed. "Eight months in fact. His daddy won't too happy about it neither. Taking on another man's baby and him still two years from finishing up at Carolina? But Malcolm said he won't gonna let her get away again, and if Mr. Johnson didn't help them, he'd quit school right then and there. Jeff's mama won't happy about it neither. She was in my Sunday school class back then before the church split last time and — no, wait a minute. It was time before last when that preacher — what *was* that man's name?"

Isabel's church seems to split up every five or six years with great drama and many hard feelings, so it's no wonder she can't keep track. Before she could go wandering down that interesting track, I said, "So Mrs. Barefoot was in your Sunday school class?"

"Yes, and it really hurt her when Sarah let Malcolm adopt Charlie and give him the Johnson name. She said Malcolm had Jeff's wife and Jeff's baby, and he was living the life Jeff was supposed to live." Isabel heaved a great sigh. "And now he's lost both of the kids."

"Huh?"

"Well, that's what it sounds like. I heard that him and Charlie don't get along so good and Charlie changed his name back to Barefoot last spring. Whoops! There goes the dinger on my oven, honey. Now what was it you called about?"

CHAPTER 4

"I don't know much about it either way. I
only know he's dead."
— *A Christmas Carol,* Charles Dickens

After hanging up from talking to Isabel, I
let Bandit out of his crate and opened the
back door so the little dog could go outside,
then I cut through the living area, circled
past our ceiling-high Christmas tree, and
headed into the bedroom, where I changed
out of my dark green wool suit with its sassy
cropped jacket and formfitting slacks into
jeans and a warm red Hurricanes sweatshirt.

The tree made me smile every time I
looked at it.

Like every other farm family around, my
brothers used to go out with Daddy and cut
a bushy cedar from the few still left on the
farm. By the time I came along, nicely
shaped ones had dwindled into virtual

extinction, so that Mother would send the boys to town to buy a fir or spruce grown on tree farms up in the mountains. Between bought trees and artificial ones, cedars have made a nice comeback along our hedgerows and back pastures, but Dwight likes to re-create the pines he cobbled together after his dad died when cedars were few and money was too tight to waste on buying a tree.

A freshly cut young pine is as scrawny and pitiful-looking as Charlie Brown's Christmas tree, but Dwight thickens it up with extra branches until it's as full and bushy as any other.

Last year, the week had been crowded with parties and festive dinners to celebrate our wedding. Dwight's ex-wife had allowed him to have Cal over the holidays for the first time since the divorce, and we had gladly dispensed with a honeymoon so that Dwight wouldn't have to miss a moment of the visit. Watching his face while he watched Cal tear into his presents was worth any number of moonlight cruises.

Then Jonna died and Cal came to live with us. Some memories of her death are blessedly beginning to fade for him, but not the memory of last year's celebration down here on the farm. He started bugging

Dwight to go cut a tree right after Thanksgiving, the minute that twinkling lights first began appearing on rooftops and doorways and the warm glow of decorated trees radiated from windows through the winter darkness.

Dwight's sister-in-law Kate keeps Cal after school during the week, and once their tree was up, the pressure was really on for ours. Rob's an attorney with a large law firm in Cameron Village and he does not share his brother's nostalgia for those pinch-penny times. The first Christmas after he and Kate were married, he bought an expensive fully wired artificial fir tree and they fastened all the ornaments on so securely that it takes less than a half hour to bring the tree in from one of the outbuildings, carefully remove its protective dustcloth, and plug it in.

Instant Christmas on the fifteenth of December.

No muss. No fuss.

"No real pine smell either," Dwight mutters.

I switched on the tree lights, added water to the stand, and breathed in the woodsy fragrance. Kate burns pine-scented candles, but Dwight's right. It's not the same.

It's like the difference between our fireplace and their remote-controlled gas logs, I thought, as I opened the damper, folded back the glass doors, and struck a match to paper and kindling. The bright flames danced up and caught the dry oak logs cut from last year's windfalls around the farm.

I heard Bandit scratch at the door, but by the time I opened it, Dwight's truck rolled up and the dog had changed his mind about coming in right then. Instead, he danced around the passenger side till Cal got out and petted him.

"Guess what?" Cal called to me, pulling a sheet of paper from a side pocket of his bookbag. "I only missed one on my spelling test!"

"Don't tell me you messed up on 'disease'?"

He laughed and shook his head. "No. 'Despite.'"

He showed me his paper and I had to laugh, too. He usually does his homework over at Kate's, but last night I had worked with him on his word list because he kept wanting to spell "disease" d-*e*-s. We had tried so hard to implant d-*i*-s that it had carried over to "despite," which he had spelled d-*i*-s, too.

I took his bookbag and he went to help

41

his dad load the cart with an evening's supply of logs.

Not that we were going to be here throwing logs on the fire all evening. Tonight was the last home game for the Carolina Hurricanes till after Christmas and we had tickets, which meant junk food at the RBC Center in Raleigh instead of a nutritionally sound supper.

Ice hockey is a relatively recent import in the South. I grew up on basketball and baseball, with an occasional high school football game thrown in whenever some of my brothers were playing. I had heard about hockey, but the televised games never grabbed me. I couldn't relate to ice skating, and the puck zipped around the ice too quickly for me to follow, but winters were colder up in the foothills of the Virginia mountains and Cal loved the game. When he came to live with us last winter, I remembered that a former client worked for the Canes. Karen was able to come up with a pair of decent seats for the second half of the season and I thought that the drive back and forth to Raleigh would let Dwight help Cal get a handle on all the changes in his life.

Then came the night that Dwight was called out on a murder case just as they were about to walk out the door. Cal tried so hard not to show his disappointment that I said I'd take him if he would get me up to speed on the rules by the time we got to the game.

It was an amazing evening — the blaring horns and the eye-blinding lights that chased themselves around the rims of the upper levels whenever the Canes scored, the enthusiasm of the crowd, the sheer grace of the skaters, and the clash of hockey sticks almost put me in sensory overload. I discovered that I could actually follow the puck, and by the time the Canes played the whole game, went into overtime, then won in a shootout, I had yelled myself hoarse and was thoroughly hooked.

This year, we had squeezed tickets for twelve games out of our budget, and tonight the Carolina Hurricanes were going up against the Florida Panthers. As soon as our most pressing chores were done, Cal put on his own red sweatshirt with the autographs on the shoulder, and the three of us headed back out to the truck. Dwight does not wear any shirts or sweaters with messages — "I got enough of that in the Army," he says — and he only allows one tiny Hurricanes bumper sticker on his truck. As a concession to us, though, he did let Cal clamp our red flags to the windows and we flapped our way over to Raleigh.

At the RBC Center, we munched on burgers and fries and watched the Storm Squad — skimpily dressed cheerleaders in fur-trimmed red Santa hats — pump up the crowd.

I couldn't help flashing on Mallory Johnson, who would never again cheer a team to victory. Dead at eighteen. At least Joy Medlin had limped away from the crash that killed her boyfriend. Even if she couldn't do the moves, she could still be part of the squad, contribute choreography and moral support.

While the Storm Squad urged the crowd to roars of welcome as the players skated onto the ice, I said a prayer to whoever might be listening to please, please keep my nieces and nephews safe in their cars; then I too was swept up in the excitement.

The game was another nail-biter. Our team scored in the first period and fended off the Panthers till the third period, when they got off a strong shot that goalie Cam Ward stopped. Unfortunately, he then slid back into the net with the puck, and the score was tied 1–1 at the end of regulation play. After an agonizing four minutes into overtime, Joe Corvo slapped a high backhander over their goalie and into the net.

Hurricanes 2, Panthers 1!

All evening, Dwight and I had avoided talking about Mallory Johnson's death in front of Cal, but when Cal fell asleep against my shoulder on the way home, I kept my voice low and asked, "Were you and Malcolm Johnson in the same class?"

"No, he was a year behind me. Jeff, too."

"I'd almost forgotten about Jeff Barefoot," I admitted. "What was he like?"

Dwight shrugged. "Nice guy. Good free-throw shooter."

"Y'all played ball together?"

"Yeah. Or rather Malcolm and I did. Jeff was second-string." He flashed the oncoming driver a reminder to dim the lights as he looked for words to describe the two friends. "The thing was, Malcolm worked harder, but Jeff probably had more natural talent. Easygoing. Better-looking, too. Guess that's how he wound up getting Sarah."

"Isabel said it was because he got her pregnant."

"Yeah, I did hear that."

"Were you surprised when she married Malcolm so quickly after Jeff died?"

"What do you mean?"

"Isabel told me that Jeff died the Christmas after they were married and that Sarah remarried only eight months later. You don't remember?"

"I was in the Army then," he reminded me. "Down in Panama. Waiting for you to grow up. And it wasn't like I was real close to them. Mama or somebody probably mentioned it the next time I was home on leave, but by then it was old news and I guess I wasn't paying much attention. Besides, the way she played those two boys against each other all through school? Once Malcolm went off to college, Jeff probably had the inside track with her. She was a cheerleader, too, you know."

"Yeah, I was a freshman then and there was a lot of talk before she finally admitted she was pregnant and had to quit the squad."

He turned off the paved road onto our long dirt and gravel driveway and eased the truck wheels over the low dikes so as not to wake Cal. "I do remember thinking it was ironic that a roofer would break his neck falling off his own roof."

"Not his neck," I said, as we parked by the back door and I gently unbuckled Cal's seat belt. "His head. He hit his head on a rock when he fell."

46

"Whatever," Dwight said and carried our sleeping boy into the house.

CHAPTER 5

It fell to Puritan Reformers to put a stop
to the unholy merriment.
— *Christmas in America,*
Penne L. Restad

Friday dawned cold and dreary with a raw,
bone-chilling dampness in the air. The sky
was gray and heavy with wet clouds. Instead
of depressing our spirits, though, the
weather seemed to heighten the holiday
mood.

"Maybe it'll snow," Cal said hopefully
when he and Dwight left to meet the school
bus.

Up in Shaysville, at the edge of the Virginia
mountains, there had been snow on the
ground for most of his Christmases. I myself
could remember only two or three late
December snowfalls here in eastern North
Carolina, so he wasn't likely to get his wish,
but at least it was cold enough to keep the

seasonal pictures of icicles and reindeer and fur-wrapped elves from looking too totally illogical.

Not that Cal was the true believer he'd been last year. More wink-wink/nudge-nudgers in third grade than second, not to mention what he must hear on the bus. Ever since Thanksgiving, he had made so many elliptical remarks about the Santa myth that I was not surprised when he looked up from his breakfast cereal this morning and came out with it bluntly.

"Mary Pat says you guys are Santa Claus."

"Me?" Dwight managed to look astonished. "You see any reindeer out back? You think my truck can fly?"

"C'mon, Dad. You know what I mean." He looked at me. "It's you and Dad, isn't it?"

I immediately hopped up to get the coffee pot, unsure whether he wanted confirmation or denial. "What do you think?" I asked him.

"I think she's probably right. That it's everybody's parents. There's no way one guy — even if he *is* magic — could get to that many houses in one night." He finished his cereal and took a final swallow of milk. "Besides, a lot of houses don't even have chimneys."

"He's got a point," Dwight told me, holding out his mug for a refill.

"True," I agreed. "If it was me, though, I'd still hang up my stocking."

"Yeah, that's what Mary Pat said."

"Just in case?" Dwight teased.

"And 'cause Jake'll notice if we don't and it might spoil his Christmas 'cause he's too little to understand. Besides, Mary Pat said we'd probably —"

He broke off, his brown eyes dancing with mischief.

"Probably what?" I asked.

He laughed. "Probably get more presents if we have stockings."

Driving over to the Dobbs courthouse an hour or so later with the radio belting out an uptempo country version of "Up on the Housetop," I was still smiling. Mary Pat certainly had Kate and Rob pegged. No way could they let it appear that Santa had brought her less than he brought Jake and R.W. But she was sweet to enlist Cal in a conspiracy to keep the younger boys from catching on too soon.

Up on the housetop, click-click-click!
Down through the chimney with a good
    Saint Nick!

50

I've heard that there are people who were so traumatized by learning the truth about Santa Claus that they would never allow their own kids to believe in him. My friends and I figured it out about Cal's age and none of us were bothered by it any more than Cal seemed to be. Like Mary Pat, we had also agreed that it might be to our material advantage to keep up the fiction since the grown-ups seemed to enjoy it so much.

As I topped the last small hill before the highway leveled off for the straight run into Dobbs, my smile was erased by another of those sad roadside memorials. A fresh new wreath of shiny green plastic holly, decorated with miniature toys and tied with a bright red bow, had replaced the orange pumpkins and yellow chrysanthemums of Thanksgiving. Come February, there would be valentines and red roses, then white lilies and purple ribbons for Easter.

Five or six years ago, a young woman and her two children had died here in a head-on collision with a drunk driver. She had been an only child, her children the family's only grandchildren. No wonder the grieving grandmother kept their memory green by placing new wreaths here every holiday of the year. I drove on past, wondering if Sarah

Johnson would soon be doing the same for Mallory.

At the courthouse, I parked in my reserved space and hoisted a tote bag full of canned goods from the backseat. Ellis Glover, our clerk of court, had placed two large, brightly decorated barrels next to the tree in the atrium lobby, one for donations to the county food bank and the other for needy children. Adding my cans to the overflow gave me a brief glow of feel-good sanctity, a feeling that was immediately replaced by guilt that it wasn't more considering how much I am lucky enough to have — the old push/pull of conscience.

(And yeah, everyone agrees that a Christmas tree in a courthouse atrium is totally non-PC, but all the ornaments are secular and Ellis calls them Yule bushes. He says he's going to keep putting them up until people start objecting. So far, no one has.)

As I headed toward the marble steps, I saw my childhood friend Portland Brewer on her way down. "You're still coming for lunch, right?" she called.

"Right, but it might be closer to one than noon," I warned her.

"Sounds like you're hoping to be done for the day by then," she said as she drew nearer.

"If the prosecution's prepared," I said. "Only five cases on the calendar."

She rolled her eyes in sympathy, knowing exactly what I was talking about. I never thought I would miss Doug Woodall, our DA who ran for governor (and lost), but in retrospect the current DA makes him seem like a combination of Clarence Darrow and that efficiency expert in *Cheaper by the Dozen.* The only reason Chester Nance, a tubby little mediocre attorney from Black Creek, got the Democratic nomination was because no one expected the Democratic coattails to reach all the way down to the district level, especially when the Republican candidate was a well-respected and competent attorney.

As DA, Doug prosecuted most of the major crime cases in superior court himself, and he had made sure that no backlog of cases built up in district court. "Trust 'em or bust 'em" was his philosophy, and his staff worked a full eight-hour day to keep up with the work. Cases were efficiently calendared and defendants who didn't come to court when they were scheduled had to show him a compelling reason for missing their court date or there would be warrants for their arrest. As a result, add-ons were kept to a minimum.

Chester Nance is way more laissez-faire. His staff is poorly prepared, he gets a half day's work out of them at best, and he himself hasn't prosecuted a single case since he was sworn in.

Judges and lawyers both were grumbling over the backlog. "Who knew there was such a steep learning curve?"

Today was no different. In the old Doug Woodall days, I could count on finishing five calendared cases in ninety minutes tops, fifty if they all pled guilty. As soon as I took my place on the bench, though, I was handed up a list of twelve add-ons by the day's ADA, a newly minted attorney who looked too young to shave, much less pass the bar exam.

Even then we were not ready to go. He spent another twenty minutes thumbing through the shucks, getting facts straight with the officers who were to testify, and even working out a couple of plea bargains — things that should have been taken care of earlier.

I tried not to drum my fingers or look impatient. The defendants and their companions, mostly black or Latino, seemed equally bored. They unzipped their heavy jackets or pushed back the hoods on their dark sweatshirts and waited stoically to be called. Off to one side was a middle-aged white woman with early flecks of silver at the temples of her lacquered black hair. She wore a cream-colored turtleneck jersey beneath a red boiled wool jacket appliquéd at the hem and cuffs with Christmas ornaments and crisp silver braid. Sharp-pointed silver snowflakes dangled from her earlobes and I caught an icy flash of diamonds when she picked a stray piece of lint from the jacket, examined it between her fingertips, then flicked it to the floor.

Ellen Englert Hamilton. She gave me a frosty half-smile when our eyes met, a smile I returned with exaggerated (and equally hypocritical) warmth. Englerts and Hamiltons have been intermarrying for so many generations that it's a wonder they aren't all congenital idiots. As a rule, both families are fanatically opposed to alcohol in any form except as an antiseptic; but every rule has an exception and every Englert/ Hamilton generation throws up at least one drunkard, which is enough to fan the flames of righteousness in the rest of the clan.

I had once dated Ellen's younger brother Rudolph until their mother decreed that a bootlegger's daughter was no fit consort for an Englert. Once I got over my indignation, I had to admit that Mrs. Englert had cause.

Her late husband had evidently been one of my daddy's good customers; and when a sheriff's deputy found a jar of white lightning in the basement after Mr. Englert died, it was Mrs. Englert who was charged with possession of untaxed liquor. Ironically, Rudolph has turned into this generation's lush and I've heard that it's all my fault for dumping him.

Go figure.

There was no way Ellen would be in this DWI court as a defendant, and I couldn't see her there as a character witness for any of the others, so what — ?

And then it dawned on me.

Of course.

Ellen is president of Colleton County's MADD chapter. Mothers Against Drunk Driving. I had heard that they were going to start monitoring judges so that they could point well-publicized fingers if any DWI charges were dismissed.

Yes, there are judges who drink and drive and who base their judgments on the old there-but-for-the-grace-of-God-go-I principle, but I'm not one of them. Nevertheless, the state has to prove its case before I'll take someone's license or give them active jail time and no MADD watchdog could make me rule differently.

The ADA finally rose to say that he was ready to begin with the State versus Salvador Garcia, an illegal alien who had started the day with five DWIs pending against him. The ADA explained that he had dismissed two of them as part of a plea bargain, which was not what I would have done, but I could understand his reasoning.

Immigration had put a hold on Garcia and he was going to be deported to Honduras anyway, so the ADA wanted to clear up all his outstanding cases here in Colleton County. Garcia seemed to speak and understand English fairly well, but because he had pled guilty to the three remaining charges and because I would be imposing jail time, I appointed an interpreter so that he couldn't later appeal on the grounds that he hadn't understood.

I could have ordered probation of the first charge, but I knew he'd be getting active time on the other two because of several aggravating factors — he had blown a .22 on one and a .21 on the other, and he had a prior conviction. Therefore I ordered five-to-sixty days for the first charge, six months on the second, and twelve months on the third. I also ordered alcohol treatment while he was incarcerated here.

When he and his court-appointed attorney

stood to hear me pass sentence, I added, "Mr. Garcia, I'm going to remain silent on these convictions, which means that they will run concurrent with each other. Had you not been subject to deportation, I would have let them run consecutively, but I'm sure ICE is very likely to send you back to your home within a couple of months."

I leaned forward until his brown eyes met mine and I was sure I had his attention. "As we all know, drinking is not a crime."

Ellen Hamilton gave an audible sniff and a flounce of her head at that comment, a reminder that if it were up to Hamiltons and Englerts, Prohibition would still be on the books.

"Drinking is not a crime," I repeated, "and being an alcoholic is not a crime. But driving drunk *is* a crime. You have a serious alcohol problem, Mr. Garcia, and whether you're here in the United States or Honduras or any other country on this planet, you need to address that before you kill yourself or someone else, which is why I've ordered alcohol treatment while you're still here."

When the interpreter finished his flow of Spanish, Garcia gave a disheartened *"Gracias"* before the bailiff led him away. I couldn't tell if he was down because he would soon be deported or because he knew he was in for a long dry month at least.

Next up was a very remorseful black man who had been stopped after a few drinks at a sports bar. He had a spotless driving record and no prior convictions. He also had a wife sitting two rows back who had made it clear that she would leave him if it ever happened again.

Because he barely registered a .09 on the Breathalyzer and there were no grossly aggravating factors, I sentenced him to a Level Five: sixty days in the custody of our county jail. I then suspended the sentence and placed him on supervised probation for six months on condition that he pay a hundred-dollar fine and court costs, obtain a substance abuse assessment, do community service, and surrender his license until he qualified for limited driving privileges.

I had a feeling he would not be back in court again, a feeling I did not have with the next eight defendants — three Hispanic males, one white female, and four black males — even though they were all Level Fives, too.

They were followed by several Level Ones, the highest level for misdemeanor DWI, and all received active time along with my hope that they would take advantage of the alcohol treatments and change their ways.

One of them — Jackson Dwayne McHenry, white, twenty-six — gave me the finger as he was being led away. I could have found him in contempt and given him more time, but I let it pass.

When all the plea bargains were out of the way, there were two trials wherein the defendants pled not guilty. I found the first one guilty but the second dodged the bullet.

He had refused to take the Breathalyzer test, "Which was his constitutional right," his attorney, Zack Young, reminded me. "The state has to prove that he was *appreciably* impaired beyond a reasonable doubt."

The officer who stopped him testified that the defendant had passed the field sobriety tests. "Not perfectly, Your Honor, but all right."

It was the same with his driving. Under Zack's pointed questioning, the officer had to admit that he wasn't all over the road, only weaving a bit inside the lines of his lane.

When both sides rested, I said, "Sir, I suspect you had more than the two beers you told us about, but that's not the evidence before me, and the law requires me to rule on the evidence, not on what I suspect. You were probably impaired and you shouldn't have been driving, but under the law, you were not *appreciably* impaired, so I find you not guilty. You are free to go."

The man immediately turned to Zack and vigorously shook his hand.

Zack's probably the best defense attorney in the district even though he likes to play the shambling good ol' boy who probably thinks a tort is a kind of turtle. His fee was going to prove an expensive lesson in the cost of drunk driving for this defendant.

Throughout the session, Ellen Hamilton had taken extensive notes in a black leather-bound notebook, and there was a look of disapproval on her face when I pronounced the last man not guilty.

She caught up with me out in the hall. "How do you know it wasn't someone weaving all over the road that caused poor little Mallory Johnson to wreck her car?" she demanded.

"I don't," I said. "Do you?"

"No, but why else would she have crashed on a straight stretch of road? *She* wasn't speeding and she sure wasn't drinking."

"I guess we'll never know, will we?"

"Don't be too sure. And if it turns out to be somebody you bleeding hearts let slide by —"

"Gosh, Ellen," I said, glancing pointedly at my watch. "I'd love to stay and talk to you about it, but I'm already late for an appointment."

No way was I going to tell her my appointment was with a baby girl who would turn one year old next Tuesday. Carolyn Deborah Brewer was bright-eyed and intelligent, but she hadn't quite grasped the concept of clocks yet.

CHAPTER 6

"That they are what they are, do not
blame me!"
— *A Christmas Carol,* Charles Dickens

Lunch was a steaming cup of tomato soup with slices of spinach quiche for Portland and me. The baby had strained carrots and spinach for her entrée and pureed peaches for dessert. Throughout the meal, we played peekaboo with my napkin and her bib till Portland threatened to send us from the table before we knocked something over.

She and Avery are both attorneys and their home is only a few short blocks from the courthouse, so I get to see little Carolyn often enough that she's not shy with me. She was born about eighteen hours after her mother walked down the aisle in a red velvet matron of honor dress last December — my brothers had a pool going as to whether or not the baby would arrive in the middle of our wedding. Like most babies, she was more interested in the paper and bow on the brightly wrapped birthday gift I had brought than in the adorable plaid taffeta dress inside the box.

I cleared away our lunch dishes while Portland put Carolyn down for a nap, then we carried our tea glasses out to the sunroom, where we could kick back and put our feet up on the large wrought iron table that was surrounded by mismatched white wicker chairs with their comfy red-and-white cushions. Trays of crisp red geraniums lined the wide low ledges beneath the windows that formed two walls of the room. Funky pots of greenery were clustered in the corners — ferns, dieffenbachia, schefflera, and a snake plant that had belonged to her mother and was now about six feet tall. Strings of small clear lights twinkled amid the plants and cinnamon scented candles gave a Christmassy smell to the air.

Table, wicker chairs, and funky pots had all been picked up at flea markets or garage sales and had been refurbished to make this comfortable room uniquely Portland's. I knew for a fact that one of those pots had come from the landfill outside town. To Avery's deep embarrassment, his wife would rather go Dumpster diving than shop in a regular store. After all these years, he still doesn't get it that Portland's junking expeditions are the equivalent of his fly-fishing — the thrill of the chase, never knowing if you're going to snag an old boot or a nice rainbow trout.

"Where has the time gone?" Portland moaned as she sank into one of the chairs and leaned her head back against the colorful cushion. Her thick dark curly hair could use a trim and her bright red nails were due a manicure, two bits of grooming that were never neglected in the pre-baby days.

"I can't believe she's going to be a year old next Tuesday. Did you see the way she pulls up now? She'll be walking by her birthday. At the rate time's flying, I'm gonna turn around next week and she'll be off to kindergarten."

I toasted my namesake's pulling-up with my glass of iced tea. "And begging for her driver's license about six weeks after that."

"Well, she can beg till she's blue in the face. Avery says she's not getting the keys to any car till she's twenty-five." Her face darkened. "Wasn't it awful about Sarah and Malcolm Johnson's daughter? Have you heard anything about funeral arrangements?"

"Not yet. I haven't even heard how it actually happened. You?"

"Not really. At the office, someone said that she'd been to a Christmas party and left early because she was getting a cold."

"Emma's on the cheerleading team and said Mallory texted them a reminder about a photography session for the yearbook on Thursday. Probably one of the last things she did before she crashed."

"Cell phones!" Portland exclaimed. "There ought to be a governor or something that would keep them from working while the car's moving."

"You invent one the kids can't disconnect or override and I'll invest in it," I told her, and added wryly, "You could put it on the same circuit as the seat belt alarm."

She smiled, knowing how much I dislike the way mine starts its annoying *ding-ding-ding* the instant the car moves. I always put it on before I get up to speed, but there are times when I can't click it right away and the damn thing gets increasingly louder, like an angry teacher shaking her finger at me for ditching school or talking back. I tried to get my mechanic to disable it, but he just laughed at me and shook his head. "Sorry, Deborah. It's connected to stuff you need to keep the motor running."

"So how are you going to celebrate?" I

asked. "You're not giving her a birthday party, are you?"

Portland shook her head. "Aunt Zell invited Mom and Dad for Sunday dinner and Avery and I are bringing the cake and ice cream. Avery's parents are driving up from Wilmington on Tuesday morning to spend Christmas with us and they'll babysit that night so we can go to the dinner dance out at the country club. What about you and Dwight?"

"What about us?"

"C'mon, Deborah!" she said impatiently. "Monday's your first anniversary. Don't tell me you're skipping that, too?"

The "too" referred to the fact that Dwight and I still hadn't had a proper honeymoon. We didn't plan *not* to have one, but between Jonna's death, his job, my work, and Cal's school, there just hadn't been a convenient time to get away.

"If you aren't going to celebrate on Monday, why don't you come out to the club with us on Tuesday?"

Dwight's so good on a dance floor that I was immediately tempted. "But won't they be sold out by now?"

"Probably, but I'll call the manager and ask him to pull up two more chairs to our table. He owes me one. Do it, girlfriend.

It'll be like old times. Fun."

I reached for my purse. "Okay. We said we weren't giving each other anniversary presents, but we haven't been dancing in ages. Take a check?"

"I know where you live, don't I?"

She told me how much the tickets would be, I wrote the check, and talk turned to Christmas plans, crowded calendars, the cards we'd sent, and the old friends we'd heard from. It was the usual lazy give-and-take of a friendship that went back to childhood.

My Aunt Zell is married to her Uncle Ash, and we both smiled when she asked if I'd received a fruitcake yet. "I cut a piece for supper last night and the fumes almost knocked me over. I thought you said Mr. Kezzie had quit making the stuff."

"That's what he tells me, but Mother once said that whiskey-making was the only thing he ever lied to her about." I shook my head. "So who knows? If he'd lie to her, he wouldn't think twice about me."

But one mention of Daddy's illicit activities led to another, and she giggled when I told her about Ellen Englert Hamilton being in my courtroom this morning. She knew about Mrs. Englert's run-in with the law over that jar of white lightning that had been found in the Englert basement, and she had been present when I dumped a full glass of cold water, ice cubes and all, in Rudolph Englert's lap after he told me his mother wanted us to cool it.

She hooted with remembered glee. "And then Dwight and Reid gave you a package of those little frozen sausages the next day."

"All the same," I said, "she thinks the Johnson girl could have been run off the road by a drunk driver. She said it happened on a straightaway. Wonder what caused her to flip over like that?"

Portland shook her curly head. "Could've been a deer or possum or something and she swerved to miss it, then overcorrected. What does Dwight say?"

"He hasn't. He'll probably get the trooper's report today, so I'll ask him tonight."

"Poor Malcolm and Sarah," Portland said, unconsciously echoing my nieces.

I was surprised to realize that she knew them fairly well since they had been older than us back in school.

"Not Malcolm so much," she admitted, "but I got to know Sarah better when her son wanted to change his name back to Barefoot. I drew up the petition for him last spring and did all the official notifications."

I was curious. "Why? What was that about?"

"The usual. Two mule-stubborn males butting heads. He was jealous of Mallory — claimed that Malcolm had never really treated him equally. And it didn't help that his Barefoot grandparents had been wanting him to do it and come live with them ever since he turned eighteen. Not that he needed much urging for the name change. I don't know what finally pushed his buttons, but he really turned against his dad. And he wasn't too happy with his mom either. He thought Mallory was spoiled. That Malcolm gave her more and let her get away with more than he ever got."

"Was he right?"

"Probably. She was daddy's little girl all right. Anything she ever wanted, he'd bust his britches to get it for her. All she had to do is look wistful, Sarah said. Just between you and me, I think she was a little bit jealous herself."

"Nobody speaks ill of the dead," I said, "but that's the first negative thing I've heard anyone say about her."

"I'm not speaking negatively of Mallory," Portland protested. "Just because Malcolm doted on her and wanted to give her the moon and a few stars doesn't mean she was spoiled. She seemed like a sweet kid and she tried like hell to talk Charlie out of changing his name, but he'd made up his mind and wouldn't back down."

She glanced at my empty glass and emptied her own in one swallow. "Let me get you some more tea."

I glanced at my watch. As always when we get together like this, I had stayed longer than I planned.

"Gotta run," I said.

Before she could urge me to stay, the baby woke up from her nap and began to cry.

"Call me," I said and let myself out.

CHAPTER 7

Chill December brings the sleet,
Blazing fire and Christmas treat.

— Traditional rhyme

While I may —

Okay, correction: while I *do* grumble about the new NutriGood store that has taken over a corner of a crossroads less than five miles from the farm, I have to admit that I like being able to stop off on my way home. Dwight likes it because he doesn't have to drive into Raleigh for the coffee beans, cheeses, and store-baked breads that can't be found in Dobbs.

Unlike me, he doesn't mind shopping for groceries. In fact, when he first proposed, one of the reasons he gave for wanting to get married was that he was tired of buying single-serving packages. I'm perfectly happy to let him be the one who keeps the pantry and freezer stocked, yet there I was that

Friday afternoon, roaming the endless aisles, hunting for the stuff we don't normally keep on hand — confectioners' sugar, candy dots, little cinnamon red-hots, and a four-pack of food coloring. Ever since they were old enough to dump sugar into flour and use a cutter on the flattened dough, my nieces and I have spent the Saturday before Christmas making fancy cookies together.

As long as I was in the candy aisle, I picked up a package of old-fashioned hard candies for the brilliant-cut glass candy dish Aunt Sister gave us for a wedding gift. Mother had given it to her several Christmases before I was born, "but now that I've got the sugar diabetes, I ain't got no use for it anymore and I thought you might like to have it, honey," she had told me when I unwrapped it last December.

One way or another, I managed to fill a basket, and as I loaded the groceries in the trunk of my car, Dwight called to say he was running a little late. "Can you pick up Cal?"

"No problem," I said, but I thought I heard something odd in his voice. "Anything wrong?"

"I'll tell you about it tonight," he hedged.

"You *will* be home for supper, won't you?" I asked.

"There by six-thirty," he promised.

The big round table in the playroom at Kate's house was littered with bits of lace, satin ribbons, colorful scraps of fabric, and sprinkles of gold and silver glitter. A cake box full of craftsy odds and ends had been upended. While Mary Pat rummaged for a second white feather, little R.W. gnawed on a set of plastic keys and watched the action from his high chair. (I've already promised him that I'll put in a good word with Carolyn when they're both a little older.)

"You're just in time to make a tree ornament," Kate said as she ushered me in.

"So I see," I said, smiling at the young woman across the table who seemed to be in charge of the scissors.

Erin Gladstone is the live-in nanny that Kate hired when she realized that she was hovering too closely over her variegated brood instead of getting back to work designing the fabrics for which she had made a name for herself in the fashion industry. In addition to Mary Pat, her orphaned young cousin who's six months older than Cal, there's Jake, her son from her first marriage, and R.W., her almost one-year-old son with Rob. This past summer, she and Rob obtained legal adoptions for Mary Pat and Jake so that all three kids now have the same last name and the older two can legitimately call them Mom and Dad, something the children had already begun to do before the adoption.

"See my wooden soldier," Cal said, proudly holding out a peg-type clothespin he had painted blue and topped with a red chenille ball above a tiny face he had inked on with a fine-pointed Sharpie. "It doesn't need a hanger 'cause his legs will let him sit on a branch."

He demonstrated on the tree that stood nearby, another artificial one somewhat smaller in scale than the large one out in the living room. This one was decorated with wood and plastic ornaments sturdy enough to survive if a ball crashed into it.

"Look at my angel, Aunt Deborah!" Mary Pat said. Her clothes peg had flowing yellow yarn hair, a tinsel halo, and a robe of white lace.

"How can it be an angel if it doesn't have wings?" five-year-old Jake asked scornfully.

"It'll have wings just as soon as I find some more white feathers," Mary Pat told him, plucking one from the pile

"So what are you making?" I asked Jake.

He had inserted a strip of green cardstock with rounded tips into the slot of the clothespin and was gluing a second one in place above the first so that it looked vaguely like an old biplane.

"A dragonfly," he told me earnestly. "These are its wings."

Kate had used red wool to make a skinny Santa Claus with a white cotton beard, and it took me right back to childhood when Portland and I had spent a whole summer making clothespin dolls. My fingers itched to dive in, but I had planned to make a beef stew for supper and I knew I'd lose track of time if I ever took the clothespin Kate held out to me.

"Sorry," I told her, "but we need to go let Bandit out and get started on supper." I smiled at Cal. "Bookbag? Jacket?"

While he gathered up his things, Kate said, "Rob and I plan to take the children to the light show over in Garner tomorrow night. Okay if Cal comes?"

"Sure," I said. "Call me and one of us will run him over."

Back at the house, Cal helped me carry in the groceries, then took Bandit out for a romp around the yard while I browned chunks of chuck with a large chopped onion. I poured off the excess grease, stirred in some flour until it was nice and brown, then whisked in enough water to cover the meat. When it came to a boil, I dropped in a bay leaf, put the lid on, and turned the heat down low. Once the meat was tender enough, I would add carrots, peas, and potatoes.

By the time Dwight got home and hung his jacket on a peg beside the door, the kitchen was redolent with those homey aromas. I stirred up some dough for dumplings, dropped them onto the surface of the stew, and put the lid back on to let them steam while I set the table and started a load of laundry.

"Erin's going to take us to Raleigh to see Santa Claus on Monday," Cal said when we sat down to eat.

"Yeah?" said his dad. "You gonna sit on his lap? Get your picture taken?"

"Maybe." His eyes sparkled with mischief.

"What'll you say when he asks what you want him to bring you?" I asked suspiciously.

"Mary Pat and me, we're gonna ask him for cell phones."

"Good luck with that," Dwight told him. "He'll bring you a cell phone about the same time he brings you a Lamborghini."

"What's a Lamborghini?" Cal asked.

"Something else you're never gonna get,"

Dwight said, tousling his hair.

He went back to the stove for a second helping of stew and Cal leaned in close to whisper, "So can we? Please?"

When he'd asked me earlier, I had said that we'd see, thinking it was really too early.

"Presents are for Christmas morning," decreed the starchy conformist preacher who lives in the back of my head.

"But Dwight will enjoy playing with it more before Christmas than after," argued the rule-breaking pragmatist who shares their housekeeping duties.

"Pleeeeze?" said Cal.

"Okay," I relented. "After supper."

By the time Dwight finished eating, Cal had carried his own plate and mine out to the dishwasher.

Dwight raised an eyebrow at so much unsolicited helpfulness. "What's happening? We expecting company or something?"

"Not that I know of," I said innocently.

"You finished, Dad?" Cal asked, reaching for his plate.

"Looks like I am whether I want to be or not," he said with a puzzled smile.

There was a metallic clash from the kitchen as tableware hit the dishwasher basket, then Cal darted back past us and into the living room. "Come sit here, Dad,"

78

he said, patting a place on the couch.

I cleared everything off the coffee table while Cal ran down the hall to retrieve the huge flat box he and I had stashed under his bed last weekend.

"Hey, what's this?" Dwight said when the brightly wrapped gift with its big red bow was placed on the low table before him. "Santa Claus come already?"

"Yeah," Cal said, nearly bursting with anticipation. "Open it! Open it!"

Happily for Cal and me, Dwight's not one of those methodical types who has to untie every ribbon or undo every strip of tape. He found a loose edge and ripped the paper away with both hands. I'm sure that he was prepared to fake pleasure no matter what it was, but his prepared smile turned to genuine delight as the picture on the box registered. It's not that Dwight had a deprived, poverty-stricken childhood by any means, but his father never made much money, and after his death, during the years that Miss Emily was finishing college and getting her master's degree, her budget had been too tight to stretch to the train set he had yearned for.

How long he would have sat there just grinning at the box is something I'll never know, because Cal was already trying to pull the lid off and show him all the wonders within. "The headlight really works, Dad, and the engine puffs smoke and we got extra tracks so it'll go all the way around the tree. We could've gotten a passenger train, but we thought you'd like a freight train better. She and I went in on it together. Do you like it? Were you surprised?"

"I like it lots, buddy," he said and swept the boy up in a huge bear hug.

Two minutes later, he and Cal were on the floor, fitting the tracks together to encircle the tree.

Several packages had accumulated beneath the drooping branches, but when I went to move them out of the way, Dwight grabbed a small flat one about the size of a paperback book that hadn't been there earlier.

"No shaking till Christmas morning," he warned me. "Especially not this one."

He and Cal shared a conspiratorial grin.

"Hey, no fair!" I protested. "I let y'all shake mine."

"Yeah, right," said Cal, who last year had rattled every present with his or Dwight's name on it till I thought he'd wear the bells and holly off the wrapping paper. "That's 'cause you cheat and put in rocks and marbles and BBs."

"All's fair in love and Christmas presents," I told him and went out to the kitchen to make a pot of coffee and check to see if the laundry was dry yet.

There was a knock at the door and Haywood stuck his head in before I could answer it.

Haywood's one of the "big twins" from Daddy's first marriage, and even though they're not identical, he and Herman are both tall and wide. (The younger set, Zach and Adam, *are* identical and are referred to as the "little twins" even though they're both a full inch taller.) Haywood's never been one to stand on ceremony and I'd have to lock the doors to keep him from walking in on us as the mood takes him.

"Hey, shug. Y'all busy?" Without waiting for an answer, he set his porkpie hat on the counter and handed me a well-wrapped package that must have weighed three or four pounds. "Aunt Zell sent y'all a fruitcake. Um, boy, that coffee sure smells fitten to drink!" He unzipped his heavy jacket. "Bet a slice of this cake would go real good with it."

I laughed. "So how many slices of Aunt Zell's cakes have you already had today?"

He grinned. "Not a crumb today." The grin grew sheepish. " 'Course now, I got to say that the two slices I had yesterday were right hefty, and Bel won't let me have any more till both the children are home, and Jane Ann can't come till tomorrow."

He gave me a hopeful look.

What the hell? Another serving of fruitcake wasn't going to affect that fifty-inch waistline any more than cutting two million out of the federal budget was going to affect the national deficit. I took his jacket and sent him on into the living room.

"Lord have mercy!" I heard him say. "What you boys got there?"

A gleeful *toooot-tooot* answered him.

It was almost nine-thirty before Haywood reluctantly left. By then I had folded and put away two loads of laundry and the train was circling the tree, headlight shining, whistle blowing, smoke puffing. A pile of pine twigs had been tossed on the fire, sacrificed to give better clearance for the locomotive. Cal turned the controls over to Dwight, let Bandit outside for a final time, then went off to brush his teeth and get into bed. Bandit had already settled in beside him when I went to check on them.

I'm not sure if he was getting less self-conscious about accepting affection, but he had quit shying away from my touch. When

I leaned over to kiss his forehead that night after tucking the blanket around him, he actually hugged me back and said, "Dad really likes that we got him that train, doesn't he?"

"He really does," I agreed, remembering how solemnly he'd handed me the twenty dollars he had saved up to help pay for it.

He reminds me of a young horse that's not quite saddle-broke. Enough sugar cubes, enough unsudden movements, and one of these days he's going to trot right over to me without any coaxing.

Or so I kept telling myself.

On the other hand, he had almost quit calling me by name, referring to me as "she" or "her" or "you" unless there was absolutely no way to avoid saying "Deborah." Dwight hadn't noticed and I wasn't going to call attention to it, but I'd be lying if I said it didn't hurt a little.

When I came back to the living room, Dwight had put a CD of soft carols on the player and turned off all the lights except for the tree itself. The last log of the evening burned low on the hearth. I slipped off my shoes to join him on the couch, lying down across his chest with his arms around me and my head on his shoulder.

Snuggling myself more deeply into his

arms, I said, "You don't have any plans for our anniversary, do you?"

"Dinner at Las Margaritas, then back here for champagne," he said promptly. "Mama's already said Cal can spend the night there."

I was touched. Dinner at that Mexican restaurant in Garner had led to his unexpected proposal.

"Sounds wonderful," I told him. "And then can we go dancing Tuesday night with Portland and Avery?"

He nodded, then murmured, "Thank you for my train." He tipped my face up for a long sweet kiss and we held each other quietly, savoring the moment. Nowhere to go, nowhere to be, just here and now, together, both aware of where this would lead but without any urgency to rush.

Eventually, he slipped his hand up under my sweater and chuckled to realize that I'd shucked my bra sometime earlier.

The log had burned down to embers before we finally pulled ourselves up, unplugged the tree, and got ready for bed.

While brushing my teeth, I remembered that odd quality in Dwight's voice when he called me before; and when I joined him under the covers, I asked what had kept him at work.

"You know how the hospitals always draw a vial of blood when car wreck victims are brought in and how they test for alcohol?"

I nodded.

"Well, when they drew Mallory Johnson's, it registered point-oh-three."

"Really?" Even though I didn't know the girl, that surprised me. "Nothing my nieces said indicated she did alcohol."

"Yeah, that's what Malcolm said, too, when he and Sarah came in yesterday to hear our findings on the wreck." Dwight reached up to switch off the lamp above his head. "When I told them her alcohol level, he went ballistic. Swore that Mallory never drank anything stronger than Coke and that somebody must have slipped it into whatever she drank at a party she went to after the game Tuesday night. Not just a little alcohol, but maybe crack or meth, too. Sarah did say that she was taking Benadryl for her cold and even a little whiskey could have intensified the effects of Benadryl, slowed her reflexes, maybe left her disoriented. That might explain why she'd go off a straight stretch of highway. I've got a deputy checking it out, getting a list of who was there and if anyone saw her add a shot of something to her Coke."

"The girls are coming over tomorrow

morning to make cookies," I said slowly. "Want me to ask if they've heard anything?"

"Yeah. Won't hurt, and it might make Malcolm and Sarah feel better to know. Right now, he's pushing us to run a tox screen on her blood sample even though that would take at least six weeks. I didn't want to tell him we don't have the budget for that. Not for a one-car accident."

CHAPTER 8

We are not daily beggars who beg from
   door to door,
But we are neighbours' children whom
   you have seen before . . .
        — "Here We Come A-Wassailing"
                 (Traditional English)

When my nieces were younger and I still lived in Dobbs with Aunt Zell and Uncle Ash, the girls would converge on Aunt Zell's kitchen the Saturday before Christmas the instant they could persuade a parent to drive them into town. More than once I had groggily answered a six a.m. phone call to hear a small voice ask, "Can I come now, Aunt Deb'rah?"

Annie Sue, Herman's youngest child, was nine the chilly December morning that Uncle Ash opened the door to get his newspaper and found her huddled on the front step nearly blue with cold. She had ridden her bicycle the few short blocks over from their house at dawn to make sure she wouldn't miss anything.

These days, the other girls don't climb out of bed much before midmorning, and Annie Sue is still the first one here even though she now has the longest drive. Her new white electrician's truck rolled into the yard as Dwight was pouring himself a third cup of coffee.

"Actually, I'm going to do some work today," she said with a grin when Dwight teased her that she just wanted to show off the truck's redesigned logo. "Reese is coming over later to help me install your new aff-sees."

"The what-sees?" I looked at Dwight.

He shrugged.

Annie Sue spelled it out for us. "A-F-C-I's. Short for arc fault circuit interrupters. Circuit breakers."

"Why do we need new circuit breakers? This house is only three years old."

"Because they weren't required when Dad wired you up. These babies will trip the breaker if there's a frayed or exposed wire and maybe keep your house from catching fire. I'm putting them in all the bedrooms here on the farm. The state requires them in new construction even though the Home

Builders Association bitched and yelled about the extra cost."

"So how much *is* this going to cost us?" Dwight asked.

"No more than sixty or eighty dollars."

I was surprised. "That's all? Then why's the Builders Association fighting it?"

"Beats me," Annie Sue said. "They're a lot cheaper than the granite counters and designer upgrades the builders are always pushing, and those don't save lives. That's why come Reese and I are doing it at cost for all the family. I'll get started here this afternoon but we have to fit it in around the rest of our work and deer season."

Dwight raised his eyebrows at that. "What's deer season got to do with it?"

She shook her head with a rueful smile. "You know Reese. He said he saw the tracks of a big buck down at Uncle Haywood's end of the long pond last weekend, so it's hard to keep him focused."

"Tell him we'll take the tenderloin off his hands," Dwight said as he picked up his keys and put on his jacket.

"Anyhow, I'll need a key so we can finish up on Monday or Tuesday when we're out this way. A lot of people are getting electrical appliances for Christmas, so we're real busy."

Annie Sue began taking courses at Colleton Community long before she graduated from high school last spring. When she passed the state test and earned her electrician's license back in the summer, Herman officially changed the name of his electrical contracting business to *Knott and Family.* He actually wanted to make it *Knott and Daughter* as a slap at Reese, who could not be shamed into buckling down and acquiring his own license, but Annie Sue wouldn't let him. Reese can pull wire as competently as most other electricians, but he's never had his little sister's flair for it nor the discipline to jump through the educational hoops, and it doesn't seem to bother him one bit to work off her license or their dad's.

Or to take off and go hunting when he's supposed to be on the clock.

Even though she's now holding down an adult job and drawing adult wages, Annie Sue wasn't quite ready to give up making Christmas cookies, and she helped me clear away the breakfast things and get out the baking utensils while Dwight and Cal went to pick up Mary Pat and Jake.

Because Kate lets Cal go there after school on the weekdays, we try to give her a break by taking the two older children on Saturdays.

They trooped into the kitchen, red-cheeked and ready to measure and mix while Dwight took our weekly accumulation of trash and recyclables to the neighborhood disposal center a few miles away. All three of them wanted to crack an egg and I tried not to wince when flecks of shell went into the bowl or when Jake's egg slipped out of his hands and splatted on the floor. After they cut out and decorated several gingerbread men, I showed them how to use drinking straws to punch holes in the stiff dough so that they could later add a loop of red yarn after baking and hang their creations on the Christmas tree.

When the cookies had cooled enough, Annie Sue helped each boy pipe his name in white icing across the fragrant chest of his best effort. Mary Pat insisted on doing hers by herself. Eventually, there would be a personalized gingerbread man for every member of the family, and these would act as place cards for our big Christmas dinner at the homeplace. This was something Mother had done when I was a child, and when I came back to Colleton County I claimed it as my own contribution to the family feasts.

By the time Seth's daughter Jess, Andrew's Ruth, and Zach's Emma arrived, the kitchen was fragrant with cinnamon, ginger, and nutmeg. They quickly shed their jackets, washed their hands, and plunged in.

Once there were no more eggs to crack, Cal and Jake soon grew bored and wandered outside to help Dwight unload the empty trash cans and recycling bins and put them back in the garage, but Mary Pat decided she wanted to hang with the girls, especially since they had brought along Melissa, my brother Robert's eleven-year-old grand-daughter.

Ruth was all around the kitchen with her digital camera, documenting our baking session for a "Christmas on the Farm" album she planned to make for Daddy. He refuses to have anything to do with computers and misses out on the uploaded photos the rest of us share back and forth. He wants color prints he can hold in his hands. Emma's our computer whiz and she and Ruth keep saying that one of these days they're going to take all the old photo albums that are cornflaking on a shelf at the homeplace and put them on a DVD.

We had finished with the gingerbread men and moved on to Mexican wedding cakes rolled in powdered sugar and heavily deco-rated sugar cookies when Haywood's Jane

Ann walked into the kitchen lugging a large navy duffel bag with a navy, gold, and white UNCG logo on the side.

"I'm not too late for the bourbon balls, am I?" she cried as the others rushed to hug her. "I got here quick as I could." There were dark circles under her sleepy blue eyes.

"You're just now getting home?" I asked, eyeing her duffel bag. "I thought you guys were due in last night."

"Yeah, well, Stevie made it, but today was the absolute deadline for one of my term papers," she confessed. "I pulled an all-nighter and almost missed my ride."

"So what else is new?" Jessica asked.

Annie Sue shook her head, but the rest of us just laughed.

Jane Ann is the family's biggest procrastinator. She's bright. She's observant. She can and will do whatever's required. But she never finishes anything until the very last minute, and too often that last minute is five minutes too late because she never allows for any unexpected delays. She spent her whole high school years doing extra work to compensate for overdue assignments, and it would appear that college had not changed her.

"Where's your car?" Ruth asked, clicking a picture of her cousin, who looked perfectly beautiful, even in a UNCG hoodie, no makeup, and her hair skinned back from her face.

"I left it in Greensboro. Something's wrong with the brakes and I didn't have time to take it in to get it fixed."

This got her more snickers from her cousins.

"Come on, y'all. Quit laughing. It's no biggie. I got a ride with some friends from Makely and they let me sleep all the way over. Besides, tired as I was, Mom and Dad ought to be happy I didn't try to drive myself after what happened to Mallory. Oh, God! I couldn't believe it when I started getting all the messages. Do they know why yet?"

Being rather golden herself, Jane Ann would of course have known a golden girl like Mallory Johnson, despite being a year ahead of her. Listening to the girls, I realized that Mallory had been part of the court when Jane Ann was named homecoming queen last year. No surprise that Mallory had been this year's queen.

As we rolled and cut, and shuttled pans of cookies in and out of the oven, my high school nieces brought Jane Ann and Annie Sue up to date — the last time each of them had spoken to Mallory, whom she'd last dated, their speculations as to why she had wrecked her car on a straight stretch of road, and whether she'd been buckled up, thrown out of the car, or crushed behind the wheel.

They described the memorial they had helped construct and place at the crash site yesterday morning and Ruth brought up pictures of the cross and wreath on her camera. "I'll upload them and send y'all the link," she promised.

"What's with the beer cans and Bojangles' box?" Jane Ann asked.

"Oh, that's just the trash that was in the ditch across from where she crashed. I picked up a bunch of it while they were doing the wreath so it'd look nice along there. People are such slobs."

Jane Ann squinted at a picture of gray with black streaks across it. "And what's this?"

"Her skid marks. She only laid down rubber for a few feet," said Ruth. "I guess she was trying to keep from hitting a rabbit or possum or something at the last minute."

"No," Jane Ann said. "It would have to be a lot bigger. At least the size of a deer or a really big dog."

She sounded so sure of herself that I was curious. "Why do you say that?"

"Because her dad hammered it into her

that you never swerve for an animal in your lane. Never. He told Mallory that too many kids flip over trying not to kill something. That they cut the wheel and then overcorrect. Before he let her get her license, he took her out on the road a few times till they found a squirrel or a rabbit or something in her lane and he made her run over it. Can you believe that? Told her not to brake and not to turn the wheel. She could take her foot off the gas, but that's all."

"Hey, that's right," Jess said. "In Spanish class this fall, she was real down about hitting a turtle that she didn't notice till the very last minute and she said the same thing. How she had promised her dad that she absolutely would not swerve around any animal in her lane. And she loved turtles."

"Must have been a deer, then," Annie Sue speculated.

Emma told of how shattered Joy Medlin was by this latest death. "She had a voice mail from Mallory right before the game and she says she's never going to delete it. She's got Stacy's last voice-mail message, too. It's so sad."

When all this talk started, I had briefly considered Mary Pat and Melissa's tender ages and whether I ought to send them outdoors to play, but they had immediately let me know that they knew all about this latest tragedy, and they were not shy about voicing their own thoughts and opinions.

"Mom told Erin that she has to turn her phone off when she's driving us," said Mary Pat.

"I'm never gonna turn mine on in the car," Melissa said.

Mary Pat looked at her enviously. "You have a phone already?"

"No, but I'm hoping they'll break down and get me one for Christmas. It's all I really want."

"Me, too." Mary Pat sighed.

(I knew for a fact that they had better chances of getting a blizzard for Christmas than their own cell phones.)

"Mallory probably did have hers on," Emma said quietly. "She texted the whole squad from the party Tuesday night."

"Were you at that party?" I asked, knowing what a tight leash Barbara keeps her two kids on.

Jessica glanced up from putting cinnamon drops on some sugar cookie stars. "What party?" She made a face. "You don't mean Kevin Crowder's party, do you?"

Emma hesitated. "All the other cheerleaders were going, but you know Mother. She always makes Lee bring me straight home

97

after a game."

"Who's Kevin Crowder?" Annie Sue asked. She and Jane Ann were the same age, but she had attended Dobbs Senior High, not West Colleton as had the others.

"He's a shooting guard on the basketball team. Has a wicked three-pointer but he's a real assh —" Jess caught herself, whether out of deference to her elderly aunt's ears or the ears of the two little ones, and changed it to "Real jerk."

"I remember him," Jane Ann said, nibbling on a broken cookie. "You've seen him around too, Annie Sue. He was at A.K.'s birthday party. Tall blond guy? Blue convertible?"

Her cousin reached for the other part of the cookie. "Acted like he was God's gift to women?"

"He's a senior this year and even more stuck on himself than last year," Jess assured them.

"Be fair," Emma protested. "He's really nice when you get to know him."

They stared at her and she flushed a bright red.

All the Knott kids have blue eyes, relatively fair skin, and hair that ranges from light brown to blond, but Emma had inherited Barbara's delicate pink complexion and her long hair was the color of spring dandelions.

"Please tell me you are not getting to know Kevin Crowder," Jane Ann said sternly.

The flush on Emma's cheeks spread across her whole face and up into her hairline.

"Oops!" I cried, reaching for a potholder. "Anybody remember when that last pan of cookies went in?"

Someone had left a nearly empty glass of milk beside the potholder right on the edge of the counter. A tiny imperceptible nudge as I picked up the potholder was enough to send it careening toward the floor.

Jess and Annie Sue both lunged for it. Spraying milk on their sweaters, it bounced off their hands toward Mary Pat, whose misjudged grab swatted it across the room where it shattered against the edge of the refrigerator.

More of a mess than I had intended, but by the time all the milk and glass were cleaned up, the sweaters sponged off, and the last sheets of cookies were out of the oven, conversation had moved on to other topics less interesting to Melissa and Mary Pat. When I brought out the bottle of bourbon to mix up those sinfully delicious bourbon balls, they wrinkled up their little noses and decided to go see what the boys were up to.

I made a fresh pot of coffee and Ruth and Emma used my food processor to turn several cups of toasted pecans into tiny bits. Jane Ann and Jessica pounded vanilla wafers into crumbs and Annie Sue measured out butter and powdered sugar.

For a wedding gift last year, the local bar association gave Dwight and me a huge ceramic bowl they had commissioned from the Jugtown Pottery over in Seagrove. The bowl is big enough to serve coleslaw to the whole family at a pig-picking, and it's also perfect for mixing up a family-size batch of bourbon balls. I drizzled melted butter over all the dry ingredients, then poured in the bourbon. A big wooden spoon passed from hand to hand as we each stirred the stiff mixture till our arms gave out.

I may have been a little too lavish with the bourbon, because when Annie Sue took her turn with the wooden spoon, she immediately began to warble:

The birds in the sky get so drunk they
    cain't fly
From that good ol' mountain dew.

When everything was thoroughly mixed and the coffee was ready, we carried our mugs to the dining table and set the big bowl in the middle so everyone could reach in, pinch off some dough, and shape it into one-inch balls. As soon as one cake box was filled, it was carried out to a workbench in the garage to chill and another took its place.

With so many hands dipping in and out of the bowl, I knew it wouldn't take long to finish, so while there were no loose-lipped little kids in the room, I said, "So, Emma. Can we assume that Kevin Crowder's house is on a straight line between South Colleton and your house?"

She stared at me, stricken, then whispered, "Who told you?"

I wasn't about to say that it was her own evasion of my first question that tipped me off, and now her guilty look confirmed my suspicions.

"Please," she said, imploring the others as much as me. "Don't tell Mother. She'll blame Lee, too, and it's not his fault. Laurie Evans broke up with her boyfriend and asked if we could drop her at the party 'cause she didn't want to ride with him and she knew we'd be going right past Kevin's house. I talked Lee into it. See, Kevin sits next to me in study hall. That's how I know him. I told him I couldn't go, but everybody was so pumped about beating South we didn't want the night to end — it really was only for a few minutes. But his parents weren't home and there were some older kids there that we didn't know and one of them was high on something, so Lee made me leave before I could even take off my jacket, but Mother will kill us if she finds out. The only reason she let me join the varsity squad was because I promised I wouldn't try to act like I was a junior or senior."

The words tumbled out in such a rush that she was almost crying, and Jessica reached out to pat her arm. "It's okay, Em. We won't tell. None of us will, will we?"

The girls all shook their heads and looked at me.

"I won't tell either," I said slowly, "but the boy that was high? Were there drugs at the party?"

"I don't *know*," she wailed. "I wasn't there long enough to even drink a Coke."

"But Mallory was there?"

"We all were. The whole squad and most of the varsity players."

"Was she okay at the game?"

"Sure. She was starting to get a cold and her voice sounded a little raspy. She did take a pill, but it was just a Benadryl tablet. And she was drinking lots of liquids to try and flush the cold out of her system."

"What about at the party?"

Emma shrugged. "She had a Coke can in her hand when we got there, and there was booze on one of the counters, but I'm sure she didn't put any in her drink if that's what you mean. Bridget's the only —"

She clapped a sticky guilty hand to her mouth as if to block the words we'd already heard her say.

Jane Ann pounced on them in disapproving surprise. "Bridget Honeycutt drinks?"

I suppose I should have appreciated the irony of the situation. Here we sat, up to our wrists in bourbon-saturated dough, and my nieces were expressing disbelief that a "nice" girl like Bridget Honeycutt had a drinking problem?

The difference, of course, was that by the time these calorie-laden little balls had ripened in cake boxes out in the cold garage for several days and I had drizzled chocolate over them, most of the alcohol would have evaporated, leaving only the flavor behind.

Some of my brothers — their dads — had abused alcohol in their younger days, A.K. was known to sneak an occasional beer, and Reese had a DWI on his driving record, but bourbon balls had never led any member of my family down the primrose path to alcoholism any more than Aunt Zell's fruitcakes had.

"Bridget's no drunk," Emma said hotly. "She couldn't drink much and still keep up with the rest of us, but she says that it helps take the edges off things."

She would not elaborate on why Bridget needed some edges blurred, but I got the impression that Jess and Ruth probably knew.

"You said you saw booze," I said. "What about drugs?"

"No!" Emma cried. "Why do you keep asking me? I told you. I wasn't there long enough to see who was doing what."

My nieces aren't dummies and it was sweet levelheaded Jessica who said, "You know something, don't you, Aunt Deborah?"

I nodded. "But you absolutely can't talk about it right now. It'll come out soon enough. Mallory had alcohol in her system when she died, and her dad seems to think someone spiked her drink or maybe even added drugs to it to make her so disoriented that she would run off a straight road on a clear night. Who at that party would do that to her, Emma?"

But Emma had immediately realized that

there would be an inquiry into that party and she had leapfrogged to what was, for her, the larger issue. "I'm dead," she moaned. "Mother will make me quit the squad. She'll take Lee's car keys and he'll hate me forever."

"Not necessarily," Jane Ann said soothingly. "If you were only there for a minute, chances are that no one really registered it."

Emma shook her head and golden hair swirled around her anguished face. "Laurie knows and so does Kevin. As soon as Uncle Dwight starts asking for names, mine's going to pop out."

Annie Sue had continued to roll bourbon balls through all this, but now she paused and said, "So here's what you do. You're going to the visitation tonight, right?"

Emma nodded tearfully.

"It'll be perfectly normal to talk about the last time you saw Mallory. You will probably cry. That's when you tell your mom how good she was at the game and how your last memory of her will be taking a sip of her Coke at Kevin Crowder's party."

"Annie Sue! I can't. She'll go ballistic!"

"No she won't," Annie Sue said calmly, "because when she asks what you were doing there when you were supposed to come straight home, you'll explain about this

105

Laurie kid and how the only reason you and Lee stepped inside was to make sure that Laurie had a way home. You got home around your usual time, right? So clearly you didn't stay. Don't make a big deal out of it and Aunt Barbara will think you did the proper thing. That she's raised two very considerate and responsible kids."

There was more cynicism in her voice than I wanted to hear, but I had to admit that she really did have Barbara pegged.

From the sudden look of relief on her face, Emma knew it, too.

Two minutes later, Jane Ann was the one in trouble with her mother when her cell phone rang and she had to admit that she had come here first instead of going straight home.

I could hear Isabel's outraged voice from the other side of the table. "Your daddy's out there pacing a rut in the yard, worried to death that you ain't come, and you're over yonder making cookies?"

"I'm coming right now," Jane Ann assured her. She clicked off and hurried to the sink to wash her hands.

Annie Sue was right behind her. "I'll drive you," she said, "but I'm not coming in to find out if you're okay."

CHAPTER 9

"Send him to jail now, and you make him
a jail-bird for life.
Besides, it is the season of forgiveness."
— "The Adventure of the Blue Carbuncle,"
Arthur Conan Doyle

I took Mary Pat and Jake home shortly before sunset and left Cal there, too, to spend the night. Kate and Rob planned to treat the children to pizza and then to a Christmas lights theme park near Raleigh while Dwight and I went to the funeral home in Cotton Grove where Mallory Johnson's visitation was being held.

As a sitting judge who has to run for office every four years, I get invited to a lot of weddings and I attend a lot of funerals. My inner pragmatist knows that it's a chance to shake hands and remind the voters that I'm in and of the community. My inner preacher worries about taking advantage of a family's emotional state.

Weddings are usually fun and I don't mind funerals for the terminally sick or nursing home elderly. These can turn into a celebration of the person's life, with more smiles than tears. Anecdotes and good memories can surface again and the survivors talk about their loved one's release from suffering or dementia. You often sense their own release from grief and exhaustion, a relief tinged with guilt for being glad that the deathwatch is over.

Funerals for adults cut down in their prime are usually sad, but they are laugh riots compared to the rituals for a well-loved child. Those are hard, hard, hard, and I knew that the evening would be a tortured ordeal for Sarah and Malcolm Johnson as they touched the hands of Mallory's classmates and were reminded over and over again that those kids were going to move on into bright futures that their own child would never see.

The visitation was scheduled for six to eight, so Dwight and I had supper first at my cousin's barbecue house, which is only four miles away.

We had to wait a few minutes to get a table and then had to share it with a couple of friends. We spent the meal catching up with them — new house, new job, new baby — and it wasn't until we were driving over to Cotton Grove that I had a chance to tell Dwight the meager facts I had picked up from my nieces.

He was sorry that Emma and Lee hadn't stayed longer at the party, "but I've put Mayleen on it," he said, naming one of the more capable deputies on his squad. "She'll get a list of everyone who stepped through the Crowder door that night. I'm pretty sure we'll wind up identifying whoever spiked her drink if the DA wants to prosecute for contributing to the girl's death. Which I doubt."

His opinion of our new DA wasn't much higher than mine. "Any good attorney can argue that it was Mallory's inexperience and the Benadryl that made her swerve for something and flip the car, not a shot of whiskey."

"Did the troopers find any dead animals at the site?" I asked.

"Nope."

"Did they look?"

"They always look. She must have missed whatever it was."

I described Jane Ann and Jess's insistence that Malcolm had drilled it into her not to brake and swerve for any small animal.

"A deer then," he said dismissively. "Or a big dog, because she certainly braked to avoid hitting something."

"And not another car?" I persisted.

"No skid marks in the other lane and only a short one in hers."

I knew that meant she hadn't seen whatever she braked and swerved for till the last minute.

We got to Aldcroft's Funeral Home a little before seven and the spacious parking lot was completely filled. Cars lined both sides of the street.

"You dressed warm enough to walk a couple of blocks," Dwight asked, "or you want me to let you out in front?"

I told him I was fine to walk, but I was wishing for fur-lined boots instead of thin heels by the time we reached the entrance. At most large funerals, the line is out the door and down the sidewalk, but tonight's temperature hovered in the thirties and everyone had squeezed inside. The line began in the front lobby, stretched all the way to the far reaches of the building, and doubled back on itself.

From experience, we knew that it would be at least ninety minutes before we could work our way to the parlor where Sarah and Malcolm would be standing next to their daughter's open casket.

Aldcroft's is the nicest of the local funeral homes. Outside, it looks like Tara, with fluted columns that sit on the stone terrace and rise to a classic pediment, all painted a dazzling white that glowed in the floodlights artfully hidden among the boxwood foundation plantings. Inside was hushed elegance, from the crystal chandelier eight feet above our heads to the thick pearl gray carpet beneath our feet. Gilt-framed portraits of three generations of Aldcroft morticians looked out from walls covered in pale pink silk.

Large floor pots of bright red poinsettias swathed in gold foil acknowledged the season, and tall white electric candles rose from sprays of holly that looked so real I had to touch a leaf to realize it wasn't. Despite the crush of bodies, there was no laughter or light talk, and the décor did nothing to disperse the funeral home smell, a mixture of air freshener and a vague aroma that I always associate with refrigerated flowers and greenery. We paused to speak in solemn tones with several people on line there in the lobby, to hug old friends or shake hands depending on the degree of kin or friendship.

Dwight's mother and his two sisters came

in right behind us. Nancy Faye and Beth had both been in school with Malcolm and Sarah. Miss Emily, of course, had been Mallory's principal, and she had also taught Sarah when she was in the eighth grade. Tonight she looked a bit drawn and tired from dealing with another student's death on top of the usual end-of-semester red tape.

Nancy Faye immediately asked Dwight to try and convince Miss Emily to go out for something to eat instead of standing for so long. "She won't listen to us."

That indomitable woman shook her head. "Stop fussing, Nancy Faye. I'm not hungry."

Dwight's sisters are dears, but they do tend to cluck over Miss Emily like mother hens at times, almost as if in competition for who can show the most concern.

Duck Aldcroft, courtly and solicitous, offered her one of the couches that lined the lobby. "Why don't you just sit down there, Mrs. Bryant, and wait for your girls to come back by?"

"Why, thank you, Duck. It's been a long day. I believe I will sit for a while."

She may have been a bit tired, but I had a feeling that she accepted his offer so she could get away from too much clucking. Either that or she wanted to take the pulse of the community, because no sooner had she crossed to the couch than several people stepped out of line to speak to her.

"She'll be worn out by the time we get back to her," said Beth as several newcomers took their places behind her and the line shuffled forward toward the back halls.

"Are you sure you don't want to have supper first?" I asked Miss Emily. "We can go and be back long before Nancy Faye and Beth come through."

"Don't listen to those girls," she said, her voice crisp with exasperation. "They think everything can be made better with food. I'm not hungry. Just heartsick for the children we keep losing."

I stopped to speak to some of my own high school friends whose children were now at West Colleton, then joined Dwight and his sisters.

As our line turned the first corner, we met Zach and Barbara inching forward with Lee and Emma. Emma's eyes were red from crying, but Barbara had an arm around her waist, so I gathered that Annie Sue's advice had worked and there would be no repercussions for stopping by that party Tuesday night.

I got a warm hug from Zach and an air kiss from Barbara, which made me glad when they turned the corner and we no longer had to make small talk.

Much of West Colleton's student body seemed to be there with their somber-faced parents, who had to be thinking that there but for the grace of God they could be the ones standing in Sarah and Malcolm's shoes.

In the next half hour, we met and passed several of my nieces and nephews and their friends, and yes, at least half of those little thumbs were texting away on the keys.

"Emma's freaking," Jessica said. "She's at the entrance of the room and she can see Mallory's casket and she doesn't want to go on in."

"She should have stayed back here with us," said Jane Ann.

"Like Aunt Barbara was gonna let her do that," said Ruth.

"Did she confess about the party?" I asked, as the line moved forward.

They nodded and Jess said, "And it went just like Annie Sue said it would."

Another corner turned and there was Ellen Englert Hamilton in full rant mode. She had her back to me and spoke in tones that were clearly meant to be heard by all around her. The teenage boy beside her must have recognized me, for he gave her a nudge, but she didn't seem to notice.

"— and then just turned him loose without even the slap on the wrist she'd given the others. Just let him go with nothing but a mealymouthed little lecture after the trooper testified that he was weaving and staggering and —"

"*Mo*-ther!" the boy said, turning beet red.

"Ah, Deborah," she said, looking not a bit embarrassed. "I was just comparing notes with some of my friends. They're MADD, too."

It took a moment to realize she meant Mothers Against Drunk Driving and not that the women behind her were angry, although from the sharp looks and frowns they were giving me, she might well have meant that, too.

"I was telling them how you dismissed all the charges against a drunk driver yesterday," she said coolly.

"And did you explain that the state hadn't proved he was over the limit?"

"Since when does a judge take the word of a drunk against the word of a state trooper?" asked one of the Englert-Hamilton clones.

"Ever since our Constitution said that someone's innocent until proven guilty," I said sweetly. "That's what it means to be a

115

judge. To decide if there's enough proof to determine guilt. Did Ellen tell you about the other dozen or so that I did find guilty?"

"But then you turned around and gave suspended sentences and probation to more than half of them," Ellen snapped back. "The only way people who abuse alcohol are going to get the message is to give them jail time every time they're charged."

"You honestly think a judge should always rule for the officer even when the evidence doesn't support him?"

"Absolutely! If there's enough for a charge, there's enough for a conviction. And a conviction should carry jail time."

"Oh dear," I said with mock chagrin. "Does that mean I was derelict because I didn't send your mother to jail when she was charged with possession of untaxed liquor?"

Except for the MADD women, everyone within earshot, including Ellen's son, grinned.

"That was different and you know it!" Ellen cried, but her cheeks were burning and she seemed only too glad to turn the next corner.

The MADD women quickly followed.

Dwight shook his head at the others, who were still smiling. "Can't take her anywhere," he told them.

Before I could pat myself on the back for my smart-alecky putdown of that sanctimonious prisspot, Patsy Denning, my fifth grade teacher, who had listened to the exchange without comment, now drew even with Dwight and me and she put a firm hand on my arm. In her low sweet voice, she said, "Don't let the messenger sour you on the message, Deborah. Even though Ellen doesn't want anybody to drink anything alcoholic ever, the organization itself has helped save a lot of lives."

She was right.

I sighed. "All the same."

"I know." Mrs. Denning's eyes shone with mischief behind her polished glasses and she squeezed my arm before the line moved on. "All the same, she's certainly her mother's daughter, isn't she?"

CHAPTER 10

Christmas is not just a time for festivity
and merrymaking. It is more than that. It is
a time for the contemplation of eternal
things.

— J. C. Penney

Eight o'clock had come and gone before we
worked our way back to the front lobby, and
a good fifty people had entered after us. It
would be well after nine before poor Sarah
and Malcolm shook the last hand, hugged
the last friend, thanked the last person for
the words of sympathy.

We found Miss Emily still surrounded by
a cluster of neighbors, former students, and
the parents of current students.

Nancy Faye and Beth had worried that
speaking to so many people would have
exhausted their mother, but I thought she
seemed reenergized when she stood up to
join us.

118

As we moved through the lobby, the modest wreaths and floral sprays from Mallory's friends gave way to more elaborate offerings and the chilly smell of refrigerated carnations and greenery grew stronger the closer we got to the main room. Malcolm Johnson and his older brother worked with their father, who owned Triple J, one of the largest insurance companies in the county. The company had been started by Malcolm's grandfather back when this was a sleepy, sparsely inhabited rural area devoted to small family farms and modest mercantile stores. With so much growth these past thirty years, business had boomed and the Johnsons were now a family of wealth and influence. Between them, Malcolm and his family belonged to most of the civic organizations and they had a large circle of friends, relatives, and important customers.

All had sent impressive arrangements.

Interspersed among the flowers were monitor screens set at eye level, and soft, solemn music issued from a single speaker. Eighteen years of Mallory Johnson's life played out in endless loops of still photographs, from her infancy to just a few weeks ago. One screen was devoted to a silent DVD of Mallory as she arrived at the homecoming game with her court, smiling

119

and waving. Her tiara sparkled beneath the floodlights and she was breathtakingly beautiful and alive.

Beside us, Miss Emily caught her breath and sudden tears filled her eyes. "Do *not* do this when y'all bury me," she whispered urgently. She clasped her daughters' hands. "You girls hear me? The pictures are sad enough, but *this!* To see her moving and laughing? Promise me you won't."

We signed the visitors' book and entered the parlor that was so crowded that it was impossible at first to see the casket. The reception line began with Sarah's family — her sister and brother, their spouses and children, and then her parents.

Next came Mallory's brother Charlie, an awkward young man who seemed to be going through the motions mechanically as I took his hand and murmured my sympathy. He appeared to be about six-three with small, closely set hazel eyes in a long narrow face. It was a pleasant enough face, but clearly Mallory had inherited all the beauty in that family. When his eyes met Dwight's, he seemed to focus, and for a moment I thought he was going to say something more than "Thank you" to Dwight's own words of sympathy, but the moment passed and we moved on to Sarah and Malcolm.

Both seemed emotionally and physically drained. Someone had brought a chair for Malcolm, who sat with hunched shoulders and responded dully to those who tried to console him. Sarah was still on her feet and she teared up again when Miss Emily reached out to hug her. I wondered how she could possibly have any tears left.

"Bless you for coming," she murmured as Miss Emily moved on to Malcolm and our turn came to speak. She took Dwight's hand. "Is there anything more you can tell us, Dwight?"

He shook his head and his words included Malcolm. "I wish there was, Sarah. Malcolm."

"You don't get it, Dwight. She never touched liquor," Malcolm said, his voice ragged with pain as he stood to face his old teammate and plead for an answer. "So how did it get in her system? How? Answer me that. Whoever did that to her is as much to blame as the person who made her run off the road, and if I ever find out who — Look at her, man! Is that the face of a drunk?"

He wrenched Dwight's arm in an angry explosive gesture that put him close enough to Mallory to touch her. They had dressed her in her homecoming gown and tiara, and whatever injuries had caused her death, her lovely face had been unharmed. Malcolm cupped that ivory-smooth cheek in his hand and his anger dissolved into despair again. "My little girl. My baby. She shouldn't be lying here. She shouldn't, Dwight." He was sobbing now. "She shouldn't. Oh, God, she *shouldn't!*"

Sarah stepped forward to put her arms around him, her own face crumpled with grief, and Malcolm's stern-faced father came from the other side. Together they calmed him down and the line moved grimly forward again. Soon we were past Malcolm's parents, his brother, and the brother's wife and adult children, then mercifully out of the parlor and back into the lobby.

Again, there were people we had to speak to as we headed for the door, but we didn't linger. Outside on the front terrace, the temperature was so near freezing that we quickly said good night to Dwight's sisters and mother and were turning onto the sidewalk when we realized that Miss Emily had followed us.

"Mama?" Dwight said.

"I'll ride home with you and Deborah," she said, giving him a meaningful look.

He was as instantly curious as I was, but she gave us both a warning shake of her head as a cluster of people passed us and murmured, "Good night, Miss Emily. 'Night, Deborah."

"Why don't you two wait here and I'll go get the car," he said.

"I can walk," she said sharply. "After all that sitting, it feels good to move my legs."

Despite her protests, I insisted that Miss Emily ride in front with Dwight, and I think she was glad to be closer to the heat vents. Dwight always grumbles because my car isn't as roomy as his truck, and with his seat pushed back as far as it would go to accommodate his long legs, I was squeezed in behind his mother.

As soon as we pulled out onto the street, she turned to Dwight and said, "Was Vicodin in Mallory's bloodstream when she died?"

"Where on earth did you get that notion?" he countered.

"Something I heard tonight," she said, confirming my earlier suspicion that she had deliberately chosen to sit where everyone would pass. "Whatever one child knows these days, they all seem to know. It's almost like one of those old *Star Trek* plots, where every mind is linked together like bees in a hive. I suppose you also know that Mallory went to a party Tuesday night after the game with South Colleton? Kevin Crowder's house? And that his parents were away?"

"And?"

"Kevin's not a bad kid. Not really. He pushes the boundaries and he gets away with it because he's nice-looking and has a glib tongue on him. He can make his parents laugh so they don't rein him in as much as they ought to." She sighed and loosened the scarf around her neck.

"Too hot?" Dwight reached for the controls.

"Not yet. What about you, Deborah?" she asked. "You getting any of this heat?"

"I can feel my toes again," I said, "so y'all make it comfortable for yourselves."

"The party," Dwight prodded.

"The party. Yes. Kevin's parents had gone over to Greensboro for the night to attend a Christmas concert. His sister's in the college chorus and she had a solo part. His mother had knee surgery back in the summer and Vicodin was what they gave her for pain. She had pretty much quit taking it, but the drive up and back bothered her knee, and when she got home Wednesday afternoon and went looking for the prescription bottle in her medicine cabinet, it was gone. It had been there Tuesday morning, because she almost took it with her and then decided that Tylenol would probably be all that she'd need. So she asked Kevin and he had to confess to the party. When they heard about Mallory, they were afraid that she might have been drinking there and that they would be liable, but he swore she hadn't and all the children I've talked to say the same. Mallory didn't drink, but if someone spiked her drink, then that same someone could have slipped her a Vicodin. They were all over the house, so any of them could have taken the pills. Kevin immediately texted everybody there and let them know what he thought of someone who would steal his mother's pills. You warm enough now, Deborah?"

I said I was and she switched off the heater fan and lowered the thermostat. "Remember, Mallory was still in a coma on Wednesday. Nobody had any idea that she'd taken anything except one of those over-the-counter cold medicines."

"Benadryl," Dwight said. "And alcohol would have enhanced its effects."

"The thing is, son, that no one's admitted spiking her Coke while she was still alive. Now that they know it might have slowed her reflexes and helped cause her to wreck the car, they certainly aren't going to come forward and confess about any pills."

She leaned her head back against the seat. "The funeral's tomorrow at three. Y'all going?"

"I probably will," I said. "You want to ride with me?"

"That would be nice. What about you, Dwight?"

He shook his head. "Sorry. I promised Cal we'd take my .22 over to the woods back of Seth's house and see if we could shoot us down some mistletoe. If we have any luck, you want some?"

"Only if you haven't shot all the berries off." There was almost a hint of her old humor in her voice.

"I'll send Cal up the tree myself if you promise to tell me whatever else you pick up from the hive mind, okay?"

"Deal," she said.

CHAPTER 11

I do not know a grander effect of music on the moral feelings than to hear the full choir and the pealing organ performing a Christmas anthem in a cathedral, and filling every part of the vast pile with triumphant harmony.
— *The Sketch Book,* Washington Irving

Most Sundays, if we get moving early enough to go to church, it's to nearby Sweetwater Missionary Baptist, the church I grew up in. The minister is earnest and not too hard-shelled, and the choir does the best it can with the talent available.

When I lived with Aunt Zell and Uncle Ash and was still in private practice, though, I moved my membership to the First Baptist Church of Dobbs for purely pragmatic reasons. Not only was it easier to get to on Sunday mornings after a late Saturday night, but this was also where many of Col-

127

leton County's movers and shakers went, and one never knew when sharing a hymnal to sing "Bringing in the Sheaves" might lead to bringing in a new client.

(What? I'm the only one who ever chose a church for other than purely religious reasons?)

The minister, Dr. Carlyle Yelvington, is a progressive liberal whose sermons don't insult one's intellect and who exhorts us to live the words, not just mouth them. But he's not the only reason I roused Dwight out of bed to go fetch Cal early enough that both could put on white shirts and ties in time to make the eleven o'clock service. I wanted some Christmas spirit, and the late-nineteenth-century stateliness of First Baptist was my provider of choice with its carved oak pews, its stained glass windows, the ribbed vaulting overhead, the richly embroidered altar cloths and choir robes, the massed greenery around the pulpit, the tall white candles, the polished brass crosses. Add in an organist and a choir who are all trained musicians, and by the time the final amen is sung I'm ready to hang up a stocking or stuff a goose.

Cal was still hopped up about the festival of bright lights he and his cousins had seen last night, especially the animated displays, and as we were getting into the car, he turned and gave the house a long consideration. "We ought to put up some more lights, Dad. Wouldn't it be really cool to have some of those tube strips like at the RBC Center, only in red and green? Or how 'bout we get one of those reindeer that the legs flash on and off like it's prancing on the roof?"

"Nothing on the roof," I said. "I don't want y'all falling off."

Cal laughed and settled into the backseat with his Game Boy and iPod, but my offhand remark must have triggered something because Dwight said, "Last night was the first time I ever saw Charlie Johnson to know who I was looking at. He really favors Jeff, doesn't he?"

"I really don't remember Jeff very well," I said, fastening my seat belt. "Anyhow, it's not Charlie Johnson anymore. He changed his name back to Barefoot."

"Yeah? When?"

"Last spring, I think. Portland handled the paperwork for him."

"She say why?"

I shrugged. "All the usual, I gather, plus he thought Malcolm made it clear which was his true child. Mallory tried to talk him out of it, so I don't think the resentment went both ways."

"All the same, maybe I'll have a talk with Charlie," Dwight said. "See if he was one of the older kids at that party."

Congregants were streaming into the church when we arrived, and Portland, Avery, and Carolyn were among them. The baby wore the lace-trimmed red plaid dress I'd given her and looked as adorable as I'd expected.

"I'll probably have to take her out before the first prayer," Portland said, "but it wouldn't be Christmas without this, would it?"

We followed them into a pew and Carolyn immediately put out her arms to me. I was flattered until I realized that she was doing it to get nearer to Cal, who was sitting on my other side between Dwight and me. Babies always home in on the children and she was no exception.

"It's okay," he whispered when the baby indicated that she wanted Cal to hold her. He's had a year of practical experience with Kate and Rob's baby and he let her balance on his knees as the rest of us stood to sing the opening hymn, "Angels We Have Heard on High."

She was quiet while the choir sang an arrangement of "Adeste Fideles" in glorious harmony, but began to squirm and fuss a little when Dr. Yelvington took the pulpit. We passed her back to Portland, who calmed her with a bottle; ten minutes later, she was sound asleep.

Cal started to take out his Game Boy, but Dwight gave a negative headshake and he put it away again and tried to look interested in what Dr. Yelvington was saying about the true spirit of Christmas.

Afterward, we sought out Aunt Zell and Uncle Ash to wish them a merry Christmas and to thank her for the fruitcake. Portland and Avery and Portland's parents were going to have Sunday dinner with them to celebrate the baby's birthday, and Aunt Zell assured me that there was enough for three more, but I had left a ham in the oven with a sweet potato casserole and we needed to get back before everything turned to charcoal.

As soon as lunch was cleared away, though, Cal began to pester Dwight to go for the mistletoe.

Mistletoe's a parasite on deciduous trees. It's spread by birds who eat the gummy white berries and then perch in the twigs at the end of a branch to clean their beaks, so it's not easy to harvest. You can't just shinny up a tree and break some off because it's usually growing out at the tips of branches too thin to support even a boy's weight. But if you have a good eye and a steady aim, you can shoot through the thick green stems and bring home enough to kiss half the county.

We're not particularly gun-crazy in my family. You'll never see an AK-47 in our houses, but most of my friends and I did grow up with utility guns. Farmers liked to keep a loaded rifle hanging on pegs over their bedroom doors where they could easily grab it if needed in the middle of the night. If any child ever touched his father's gun without permission, I never heard about it.

Daddy gave each of the boys a simple bolt-action .22 as soon as he thought they could handle the responsibility. Seth got his at ten; Will was fifteen. He taught us to respect both the gun's danger and the life of whatever animal we killed. That last was rammed home to me the day Adam and Zach shot a couple of brown thrashers down at the edge of the woods when they were eleven.

"I ain't gonna give you the licking you deserve," Daddy told them when he found the little corpses and brought them up to the house. "Not this time. But you boys ever kill another songbird, you're gonna clean it and cook it and eat every last bite of it. You hear me?"

All through my teen years, I enjoyed trailing along behind my brothers and their dogs on a frosty moonlit night to hunt for coons and possums with my own little single-shot .22, and I got pretty good at plinking cans and shooting the paper targets the boys pinned onto hay bales, but when Dwight unlocked the gun case in our bedroom that afternoon, I had to admit that I couldn't remember the last time I'd fired it. My brothers don't hunt much anymore and their children don't seem very interested either. Reese is about the only one in the next generation who wants to bag a couple of deer every fall.

Dwight and Cal had changed their suits and ties for jeans and flannel shirts as soon as we got home. Even though I was going out again, I hadn't wanted to get ham grease on my red wool suit, so I had changed into a long blue zip-up robe. Now I sat cross-legged on the edge of the bed to watch as Dwight tucked a box of cartridges in his jacket pocket and took out his .22 Remington with its 3× scope. Although Cal had lived with us for almost a full year, this was the first time he had seen the gun case unlocked and he was surprised to learn that the second, smaller .22 belonged to me. I gathered that Jonna hadn't approved of guns and wouldn't have them in the house. He hadn't even been allowed cap pistols or a BB gun. As so often happens when something is forbidden, his fingers clearly itched to hold one.

"If you want to start teaching him how to shoot," I told Dwight, "take mine. It'll fit him better."

Cal's eyes widened with excitement. "Can we, Dad? Please. Can we?"

"You sure?" Dwight asked, and I knew he was asking about more than the use of my gun.

"Nine's about when Daddy started you boys, wasn't it?"

"Yeah," he said slowly, "I guess it was."

I reached over and took Cal's arm and turned him to me until we were face-to-face and our eyes were level. With my hands on his shoulder, I said, "This is serious, Cal. A gun is not a toy. You've got to listen to your dad, pay attention to what he tells you, and do exactly what he says, okay?"

Instead of pulling away from me, he nodded solemnly. "Yes, ma'am. I will. I promise."

"Good. If you keep that promise, then when Dad says you're ready, you can have my gun to keep."

"Honest?" In his sudden excitement, he gave me such an exuberant hug that I fell back on the bed and he fell on top of me, which struck us both as hilariously funny. Especially when Bandit jumped up on the bed and started licking our faces.

As we untangled ourselves, I realized that for once, he wasn't self-conscious about having hugged me in broad open daylight, and I doubted that I'd get a better present this whole Christmas season.

Laughing and chattering in anticipation, he ran to get his own jacket, Bandit dancing at his heels.

Dwight shook his head at me. "I hope you're right about him being old enough."

I lay back on the pillows. "It's like the birds and the bees," I teased him. "If you don't teach him at home, he's going to pick it up on the school bus or on the street."

He leaned down to kiss me just as Cal reappeared in the doorway.

"Oh, jeez," he said. "Y'all aren't going to get mushy now, are you?"

Dwight gave him a scowl that didn't fool

either of us. "Aren't you supposed to knock first?"

"Not if the door's open. She said only if it's closed."

So I was back to being "she"?

Perplexed, I kicked them both out so I could get dressed for Mallory Johnson's funeral.

CHAPTER 12

*The grasp, though gentle as a woman's
hand, was not to be resisted.*
— *A Christmas Carol,* Charles Dickens

Although attendance was considerably less
than at the funeral home the night before,
the church in Cotton Grove was standing
room only by the time services started.
Fortunately, Miss Emily and I had arrived
early enough to get seats on the aisle.

The front left pew was occupied by the
honorary pallbearers, the school's cheerleading squad dressed in their red-and-gold
winter uniforms — long-sleeved jerseys,
short skirts, and flesh-colored tights. Joy
Medlin led them in on crutches, her pretty
face so pinched with pain that I found
myself thinking that this is what she would
look like at forty when the first flush of
youth was gone for good. Her face was a
reminder of how narrowly she herself had

escaped death only two months ago.

"Lucky to be alive," everyone said of the four teens who had not died in that car wreck. I wondered if the parents of the brain-damaged child still in a coma felt that way.

At three o'clock precisely, Duck Aldcroft and his assistant entered and closed the lid on Mallory's coffin. There were audible sniffs and sobs from the girls.

Moments later, the minister gave us the signal and we all rose as her parents and family were escorted down the aisle and seated in the right front pews. They were still somber-faced and grieving, but time had begun to do its work. Sarah looked resigned today and Malcolm's shoulders were straight as he sat down beside her and put his arm around her. Of the three of them, Charlie was now the one who seemed to be suffering most, as if it had only just fully sunk in that his sister was gone for good. I noticed that he left a small space between himself and Malcolm. No comfort for him there.

Mercifully, the service was short and formal. No tearful tributes from her friends, no failed attempts to make us smile by recounting humorous things Mallory once said or did, no popular songs to make her parents remember how she sang along with them.

A final prayer, then the coffin began its sad journey back down the aisle to the cemetery on the edge of Cotton Grove. The cheerleaders walked two by two out to the waiting cars, and then the family, followed by a general exodus of the rest of us.

When we got outside, we did not linger to talk. A chill rain had begun to fall, a rain that froze as soon as it hit the concrete walkways. I hadn't brought an umbrella and neither had Miss Emily.

"Do you want to go to the cemetery?" I asked.

She shook her small head decisively. "No, let's go home."

Once in the car with the heater running, though, we had to wait to get out of the parking lot because precedence went to those cars that would follow the slow-moving hearse out to the cemetery.

Like me, Dwight's mother had noticed the lack of warmth between Charlie and Malcolm and she commented on it while we waited. "I wonder if it's not because he looks so much like Jeff. There was always such a rivalry between those two boys when they were in school — over basketball, over Sarah."

"Before my time," I said, watching my wipers push wet ice granules off the windshield. "Dwight says that he had more natural ability than Malcolm but that Malcolm worked harder."

"True. Malcolm was always more focused, while it was easy come, easy go with Jeff. He had a sweet personality, though, and could charm his way out of trouble, whereas poor Malcolm never got away with anything, especially with that father of his. Shelton Johnson was a bully when we were in school together and he bullied Malcolm until Malcolm finally stood up to him about marrying Sarah. Malcolm had to struggle to make Bs. Jeff could have made straight As, but Cs were enough to let him play ball. Even then, he wouldn't work hard enough to make the starting lineup. I wasn't one bit surprised when I heard he'd fallen off that roof and killed himself. Everything came so easy for him, I'm sure he didn't think twice about the possible consequences of stringing lights in the dark on a steep roof. Sometimes I used to think that the only reason he went after Sarah was because he knew Malcolm wanted her so badly and he was jealous."

"Jealous?"

"Only human if you think about it. Malcolm's family was solid middle class. Jeff's daddy was a roofer. Malcolm was bound for Carolina and a white-collar life; Jeff was going to have his own truck and a hammer."

"But if they were best friends — ?"

"Best friends? Certainly they hung out together, but looking back on it, I have to wonder if it wasn't a case of 'keep your friends close and your enemies closer.' They may have liked each other at the start, but once Sarah came into it . . ."

"And she chose Jeff," I said. "That had to've hurt Malcolm."

Miss Emily shook her head. "I don't know if it was a matter of choosing Jeff or just that he was here and Malcolm was in Chapel Hill and Jeff sure could charm a smile out of a stone statue. Couldn't charm his way out of marriage, though, once Sarah came up pregnant."

"Did he want to?"

"Not really. To do him credit, I think he liked being married and he was certainly proud as a peacock when Charlie was born." She smiled. "He even gave *me* a cigar."

I laughed and put the car in gear as the last of the funeral procession left the parking lot. "I bet you smoked it, too."

She cut her bright eyes at me. "I didn't inhale, though."

Once out of the church parking lot, I drove a few blocks, then turned onto a street that was a shortcut over to the road home. I cornered just a little too sharply and felt the car fishtail. Luckily, there were no other cars near.

"Sorry about that," I said. "It's slicker than I realized."

"I'm in no hurry," she said mildly.

Considering that she's gotten more than one speeding ticket the way she floors her old trademark TR, I bit back the remark I could have made and said, "Tell me about Mallory. I keep hearing how perfect she was, and yet she could have spiked her own drink or stolen the Vicodin as easily as any other kid at the party, couldn't she?"

"In theory, I suppose," Miss Emily said, "but I never heard that she did drugs or touched alcohol, and I do hear things, Deborah."

If there was a touch of pride in her tone, she had earned it. From all I've heard from my nieces and nephews, very little goes on at West Colleton that Emily Bryant doesn't know about in time to do something if something needs doing.

"Did you hear whether Charlie was one of the older kids at the party?"

She shook her head. "Was he?"

"I don't know. That's why I'm asking. Or rather that's what Dwight's going to be asking. Somebody had to have slipped something in her drink can."

"Surely not her own brother," Miss Emily protested.

"He was jealous of her, wasn't he? Sounds like she came first in that family. Jessica told me that she was set to go to Carolina in the fall and that Malcolm planned a trip to Spain as her graduation gift. Charlie goes to Colleton Community College. Wonder what his graduation gift was?"

"Not a trip to Spain," she agreed.

"So there's at least one person who didn't think she was as perfect as everyone says."

"Two persons," my mother-in-law said quietly.

"You?"

"It sounds so awful to say this when right this very minute they're getting ready to lower her into the grave. It's like I'm throwing a shovelful of dirt on her coffin myself."

"But?"

"But no, Mallory Johnson didn't actually walk on water. She was everything you've heard — pretty, talented, intelligent, good

143

student, a friendly word for everyone. Sweet and thoughtful. Polite to her elders —"

"Didn't kick small animals or pull wings off flies?" I added cynically.

"Actually, she may have done a little bit of wing-pulling, but so subtly the poor fly didn't realize it was happening till it dawned on her that she could no longer fly."

"That's too metaphorical for me," I said. "Plain English, please?"

The windows were as fogged up as her words and I switched on the defroster. As the windows cleared, so did her meaning.

"Mallory could have had anyone she wanted, but she didn't want a steady boyfriend, which is not unusual these days. The kids don't pair off the way they still did when you and Dwight were teenagers. That doesn't mean there can't be some rather intense relationships within the group, and Mallory liked to mess with those. She was very open about it. Claimed she was just a little ol' tease who couldn't stop herself from flirting with every boy around, like it was all a joke. And because she didn't take it seriously, nobody else was supposed to. But sometimes the boys would be so dazzled, it spoiled them for whatever more ordinary girl they'd been perfectly happy with before."

I suddenly remembered Jess's quiet "Tell me a single guy in this school who *didn't* think she was hot."

"I think she enjoyed being Little Miss Wonderful just a little too much," Miss Emily said. "She worked hard at it and I daresay most everyone thought she *was* wonderful, but every once in a while I would catch a sense of . . . I don't know. Smugness? No, that's not the right word."

"Egotism?" I suggested.

"No." She was silent as the windshield wipers swept back and forth in front of us. "Complacency," she said at last. "That's what it was. Complacency."

When I got home, before taking off my coat and barely saying hey to Dwight, who was on the phone, I went straight to the dictionary on my desk: *"complacency: self-satisfaction accompanied by unawareness of actual dangers or deficiencies."*

CHAPTER 13

"Tell me what man that was whom we
saw lying dead?"
— *A Christmas Carol,* Charles Dickens

When I walked back into the living room,
unbuttoning my coat and fluffing my damp
hair, Cal was lying on his stomach beside
the tree to read a book and watch the train
go around. Dwight was still on the phone,
getting his Sunday afternoon update from
the various divisions within the Colleton
County Sheriff's Department. Learning
who spiked Mallory Johnson's Coke was
only one item on a very long list.

I knew that the narcotics squad was hoping to find and bust up a meth lab that was
thought to be operating somewhere near
Widdington, a little town east of Dobbs,
but so far that hadn't come off. A routine
traffic stop on the interstate had netted an
embezzler wanted in New Jersey, and New

Jersey was sending the paperwork down to begin the extradition process. Last week, a fire had destroyed one of those McMansions in an upscale housing development near Pleasants Crossroads. At first, everyone blamed a shorted-out plug on a Christmas tree. Now the experts were calling it arson, so ATF would be poking around in the ashes.

The owner had recently lost his job and was behind on his mortgage payments. The house was well insured.

"We're probably gonna see a lot more of this if the economy doesn't pick up," Dwight said.

Due to the icy roads, there were the usual number of fender benders. Three wise men had been stolen from the Christmas display in someone's yard, eight mailboxes had been smashed along a backcountry road down near Makely, and a chain-link fence had been cut open at the rear of Welcome Home, a building supply store outside Cotton Grove. There not being much call for lawn and garden items in the dead of winter, the owner could not say for sure exactly when it happened, but he was missing three push mowers, four one-hundred-foot garden hoses, a generator, and a concrete statue of Jesus.

147

Dwight shook his head in amusement as he repeated that last to me. "Who steals Jesus?"

"Any luck with the mistletoe?" I asked, pausing in the archway between the living room and dining area.

Cal giggled as Dwight put away his phone and stood to give me an exaggerated kiss. I looked up and there hanging from the arch was a healthy sprig of green. It still had a few glistening berries on it. You're supposed to pull one off every time someone gets kissed, and when all the berries are gone, no more kissing.

I left those berries right where they were.

"Dad was awesome," Cal reported. "We got enough for Grandma and everybody else. Lots of berries, too."

"How'd *you* do?" I asked.

"Pretty good. I hit the can the first time."

"He's got a good eye," Dwight said, smiling at his son. "We dug some cans out of Seth's barrels for target practice. Too bad I took all our trash to the dump yesterday."

As Cal chattered on about how amazing the whole experience had been, I made a mental note to buy a pad of paper targets for an extra Christmas gift. And maybe I'd get Robert or Andrew to sell us a few bales of hay and deliver them to the far side of

the pond. When Daddy was teaching us to shoot, he always made a point of setting up our targets on a downward slope so that there was no danger of the bullets traveling anywhere but into the ground. I figured Dwight would want to do the same with Cal.

And that reminded me: maybe Dwight would appreciate finding a box or two of extra cartridges under the tree if his own were going to be digging themselves into hay or dirt. Something else to add to that mental list.

Outside, that mixture of sleet and freezing rain continued to fall as twilight faded into darkness. Supper was a salad and toasted ham and cheese sandwiches, and I diced a little ham over some greens to take for my lunch tomorrow so that I could go shopping during my lunch recess.

"Long as you're making lunches," Dwight said, "how about fixing me a sandwich? Tomorrow's shaping up to be real busy."

"And both of you do remember what tomorrow is, don't you?" I asked.

"Tomorrow? December twenty-second?" He tried to look as clueless as Cal, who was shaking his head. "Is there a Hurricanes game? An eclipse of the moon?"

I laughed. "No, and it's not the opening

of snipe season either."

"There's no such thing as snipes," Cal said. He got up to check the calendar that hung on the side of the refrigerator. "Hey, winter begins today? I thought that was before Thanksgiving." His finger moved to the next square. "What's Ha-NOO-ka?"

"Hanukkah? The Jewish festival of lights," I explained and gave him an encapsulated version of the Maccabees, the miracle of the oil that lasted eight days, and the symbolism of the menorah.

"We're going to celebrate that tomorrow?"

"No," Dwight said. "Think about it, buddy. What were you doing this time last year?"

A sudden grin lit his freckled face. "Oh yeah. Y'all got married!" He paused and looked at us. "I guess I'm spending the night at Grandma's again?"

"You got it," his father said.

Because there was no school for him the next day, we put another log on the fire and watched a Christmas special that lasted till ten. Eyelids drooping, Cal didn't argue about going to bed, and I was ready for pajamas myself.

But Dwight was worried about his young trees, so we bundled up and went out with flashlights and hiking sticks to knock ice off the tender new twigs of the dogwoods and crepe myrtles he'd planted the length of our driveway before the weight of the ice could bow them down and snap the branches.

Pine branches at the edge of the woods were sagging almost to the ground. It's like dipping candles. Rain coats the needles, then freezes. More rain, another coat of ice. If the rain continued, by morning each pine needle could be glazed in a quarter-inch thickness of ice. Multiply that by the number of needles on a pine tree and their combined weight would leave the ground littered with snapped branches.

We walked along the drive, gently tapping the trunk of each small tree, and shards of ice tumbled down like broken glass. The wind and rain tore at our exposed faces and I was glad when Dwight's phone rang a few minutes after we got outside, so that I could retreat to the house before I was chilled to the bone.

I headed straight to our bathroom, shed my clothes, and stood under the hot shower till my circulation returned to normal. I had expected Dwight to join me, but when I walked back into our bedroom, he was still wearing his hat as he took his pistol out of the gun safe in his closet and buckled it on.

His badge was clipped to his jacket.

"What's happened?" I asked.

"Trouble with one of the Wentworths again. Two bodies out at a trailer on Massengill Road. No ID yet. Don't wait up for me."

CHAPTER 14

Foggier yet, and colder! Piercing,
searching, biting cold.
— *A Christmas Carol,* Charles Dickens

Major Dwight Bryant — Sunday night, December 21

Dwight reached the end of his long driveway and turned onto the hardtop that ran past the farm. *A dark and stormy night,* he told himself with grim humor.

Literally.

It was the dark of the moon so there was nothing to lighten the sky behind the solid gray cloud cover overhead. Rain mixed with sleet beat against the cab of his truck. Tree limbs sagged out over the narrow two-lane road, and the road itself was coated with ice. He was thankful for four-wheel drive, but mindful that even four-wheel drive is not much help if all four wheels are on ice.

Massengill Road was less than seven miles

153

from the farm, but it took him almost fifteen minutes to get there without sliding into a ditch whenever the truck fishtailed on a curve. Fortunately, it was all back roads and he met less than half a dozen vehicles on the way. They too were inching along cautiously.

There was no real need to look for a street address once he was in the vicinity. He could have followed the glow of blue and red lights that bounced off the low-hanging clouds, but the faded numbers on a rusty, dilapidated mailbox confirmed that this was indeed the dirt lane that would lead up to the house trailer occupied by one of the Wentworths.

The lane was rutted and almost washed out in places, but his tires grabbed the dirt with confidence and he easily reached the top of the rise, where he circled past two prowl cars and pulled in beside Detective Mayleen Richards's truck, which was parked next to Deputy Percy Denning's crime scene van. A red two-door Honda Civic and a black Ford F-150 pickup were nosed in next to the right side of the trailer.

Floodlights had been set up around the front of the mobile home and they illuminated the two forms covered in plastic sheeting that lay on the bare ground.

With her flaming red hair tucked inside the hood of her dark blue parka, Richards squatted off to one side and just beyond the yellow tape to watch while Denning sheltered under an umbrella and videotaped the whole area. She held a powerful flashlight in her gloved hands and played the beam at an angle as she slowly swept the yard. The ice-coated dirt sparkled in the rain and made it hard for her to distinguish what was there.

"On your left!" she called to Denning. "Is that anything?"

Being careful where he stepped, Denning moved over to the small brass object pinpointed by her torch and said, "Good eyes, Mayleen. Our first shell casing."

It lay just inside the cordoned-off area and Denning documented it in relation to the sheeted bodies a few feet away, then leaned in for a close-up. Deputy Raeford McLamb placed a marker on the dirt and carefully bagged and tagged the casing.

"Only one casing?" Dwight asked Richards when he was near enough to be heard.

She continued to sweep the area inch by inch with the angled beam. "Only one so far, sir. We're beginning to think the shooter cleaned up after himself." She paused. "Or herself. Seems to have missed that one,

155

though."

"Who called it in?"

In the cold night air, their breath sent out little puffs of steam when they spoke.

Richards stood and pointed her torch toward a light blue pickup parked beyond the floodlights on the edge of the scruffy yard. "His name's Willie Faison. He blew a point-ten when the responding trooper got here to check out his story. Says that Jason Wentworth owed him some money and he came by to collect it and found him lying there on the ground near his brother."

"He make a positive ID?"

"Sounded positive to me. Jason and Matt Wentworth."

Denning had finished with the exterior and had moved on toward the trailer itself. Dwight noted that the dwelling was dark and that the door was ajar. A cheap plastic wreath of white holly leaves sprinkled with silver glitter hung on the door. Denning seemed to be paying particular attention to the steps and the floor of the entryway.

"What are you seeing, Denning?" Dwight called.

"Not sure, Major, but it looks like someone tracked dirt in after it started raining."

Dwight lifted the yellow tape and ducked underneath. He, too, watched where he was walking and took care to step in the tracks already made by his deputies. Richards followed. He turned back the sheeting on the nearer body. The youth had fallen on his back and his right hand rested on a large bloodstain over his heart. A thin layer of ice had crusted over his face and clothes. Between the icy rain and the floodlights, the eyes of the green viper tattooed on the back of his hand seemed to glisten with life.

Dwight remembered that tattooed hand reaching for his pistol only a few days ago at West Colleton's Career Day. Afterward, Deborah had remarked that it was probably only a matter of time before this kid showed up in her court, just like his brothers before him.

No chance of that now.

He pulled the sheet back over the boy and turned to the second body. This one lay facedown on the frozen ground and had apparently been shot twice in the back. He, too, had been lying exposed long enough to be covered in ice.

"Looks like he was trying to run away," Mayleen Richards said.

Both victims were dressed in boots, jeans, flannel shirts, and pullover sweatshirts. Neither wore jackets.

"I'm guessing someone pulled up in front

157

here, honked the horn, waited for them to come out, and then gunned them down."

"Tire tracks?" Dwight asked. "Shoe tracks?"

"Far as we can tell, just Faison's," she said, illustrating with her torch where tires had circled close to Matt Wentworth's body. "He says he saw them lying there when he drove up and he got as near as he could without getting out of his truck. Soon as he realized they were both dead, he pulled up over there, then went inside to call 911 because his cell phone died on him yesterday. Or so he says. And of course, the trooper drove in over Faison's tracks."

A wisp of red hair had escaped from her hood and was now glazed with ice. She hunched deeper into her parka and shook her head pessimistically.

"It's too soon to tell when they were shot. If it happened this afternoon, the rain probably washed away any tire marks."

"Rigor?"

"Hard to say," she replied. "They're well on their way to being frozen like a side of deer meat."

"Well, let's see what Faison's got to add to all this."

By now, the rain had finished changing over into sleet and the wind had picked up

158

so that icy granules stung their faces as Dwight led the way over to the Toyota pickup truck. There was a dent in the door on the driver's side and the rear bumper sagged as if held on by baling wire. He rapped on the door, but there was no response from the man inside. He pulled open the door and saw Faison seated upright with his head back against two rifles that rested on the truck's gun rack. Loud snores reverberated off the cab's hard surfaces and the smell of beer hit them in the face. Three empty cans lay on the floor by Faison's feet and his hands clutched a fourth can even though it emptied itself across the man's jacket and pant legs.

"I'm guessing that no one thought to check whether he had more beer with him," Dwight said mildly.

"No, sir," Mayleen said.

From the embarrassment in her tone, Dwight knew that her face was probably flame-red.

"Not your fault," he said kindly. "That was the trooper's job."

He summoned that officer over and showed him the results of his sloppiness. To the young officer's credit, he didn't try to make excuses.

"I understand he blew a point-ten?"

159

Dwight asked.

"Yessir."

"So you'll be charging him with a DWI?"

"Yessir. I got here fifteen minutes after it was called in. He was here by himself, behind the wheel, with his keys in the ignition and the motor running to keep the heater going. No reason to think he hadn't driven himself here. And even if he'd drunk something else after calling, I didn't think he had time to get that drunk. I did flash my light over the interior, but I didn't see any cans, empty *or* full."

"You do a field sobriety test?"

"No, sir. Those bodies were my primary concern."

"What about his truck box?"

Embarrassed, the officer admitted he hadn't checked.

Dwight reached over and pressed the catch on the metal box clamped onto the truck bed directly beneath the cab's rear window. Inside were an assortment of plumber's tools — wrenches, pipe putty, a rusty plumbing snake, a heavy-duty flashlight with a broken lens, pipe clamps, and several elbow joints in various diameters. On top of those lay a billed cap in fluorescent orange, and an empty twelve-can beer carton.

"Your first homicide scene?"

"Yessir."

"Don't worry, son," Dwight told him. "I'm not going to write you up on this. You were probably concerned with securing the scene and calling in your report."

"Thank you, sir."

"Just take him in, book him, and see that he's sober by the time I get there in the morning."

"Yessir!"

It took three officers to pry Willie Faison out of the truck and into the backseat of the patrol car. As the trooper headed back down the lane, he had to pull aside for the EMS truck that had arrived to transport the bodies to the morgue.

Before they were loaded onto the truck, the contents of their pockets were bagged. Both had died with their wallets and car keys in their pockets.

"So robbery wasn't the motive," Dwight said, stating the obvious.

A strong odor of cigarette smoke was the first thing they noticed when they stepped inside the trailer. Next was the way at least one piece of clothing seemed to be draped over every chair. Neatness did not seem to be a virtue of the Wentworth brothers,

which made it hard to tell if the place had been tossed or not. In the living room, a wastebasket overflowed with beer cans, cigarette butts, and fast-food cartons, and the coffee table in front of the television was covered in more of the same.

The television was on and tuned to one of the outdoor hunting and fishing channels, and the ceramic gas bricks of a wall unit glowed red hot to compensate for the open door, but no lamps were lit, which probably meant that the shooting took place before dark.

"Let's have some light," Dwight said and flipped a switch.

The place seemed to have been furnished in castoffs. It reminded Dwight of the trailer where Deborah's nephew Reese lived: same mismatched flea-market furniture, same La-Z-Boy recliner, same big-screen plasma television. To be fair, though, Reese kept his place a lot cleaner and slightly less cluttered.

"Both brothers live here?" Dwight wondered aloud.

"Only one bedroom with one double bed," Denning reported from the rear of the trailer.

"Somebody get me an address for the parents. I know they live in Cotton Grove, but where?"

Richards opened the younger boy's wallet and read off the address on his driver's license.

"That sounds about right," Dwight said, heading out to the kitchen that was as cluttered as the rest of the trailer.

If anything was missing, it wasn't instantly apparent, and just as he reentered the living room, the television screen went black, as did the lights.

They waited a few minutes to see if the electricity would come back on, then Raeford McLamb shook his head pessimistically. "A tree's probably down across the power line."

Except for their flashlights and the portable floodlights, they would have been in total darkness, so they went back outside. As they passed the Honda and the pickup, Dwight said, "Y'all check out the vehicles yet?"

Upon receiving negatives from McLamb and Richards, he opened the door of the Honda. The door was frozen to the frame and he had to brace one foot against the car to wrench it open. A rabbit's foot and a pair of fuzzy green dice hung from the rearview mirror and schoolbooks were piled on the front passenger seat.

"Must be the younger kid's," said

McLamb.

They found a flat plastic baggie with about an ounce of marijuana under the floor mat. Other than that, the car yielded nothing immediately useful.

Same with the truck, but Dwight noted a gun rack. "Anybody see a gun inside?"

"I'll take another look," Mayleen Richards said.

The truck box on the pickup was locked and Dwight called for Jason Wentworth's keys. A half-inch sheet of ice went flying when the lid was lifted. Inside were some ropes, a tow chain, a bottle of motor oil, another of washer fluid, a nail apron with an assortment of rusty nails in the pockets, a hammer, a crowbar, a large monkey wrench, a bolt-cutter, a new-looking three-foot aluminum level, and a set of Allen wrenches in a shrink-wrapped orange plastic box that had never been opened. If these were the tools of the victim's trade, they were hard-pressed to decide what that trade might be.

"A jackleg handyman?" McLamb hazarded, stamping his feet to get some feeling back in his toes.

Richards came back and reported that there was no long gun in the trailer, but she had found a handgun in a drawer in the bedroom — a .38 special, fully loaded. "Lying there in plain sight if anyone opened the drawer."

They all knew that guns and televisions are the most commonly stolen items when a house is burglarized. This was looking less and less like a burglary gone wrong and more and more like deliberate murder where the only things taken were two lives.

"There's a little shed out back," McLamb said. "Why don't I take a quick look?"

He disappeared around the corner of the trailer and Dwight said, "I guess we're about through here for the night." He told Denning to take the two rifles from Faison's truck and process them. "Make sure one of them's not our murder weapon."

He turned to Richards and said, "Station one of the uniforms here. Tell him he can sack out on the couch inside if he wants as long as the doors are locked. No one's to come in except on my say-so."

Mayleen started to go, then hesitated. "Sir, you want me to notify his people?"

He gave her a tired smile. "Yeah, I'd love to hand it off to you, but I'd better do it myself. You go on home and thaw out."

At that moment, they heard McLamb call, "Hey, Major! Back here."

They followed the sound of his voice to a

ten-by-ten utility shed backed up against the rear of the trailer.

"Look what I found!" he crowed and flashed his light across three brand-new push mowers, several garden hoses, a small generator, and an array of power tools still in their original boxes. "I guess we know now what sort of work Wentworth did."

Dwight shook his head. "Wonder what he did with the Jesus statue?"

CHAPTER 15

At Christmastide, we must, directly or even by omission, . . . square our hopes with reality.

— *Christmas in America,*
Penne L. Restad

Major Dwight Bryant — Sunday night,
December 21 (continued)
Midnight and Dwight was a mile down the road before he began to see lights in the houses he was passing.

Bound to be more power outages tonight, though, he thought.

The sleet seemed to be lessening, but the accumulations on the ditchbanks glittered when his headlights lit them up, and more tree limbs would be falling, if not some trees themselves.

Cotton Grove sprawls along the banks of Possum Creek, a few miles north of the Knott farm and twenty-five minutes due south of Raleigh. The four-block-long mercantile center almost dried up before the state's population surge encouraged the town to turn the creek frontage into a park and bill itself as a place of small-town values (whatever those were) within easy reach of big-city attractions. Stores were restored to their 1920s look, ornamental iron street-lights were installed, and fast-growing crepe myrtles were planted along the sidewalks. The original oaks and maples that once nearly met overhead had been cut down forty years earlier when the streets were widened in the town's first attempt at revitalization.

These days, Main Street was one-way so that more nose-in parking slots could be created for shoppers drawn to the new businesses. During the early evening hours, tasteful wreaths trimmed in clear twinkle lights hung from each lamppost. A tall Christmas tree sat in the center of the park and kaleidoscopic reflections of its multicolored lights shimmered on the surface of the slow-moving creek. To save on energy costs, both sets of lights were turned off at ten when the last restaurants closed.

The old modest Craftsman bungalows that filled in around the business section had been snatched up and restored. Leafless wisteria or rambling roses now climbed the porch railings. In summertime they would flower and their hip new owners would brave the heat and sit out on the porches in their wicker rocking chairs to sip iced tea and try to look like natives. Here on this wintry night, a few houses had left their decorative lights on, and more than one roofline dripped with a fringe of electric icicles that were now coated with real ones.

Further out from the center of town, Craftsman gave way to cheap clapboard and asbestos siding, and although the yards were marginally larger, they lay along narrow side streets that were nothing more than clay and gravel. The address listed on Matt Wentworth's license proved to be a small board-and-batten ranch-style house in no worse condition than its neighbors. In fact, it struck Dwight as being a little neater, a little better cared for. A bush beside the front door sported multicolored Christmas lights, but the house itself was dark.

This was the worst part of his job, waking survivors out of a sound sleep to tell them bad news. Victor Wentworth had served a couple of prison terms for armed robbery and deadly assault, but even jail-hardened criminals can have parental feelings.

There was a doorbell and it actually

worked for he could hear it pealing somewhere inside.

A narrow slit in the curtains drawn over the front windows let him see that someone had switched on a light. A moment later, a light over the windowless front door came on and a woman pushed back the curtain and looked out at him.

"Who is it?" she called.

"Colleton County Sheriff's Department," he said, holding his badge so that she could see it.

"What do you want?"

"Ma'am, if you could open the door?"

She motioned for him to hold his ID closer, and after she had studied it carefully, she let the curtain fall back into place and he heard the door being unlocked.

"Mrs. Wentworth?" he asked.

"Yes. If you're looking for Victor, though, he's not here."

The door led directly into the living room and she gestured him toward a chair, then picked up a half-smoked cigarette from a nearby ashtray that was otherwise immaculate, lit it, and inhaled deeply. A hint of air freshener covered up the smell of smoke and he couldn't help noticing how tidy the room was. A small artificial tree stood in the corner and a few wrapped gifts were piled around the base.

"I've not seen him since the week before Thanksgiving and all I want for Christmas is to hear that you've found him and put him under the jailhouse."

She was barefooted and wore an oversized Duke sweatshirt that came down to midthigh. Rather shapely thighs, actually. Midforties, he guessed, with shoulder-length brown hair that was streaked with gray. Her face had the worn quality of someone who had smoked too many cigarettes and stayed out in the sun too long.

"Why would we do that, ma'am?"

She sat down on the blue couch across from him. "Aren't you here about those checks he stole?"

She did not speak with a Southern accent and her diction was better than any of the Wentworths he'd dealt with in the past eight years since coming back to Colleton County to be Sheriff Bo Poole's second in command.

"Sorry, ma'am. I don't know anything about stolen checks."

"You're not working with the Raleigh police?"

"No, ma'am. I'm here about your sons Jason and Matt."

"Stepsons," she said. "What've they done now?"

"I'm sorry to have to tell you this, but they've both been killed."

All the color drained from her face, leaving it a pasty gray.

"How?"

He didn't sugarcoat it.

She crushed the cigarette out in the ashtray and leaned her head back against the couch to listen silently. When he finished, she said, "Those poor little bastards. I hope to hell he's satisfied."

"Ma'am?"

"Victor. I knew his first wife died, but he didn't mention any kids till after I married him. He'd already kicked Hux out of the house, but Jason was thirteen and Matt was eleven. All three of those boys were wild as turkeys and Hux was just plain mean. Had a nasty temper, but Jason and Matt could've been saved. I wanted to be a mother to them, but Victor wouldn't back me up. He let them get away with murder and just laughed at me when I tried to give them some discipline. He disrespected me and let the boys diss me, too."

She opened a drawer in the coffee table, took out a crumpled pack of menthol cigarettes, and lit one. "Of course, it didn't help

172

that I was still drinking back then. I know I'm partly to blame, but I found Jesus and I've been sober for three years now. I tried, Major Bryant. I really tried. It was probably too late for Jason, but I thought I was starting to get through to Matt. He wanted to quit school and I talked him out of it."

She glanced at the slender little tree in the corner. "I got him some new clothes and that cell phone he's been dying for. The one with a slide-out keyboard." Tears leaked from her eyes and glistened on her cheekbones. "And he put something under the tree for me last week. First time ever. Oh, damn you, Victor Wentworth! All three of your sons killed? I hope you fry in hell!"

A box of tissues sat on one of the end tables and Dwight got up and brought it to her.

"Thanks," she said, "but I'm okay now."

She wiped away the tears, pushed her hair back away from her gaunt face, and stood up. "I'm going to make a pot of coffee. You want some?"

"Yes, please. And I wonder if I could look at Matt's room?"

"Down the hall, on the left," she said, gesturing with her chin. She set the tissues back in place and went out to the kitchen.

Dwight opened the door she had indicated

and found a perfectly normal teenage room — unmade bed, clothes piled on the chair and dresser top, posters of rock groups that had appeared at local concerts taped to the walls. On the single bookshelf over a cluttered desk were a paperback dictionary, a West Colleton yearbook, some comic books, a cigar box that held a handful of arrowheads, a go-cup half full of pennies, and a Little League trophy with his oldest brother's name engraved on the brass strip.

The only time Dwight had seen Hux Wentworth was when that young man lay dead on a bathroom floor, shot down by the kid he had terrified when he crashed through the locked door.

He took down the yearbook and found Matt Wentworth's picture among last year's freshman class. As he had suspected, the kid had flunked his first attempt at freshman year. When he started to put it back on the shelf, a newspaper clipping fell out. It was a picture of Mallory Johnson and her court from a feature story about West Colleton's homecoming game that had run last month in the *Clarion,* Cotton Grove's little weekly newspaper.

The desk had two drawers and Dwight found more comic books, a comb, pencils and pens, a deck of playing cards, some dice, old school papers marked in red, some snapshots of the boy standing proudly by his Honda, and, at the very back of the second drawer, an unopened package of condoms.

The package was crumpled, as if it'd been kicking around in that drawer for at least a year, and Dwight wondered if the kid had ever gotten lucky before he died.

A bedside table held an alarm clock, a lamp, and a radio that played tapes and CDs. Inside the drawer were a stack of CDs, all rap except for a surprising one of traditional Christmas carols. Underneath lay a small plastic folder. He opened it and frowned. One side held the boy's picture, the other a picture of Mallory Johnson. Both were head shots and appeared to be last year's school pictures.

He carried the pictures and the newspaper clipping out to the kitchen, where Mrs. Wentworth sat at the table, stirring sugar into her coffee. A second mug awaited him.

He thanked her, took a sip of the strong black brew, and said, "Can you think of anyone who would do this to the boys?"

She shook her head. "I haven't seen much of Jason this winter. He came for Thanksgiving. I tried to make it nice for them. With Victor gone, it was a good day. He *was* working for a roofing company, but Matt said he got fired right after Thanksgiving. They accused him of stealing copper pipes out of some of the houses they worked on, but they couldn't prove it. Matt said he was drawing unemployment."

"Matt say if he or Jason had any enemies?"

Again, that shake of her head.

"What about friends?"

"There was a Barbour boy that came here once in a while. Nate Barbour. That's the only one I ever knew. And he had a girl-friend, but I never met her."

Dwight spread the pictures on the table between them.

"Were they friends?" he asked.

"Friends?" Mrs. Wentworth smiled indul-gently. "That's Matt's girlfriend. They've been going together since October."

Dwight tried to keep the incredulity out of his voice. "Mallory Johnson was your stepson's girlfriend?"

"Is that her name? He wouldn't tell me." She pulled the news clipping closer and frowned in concentration as she read it. "She was homecoming queen?"

With her finger, she traced the words beneath the picture. " '. . . daughter of Mr. and Mrs. Malcolm Johnson.' That the same Malcolm Johnson that has the insurance

company?"

Before Dwight could nod, she said, "No wonder he didn't want me to know her name. He said her parents didn't like him and — Omigod! That's the same girl that wrecked her car last week and died a couple of days later!"

"Yes."

"I saw her picture in the paper, but I never connected it to this picture. Of course, I only saw it that once before he put it away." Tears filled her eyes again. "So that's why he was so torn up these last few days. Those poor, poor kids."

Dwight cradled the mug in his hands and said, "Tell me about them."

"I don't really know anything. Matt didn't talk about her much. It was a couple of months ago. I went into his room to ask him something and he was sitting on the edge of the bed putting her picture in this folder. I asked him who she was and first he told me it was none of my business, but I asked was she his girlfriend and he said yes, but she hadn't finished breaking up with her old boyfriend yet and they had to keep it a secret."

"You say he was upset these last few days?"

She nodded. "And Thursday night, he

didn't go to work. He was in his room when I got home, and when he came out to use the bathroom, his eyes were red. I thought he was coming down with something, but he yelled at me to leave him alone, so I did. He wouldn't say what was bothering him and I never put it together that the Johnson girl who died was the girl in that picture."

"Did he go to school last Tuesday?"

She nodded. "And then he went to his job at the Food Lion. He spent the night at Jason's so they could get up early Wednesday morning to go deer hunting. Jason has a friend that has a deer stand over in Johnston County — Willie Somebody-or-other — and they needed to be in it before the sun came up." Her smile was rueful as she drained the last of her coffee and got up to top off their mugs. "Only thing you can get a teenage boy up that early for."

Dwight covered his mug with his hand. Any more and he'd never get to sleep tonight. "So Matt ditched school on Wednesday?"

She shrugged. "I know, I know. But he said they never really did anything the last few days before Christmas and he promised to go on Thursday and Friday, so I didn't fuss. You have to pick your battles."

"Do you know where he was Tuesday night?"

"I told you. He would've worked till nine, then spent the night at Jason's."

"He didn't go to a party with Mallory Johnson?"

She looked uncertain. "I don't know. No, probably not, because she was alone in her own car, right? If they were together that night, they would have been in his car. Unless they were trying to keep her family from knowing?"

"Mrs. Wentworth, are you absolutely sure they really were seeing each other?"

She looked at him indignantly. "Why? Because she was a rich Johnson and he was a Wentworth? Matt was a nice-looking kid, Major Bryant, and he could be real sweet when he wasn't trying to out-tough his brothers."

"He was sixteen. A freshman. She was eighteen and a senior. She was an honor-roll student headed for Carolina. He wasn't."

"We didn't talk a lot," she said slowly. "Heck, we didn't even see each other a lot. I get home from work around five-thirty. He worked from five to eight or nine, depending on how busy they were, and he didn't always come straight home. Week-

179

ends, he'd be out with her or Jason. I did ask him last Saturday if he was still seeing her and he said yes. It was her birthday and he'd given her a necklace and took her to see the new Tom Cruise movie."

"Which night was that?"

"Friday. Friday, a week ago."

Dwight wrote down the date, the name of his friend, and the location of the grocery store where Matt Wentworth worked as a bagger several nights a week.

"When did you last see him, ma'am?"

"Friday morning when I left for work. He was getting dressed for school."

"What about Jason?"

She frowned and knitted her brows in an effort to remember. "Sorry. I know he came by one evening since Thanksgiving, but I can't think exactly when."

"I don't suppose you remember who it was that Jason worked for?"

Her answer surprised him. "Barefoot Roofing here in Cotton Grove."

A few further questions added nothing to his picture of either boy. Dwight stood up to go, but Mrs. Wentworth sat there numbly as the ramifications of the murders sank in. "I guess it'll be up to me to bury them," she said.

CHAPTER 16

It was a clear morning with the sun not yet high over the horizon . . . everywhere around was an unbroken carpet of thick snow. The world looked very pure and white and beautiful.
> — "The Adventure of the Christmas Pudding," Agatha Christie

I had been asleep almost three hours when I awoke to realize that Dwight was trying to ease himself into bed without disturbing me.

I turned over and reached for his hand. "It's okay, love, I'm awake."

"Sorry," he said, and put out his arm to draw me nearer.

"What happened tonight?" I asked.

"Remember the kid at school the other day? The one with the snake tattooed on his hand? Matt Wentworth. He and his brother were the victims."

"Jason Wentworth," I murmured.

"That's right. I forgot you said you had him up on a hunting violation this fall. You confiscated his gun, didn't you? That's why we didn't find one tonight."

"You expected one?"

"His stepmother said he went hunting Wednesday."

"Without a license?" I could remember the case, I could remember that the young man was angry at losing his gun and his license. What I couldn't remember was his face, and that made me sad.

He described the deaths of the Wentworth boys, their stepmother's reaction to their thrown-away lives, and Matt's claim that he had been hooked up with Mallory Johnson. When he finished, he was silent for a moment, then said, "On the way home, I got to thinking about what I was doing at that precise time last year."

"At one-thirty in the morning?"

"Yeah."

"Weren't you asleep?"

"No. Cal and I were bunking at Mama's. In the room Rob and I used to share. He was asleep, but I was wide awake, thinking about you. Us. Wondering what our life was going to be like. Wondering if Jonna would let me have Cal more and if that really was going to be okay with you."

I started to protest, but he tightened his arm around me.

"You don't have to say it, Deb'rah. I know you love him. It isn't how we wanted to get him, but this hasn't been a bad year, has it?"

"*Bad?* Oh, Dwight, do you really have to ask?" I hugged him hard. "It's been the best year of my life."

"And we've been on the same page with Cal, haven't we? I mean, he doesn't sass you, does he? Or disrespect you?"

"Of course not."

"And you do know I'll always back you up?"

I pulled away from him and propped myself up on one elbow so that I could look him in the eye. "Listen to me, Dwight Bryant. Cal is no Matt or Jason Wentworth and you are certainly no Victor Wentworth, okay? He may answer me back once in a while, but it's no more disrespectful than when he answers you back. It's totally normal and I don't take it any more personally than you take it when I bitch at you."

He smiled. "You don't bitch at me."

"Yes I do," I told him. "You just don't notice."

Next morning, I awoke at dawn to blue

skies and a rising temperature. As we feared, some of the new little trees were bent double and pine limbs at the edge of the woods were touching the ground. But the icicles hanging from the eaves of the house were melting fast, and according to the radio, our forecast was for temperatures in the high fifties by Christmas Day.

I put the coffee on, then drove Dwight's truck down to the mailbox for the newspaper. I should have worn sunglasses. Once the sun hit all that ice, it was eye-dazzling. A warm west wind was blowing and every gust that hit the trees sent a shower of ice tinkling down like slivers of broken crystal. I found myself trying to remember a Navaho chant I once read in a Tony Hillerman book:

Beauty before me.
Beauty behind me.
With beauty all around me, I walk.

Yes!

Dwight was dressed for work and pouring himself a mug of coffee when I got back, and he poured one for me. "Happy anniversary," he said. "What's it like out there?"

"Glorious! Put your jacket on and grab

your sunglasses and let's go for a quick walk."

"I really need to get moving," he said, but he followed me outside anyhow.

We keep a selection of hiking sticks propped in a corner between the porch and the house outside, and we each took one to help us keep our footing on the ice. The coffee was strong and hot and steam rose from our mugs as we walked down the drive, following the ruts I'd broken in the ice with the truck. As I might have predicted, Dwight wanted to tap his stick against the young crepe myrtles and dogwoods, and with each gentle blow, so much ice fell that the trees slowly began to right themselves.

Before we'd gone very far, we heard Cal call, "Hey, wait for me!"

He had put boots and a jacket on over his pajamas. With Bandit racing back and forth between us, he grabbed a hiking stick and soon caught up with us. Whacking the trees and watching the ice shower down delighted him.

When we circled back around the house toward the pond, Cal ran along the side of the garage and used his stick to knock down a long line of icicles. At one point, he slipped, fell into a spirea bush, and spooked a rabbit none of us realized was there. Bandit let out an excited yelp and immediately streaked after it. The rabbit beat him to the woods and both animals disappeared into the underbrush.

The pond was frozen all around the edges, but the pier had begun to absorb the sun's heat and a flip of a stick was enough to send long sheets of ice off the boards and into the water.

Eventually, Dwight looked at his watch and reluctantly turned back to the house.

"Yeah, me, too," I said.

"Awwww." Cal looked at us wistfully. "I wish y'all didn't have to go to work."

"Sorry, buddy," Dwight said and whistled for Bandit.

The dog came, but he was dragging his heels, too. I knew how he felt. I wasn't ready to go get in my crate either.

An hour later, car keys in hand, I was taking my lunch salad out of the refrigerator when the phone rang.

"Deborah?"

"Barbara?" We talk on the phone so seldom, I almost didn't recognize her voice.

"Oh, good," she said. "I was afraid you'd already gone, too."

"Cal and I were just about to walk out the

door," I told her. "What's up?"

"Has Dwight left for work yet?"

"About forty minutes ago."

I heard a disappointed sigh. "Is there something I can do?"

"I hate to ask you," she began, and from the tone of her voice I knew she really did hate having to ask me whatever it was, "but Zach's already at work and Emma and Lee have gone Christmas shopping in Raleigh. I went out to start my car just now and it won't turn over, so I'm wondering if I could ride with you to Dobbs this morning."

"Certainly, but don't you want to let's see if we can jumpstart it?"

"You know how to do that?"

"Sure," I said, amused by the surprise in her voice. I mean, what's so complicated about attaching battery cables?

"That's all right. I'll let Zach do it when he comes home. The thing is, I have a meeting with some of the county commissioners in less than an hour and I just can't take the time to worry with this car."

"No problem," I told her. "I'll pick you up, we'll drop Cal at Kate's, and be at the library in plenty of time."

Cal had already put Bandit in his crate with a new strip of rawhide and he slung his duffel bag into the backseat of my car and crawled in after it. The children were off from school until after New Year's, but this morning was a final work day for the teachers, so Miss Emily was going to pick him up this afternoon and keep him overnight.

Barbara was looking at her watch and pacing back and forth when we got there, and she had the door open almost before I brought the car to a full stop.

"I really appreciate this," she said, fastening her seat belt. "Today's my last chance to try and talk the commissioners out of cutting county funds to the library."

She greeted Cal, who responded shyly. Of my five sisters-in-law who live out here on the farm, she's probably the one he knows least, but she made an effort and by the time we reached Kate's, he was chatting normally. In response to one of her questions, he even confided that while he had enjoyed the Harry Potters, he really liked the Ender books better.

Because Barbara was in a fidget, I didn't linger at Kate's; just dropped a kiss on Cal's head when Kate came to the door and told him I'd see him tomorrow morning, "but call if you need us, okay?"

"Okay," he said cheerfully.

"You and Dwight have something on for

tonight?" Barbara asked, as we headed for Dobbs.

I knew she was only making polite conversation, but it beat riding in silence.

"Just dinner," I said. "It's our anniversary."

For some reason, that surprised her. "Has it really been a whole year?"

"Time flies when you're having fun," I said lightly.

She let that pass. "Cal seems like a bright little boy. A real reader, too."

I told myself that she didn't mean to sound insulting. "He takes after his grandmother," I said. "Miss Emily loves books."

"I know. Every time the bookmobile goes out to the school, it always takes a stack that she's requested. She probably goes through three or four a week."

"Guess I won't try to give her books for Christmas, then. But maybe you can help me about Cal. I bought him *Old Yeller.* What else do you think he'd like?"

"*Old Yeller*'s good. Has he read *To Kill a Mockingbird* yet?"

"Isn't that too old for him?"

"Not really. Sounds as if he's reading well above grade level."

"I don't mean that. I mean, won't the issues of race and lynching go over his head?"

189

"You'd be surprised. He's ten, right?"

"Nine and a half."

"Third grade?"

I nodded.

"He rides a school bus, Deborah. He has to have heard the N-word and probably a lot of worse racist language besides. *Mockingbird* could be a great springboard for you and Dwight to talk to him about it."

"Okay," I said. "I'll add it to my shopping list. Thanks."

The weather and the dazzling ice carried us for another mile or two, making me ever more conscious that this was about the longest one-on-one conversation Barbara and I had ever had. Lacking anything else, I said, "How's Emma doing after yesterday?"

She sighed. "That was really hard for her. Hard for all the girls. To put on their uniforms and walk in together, and then out at the grave — ? You didn't go to the interment, did you?"

"No."

"It was dreadful. Her parents had arranged for each girl to have a red and a yellow rosebud. They had to sing the West Colleton fight song and then lay their roses on her coffin. It was ghastly. Those girls can never again sing that song without thinking of Mallory. It really wasn't fair of her dad to

may have spiked her drink at a party."

"A party that she should have left as soon as it became clear that the parents weren't at home. Thank goodness Lee and Emma didn't stay a minute longer than they had to."

"They're nice kids," I said as we reached the outskirts of Dobbs and turned onto the main street. "You and Zach have done a good job with them."

"Well, thank you," she said, sounding slightly startled by the compliment. "It's a fine line we parents have to walk these days, isn't it? Too easy and they have no standards. Too hard and you either crush their spirits or turn them into liars and sneaks."

"Seems to me y'all've found the right balance," I said and realized that I meant it. She might come down a little stricter than I would, but it didn't seem to have hurt Lee or Emma. "I just hope Dwight and I can find that balance with Cal."

"You will. You're good with kids. The way you do things with them. The cookies. Letting them come over and swim and fish and tramp through your house to use the shower. No wonder they're —"

She broke off abruptly.

"No wonder they're what?"

"Fond of you," she said quickly. "All the

kids are."

I was pretty sure that wasn't what she had intended to say, but it still made me smile. "I'm sorta fond of them, too."

"The nice thing is that you can show it."

There was such a wistful note in her voice that it drew me up short. Before I could respond, she gave a rueful laugh. "I guess I've always been a little jealous of that."

I didn't know what to say. Jealous of *me?* When all this time I thought she was being judgmental and disapproving?

We passed the courthouse and I pulled into the narrow alley that led to the library's parking lot. As I stopped the car at the rear entrance, she started to thank me and I put out my hand. "Good luck with your meeting."

"Thanks. And thanks for the ride."

"My pleasure," I said honestly. "I'm sort of glad your car conked out on you this morning."

She laughed. "You know something? I am, too."

CHAPTER 17

Now, being prepared for almost anything, he was not by any means prepared for nothing.
— *A Christmas Carol,* Charles Dickens

Colleton County Sheriff's Department —
Monday morning,
December 22

Bo Poole leaned back in his black leather chair and listened as his chief deputy filled him in on the shooting deaths of the two Wentworth brothers.

There was a time when the news media would have been all over this story. An *N&O* reporter and a photographer would have trundled out from Raleigh, a helicopter from one of the local TV stations would have hovered over the sheeted bodies, and there would have been at least one stringer for the little county newspapers out at the site before the EMS truck got there.

Whether the lack of coverage was due to layoffs in staff, the high cost of helicopter fuel, last night's foul weather, or simply that the deaths of two petty criminals were not worth more than a few inches of newsprint and a scant thirty seconds in the roundup of local news, the department's spokesperson reported that her online posting of the bare facts had triggered only a couple of phone calls from the media.

"Richards and Dalton are over there now to see if we missed anything last night, and McLamb's gone to the autopsy," Dwight Bryant told his boss, a small trim man with thinning gray hair and sharp bright eyes that missed nothing. "Someone from Welcome Home is going to meet them at the trailer with serial numbers and invoices to ID their stolen merchandise."

"How's Mayleen working out as a detective?" Bo asked. "Her daddy's still mad with me for giving her a job. Thinks she wouldn't be hooked up with that Mexican if I'd turned her down."

"I'm glad you didn't. She's an asset. Good with computers, pulls her weight without grumbling"

"Her personal life doesn't get in the way?"

"Now, Bo, you know well and good I don't get into that unless it does get in the way. I do know it hurts her that her family won't accept Mike Diaz, but she doesn't talk about it unless someone asks."

"He good to her?"

Dwight shook his head. "Tell you what. She should be back before lunch. Want me to have her stop in here and catch you up on her private business?"

Bo laughed. "Okay, okay. So what about this Victor Wentworth?"

"I've got a call in to Wake County to see if they have a warrant out for him. Not that he's of concern to us on this."

"No, but it's always good to know," the sheriff agreed. "Hound dogs like the Wentworths always come crawling back under the house. Wish I could find it in my heart to feel sorry about his boys, but you know good as me, Dwight, they were gonna wind up a drain on the county one way or another."

He thumped the files he'd had his secretary pull. Both boys had records. Jason's was longer, of course. Hunting deer illegally, two speeding tickets, a DWI, a conviction for petty theft, another for assault, and he was currently out on bail awaiting trial for yet another assault. Nineteen years old and he had already been a guest in their jail. With his record, if he had been found guilty for this second assault, he could have pulled real prison time.

At sixteen, Matt had only three citations as a non-juvenile: one for speeding, one for underage drinking, and one for an altercation in the West Colleton High School parking lot.

Bo sighed. "Maybe Miz Wentworth was right. Maybe she could've stopped him from walking down the same road as his brothers, but I never met a Wentworth I thought I could trust. You?"

"No," Dwight admitted. "But they keep on getting themselves killed, we're gonna run out of Wentworths. And whoever shot these two is just as bad, so we need to find him."

"Any connection to the Johnson girl's death?"

Dwight shrugged. "I'd really be surprised if he was actually hooked up with her. Mayleen's interviewed some of the kids and got the names of everyone at the party. His wasn't one of them. But he did tell his stepmother that she was his girlfriend, and he was as upset after her death as if she really was. Now they're both dead. Coincidence?"

"I never much cared for coincidences," Bo said.

"Me either. I called my mother first thing this morning. Matt was still a student there. She's going to pull his attendance record for me. See if he was in school on Friday. I don't see how the deaths are related, though. It's more likely that one of them pissed off the killer and Matt was upset because he knew this was coming down the pike toward them."

"Which one was the primary target?"

"Too soon to know," Dwight said. "But as long as we're talking coincidence, the older Wentworth boy, Jason? Up until Thanksgiving, he worked for Mallory's half brother's grandfather. Her mother's former father-in-law."

"Anybody talked to him yet?"

"Who? Nelson Barefoot?"

"Naw. The half brother, what's-his-name."

"Charlie? No. I thought I'd try to get up with him after I talk to Willie Faison. See if there was another reason Faison was at the Wentworth trailer besides what he told the trooper before he passed out."

"Be real nice if we could get this all wrapped before Christmas," the sheriff observed.

Dwight grinned. "And here I thought you were too old to still believe in Santa Claus."

■ ■ ■ ■

Downstairs, he had the duty officer bring Willie Faison to an interview room, and he looked the young man over carefully when he came in and took a seat across the table.

Twenty years old. White. No visible tattoos or piercings. Black hair, slender build, an inch or two under six feet. Unmarried. No priors. Currently employed as a plumber's helper in a small three-man company in Cotton Grove. Despite registering a .10 on the Breathalyzer at the scene of the shooting, the only issue was his age, and even if Ellen Englert Hamilton were sitting in the courtroom, he would receive no more than a suspended sentence. If he could afford the services of a halfway competent attorney, he might even avoid that. With four empty beer cans in his truck, it could be argued that he had not drunk a thing until after finding the bodies.

Hell, it might even be true.

On the other hand, he was a full year away from the legal drinking age.

With the vitality of youth, Faison was clear-eyed and rested after his night in lockup. Dwight advised him of his Miranda rights and he immediately waived them because he was anxious to be released so that he could get to work before his boss docked his wages. He was also still reeling from finding his friend Jason and Jason's younger brother lying dead on the frozen ground. "I'd been calling him all weekend 'cause I wanted my stuff back and —"

"Stuff?" Dwight asked him.

"I mean, my money. The money he owed me."

"No, son," Dwight said mildly. "You said stuff. What stuff?"

The young man shrugged. "He borrowed some stuff from me."

Dwight waited while Faison's unease became more apparent.

"A jacket and a pair of coveralls," he blurted out. "I wanted 'em back."

"What else?"

"That's all," he said, not quite meeting Dwight's steady stare.

"Why didn't you take them when you went inside the trailer to call 911?"

"I don't know. I guess I was too freaked. I mean, they were out there on the ground in the freezing rain. For all I knew, whoever did that could have still been hanging around. I just wanted to get out of there and get back in my truck. What was so wrong about that? I could've just driven off, but I didn't. I waited till the trooper got there, and what's the first thing he does? Makes me blow in that damn Breathalyzer with Jason and Matt blown to kingdom come. Where's my truck anyhow?"

"Calm down," Dwight told him. "Your truck's still out at the trailer and I can have someone drive you out to get it. First, though, I need you to answer some questions and write out a statement."

"And who's gonna write me an excuse for my boss?" young Faison grumbled, but in the end he was cooperative.

He described how he and Jason Wentworth had been friends since grade school. They fished and hunted together, played poker and pool with some other guys from Cotton Grove — he wrote down their names. Yes, Jason could be a horse's ass at times, but on the whole, he was a good guy to watch your back. "Everybody liked ol' Jase."

"What about that assault charge?" Dwight asked him.

"The guy that swore out a warrant on him? Hell, he was the one threw the first punch. Jason was just defending himself."

"What about the things in the shed back of the trailer?"

Faison frowned. "What things?"

"The lawn mowers and tools y'all stole

202

from the Welcome Home store."

"No way, man! That was nothing to do with me."

"You knew about it, though, didn't you?"

"Not till last week when he wanted me to help him sell it. He thought some of the guys on my crew would want to buy a cheap push mower. Look, yeah, maybe I used to do stuff like that with Jase, but not anymore. I got a good job and a girlfriend. My aunt says we can live with her till we can get a place of our own."

"When did you last see him?"

"Monday when he came by and I loaned him that cold-weather gear."

"Not since then?"

"Not to see. I talked to him on the phone Thursday night. He said he'd drop my things off on Friday, but he never showed or called or nothing. I kept calling, but he wouldn't pick up."

He finished writing out his statement about finding the bodies around ten, dated and signed it, then slid it back across the table.

"I hope y'all locked my truck and left somebody out there to guard it. It's got my tools and my guns."

"About those guns," Dwight said.

Faison was instantly wary. "Yeah?" he

203

asked cautiously.

"I had them brought in so we could examine them more closely. We're not going to find that one of them is the gun that shot those two boys, are we?"

"Hell, no! No way in this world, man!" He pushed his chair back till he almost banged into the rear wall in an abrupt and involuntary denial.

"So tell me about them," Dwight said.

Faison's jaw tightened in mulish denial. "Nothing to tell."

"Fine. We'll just wait and see what my detective finds to tell me. I'll let the officer know you're ready to go back to your cell."

"Wait a minute! Don't I get a phone call?"

"Sure. You want to call your mama or your boss or your attorney? 'Cause it looks like you're going to be here for a while."

The youth slumped back in his chair. "Okay, okay. I loaned Jason one of my rifles to go deer hunting. Big damn deal. He saw a big buck last week and wanted to bag it before the season ended."

Dwight gave a cynical shake of his head. "He was worried about the end of deer season when he shouldn't have been hunting in the first place? He'd already lost both his own gun and his hunting license."

"That's why he needed to borrow mine.

My gun, I mean. Not my license. I wouldn't give him that."

"Matt told his stepmother they were going to use his friend Willie's deer stand over near Clayton. Your stand?"

"Huh? No, I don't have no stand."

"So you weren't with them Wednesday morning?"

Faison stared at him blankly. "Wednesday morning?" he said slowly. "No, man, I was working all day Wednesday."

Dwight had the feeling that he was missing something, but Faison had settled on that story. He had lent Jason a rifle and that's why he was out at the trailer last night. The gun and the hunting cap were all he'd taken from the place. He hadn't seen Jason since he borrowed the gun on Monday, honest, and now could he please make that phone call?

Dwight instructed the officer to take Faison before the magistrate on duty and get her to set his bail. "And then let him use the phone."

With a little luck, Willie Faison could still get in half a morning's work.

Back upstairs, Dwight stuck his head into the room that Percy Denning had fitted up as a lab so that not every single piece of evidence had to go to the SBI's lab in Garner. "You can compare the prints on Faison's guns with those of the two victims," he said. "Faison says he lent one to Wentworth. And anything on the shell casing you found?"

"It's a .32. We'll have to wait and see what the ME finds in the bodies."

A handgun then, and not a rifle.

"Richards called. She and Dalton just dug a slug out of the side of the trailer that's consistent with the line of fire. Says it looks like a .32 to her, too."

"Jason Wentworth have a cell phone?"

"I didn't see one. Want me to call Richards and ask?"

"Yeah. And check if there's a land line. See who called him the last few days."

He started to leave, then paused. "What about the Johnson girl's phone?"

"Not much on it. She must have cleared its memory earlier that evening. We've asked for the records, though, and the company's promised to email them to us today."

"When they come, see if any of the called numbers correspond to a phone connected with Matt Wentworth's name, okay? He told his stepmother that Mallory Johnson was his girlfriend."

Denning rolled his eyes. "In that case,

there'll be at least eight or ten calls a day to him."

Dwight grinned. Denning had a teenage daughter.

Twenty-five minutes later, after making a few phone calls of his own, Dwight turned into one of the older neighborhoods on the edge of Cotton Grove. This street had attractive, well-maintained homes, each on a spacious landscaped lot, each surrounded by mature oaks and maples. Unfortunately, last night's ice storm had laid one of those tall oaks across the roof of a two-story brick house and there was a gaping hole where one of the branches had broken into the attic.

Dwight pulled in behind a truck whose panel door read "Barefoot Roofing Company" and got out to join the group of people who stood watching as a man with a chainsaw cut up a tree that would easily measure two feet in diameter. He expected to recognize Nelson Barefoot from his high school years of playing basketball with Jeff Barefoot, and he was fairly certain that one of the men was an adjuster from Triple J Insurance, but he was surprised when the owners of the house turned as he approached and greeted him by name.

"Well, hey, Dwight!" Diane Hobbs called above the ear-piercing whine of the chain-saw. "You come to watch the fun?"

Her husband, Randy, an older man and a former magistrate, stepped forward to shake his hand. "Haven't seen you since my retirement party, young man," he said loudly. "How's life at the courthouse these days?"

"Not half as exciting as this," Dwight told him, gesturing toward the roof and the tree that was rapidly becoming a pile of firewood and sawdust. The clean acrid smell of freshly cut oak drifted on the morning air.

"Did you ever see such a mess?" asked Diane, who had a closer acquaintance with the tall deputy.

Abruptly, the chainsaw went silent as the workman paused to stack the logs he had cut from the branches and to roll the larger rounds out of his way.

Petite and bubbly with brown hair and snapping brown eyes, Diane Hobbs was the hygienist at Dwight's dentist. Twice a year, he leaned back in that padded chair and opened wide so that she could poke around with a pickax and jackhammer and scold him for not flossing twice a day. "And don't think I can't tell, mister."

Up on the roof, one of Barefoot's men was clearing away the fast-melting ice while another used a broom to sweep aside the water before it could drip into the attic and soak through the ceiling below.

"That's our bedroom there on the corner," Diane said, loosening the buttons of her bright red jacket as the sun warmed up the morning air. "When that tree hit in the middle of the night, I thought we'd been bombed or something. Thank goodness the weather's supposed to stay mild and sunny through the weekend. It won't feel much like Christmas, but at least our bedroom won't get soaked. And this nice man's going to make it all good as new by Christmas morning, aren't you?"

She gave Nelson Barefoot a winning smile, but he was not willing to commit to her agenda.

"Now, honey," said Randy Hobbs. "You know that Carl here's got to give us an insurance estimate first."

"I do know that," she said sweetly, "but *you* know it's got to be done no matter what Carl's estimate and you also know Mr. Barefoot's the best roofer in the county, and we don't want to mess around with second best, now do we?"

Amused, Dwight watched Diane finish wrapping her husband and Nelson Barefoot around her little finger and heard the big gruff man allow as how he reckoned he could get on it tomorrow or the next day.

"We'll let the sun finish drying it good today," he said, "and I'll send one of my boys over this afternoon to put a tarp over it from the ridgepole down so y'all won't have to look at the stars tonight."

"Stars?" Diane glanced at her husband. Her face was serious, but her eyes sparkled with mischief. "Long as the hole's already there, honey, why don't we let's put in a great big skylight so we can lie in bed and watch the moon?"

"Moon?" Randy yelped. "Skylight?"

"Oh, no, now, Miz Hobbs," Barefoot said, tilting his brown felt hat back on his head. "There's no way I can put you in a skylight before the first of the year and you're not gonna want to live with that hole that long, are you?"

"I guess you're right," she said, feigning reluctance to give up the idea. "So you'll definitely be here tomorrow to fix it back the way it was?"

"Yes, ma'am."

As Barefoot moved away to speak to his men, Hobbs said, "You wanted to ask me about something, Dwight?"

"Actually, I'm here to talk to Mr. Barefoot," Dwight said, turning to follow the

210

roofer, "but it's been good to see you again. Hope y'all have a nice Christmas."

"You, too," they said and went to help the woodcutter clear away some of the smaller branches.

"Did you say you wanted to see me?" the roofer asked, pausing until Dwight caught up with him.

Before Dwight could reply, the shriek of the chainsaw split the air again and Barefoot motioned for Dwight to follow him around to the back of the house where they could hear each other's words.

They sat down on a low brick wall that edged the rear terrace. Barefoot pulled out a pack of cigarettes and offered it to Dwight, who shook his head.

"Never picked up the habit?" the older man asked. "Good for you. I've tried to quit a hundred times and just can't seem to do it."

He took his time lighting the cigarette with an old-fashioned kitchen match. As the smell of sulphur and tobacco smoke drifted between them, he looked Dwight up and down. "I heard you were back and working for the sheriff."

"Eight years now," Dwight agreed.

"That long?" He inhaled deeply and let out a thin stream of smoke. "Heard, too, that you married Kezzie Knott's daughter."

"Yes, sir."

Barefoot took another slow drag on his cigarette. "Been a long time since you and Jeff played ball together. You still have that hook shot?"

Dwight smiled and shook his head. "Don't have much time for that anymore."

"Too bad. I guess you know about Jeff?"

"Yes, sir. I was real sorry. Must have been rough on you and Mrs. Barefoot."

"And Sarah. Been thinking about her a lot this week. Losing Jeff and now losing her daughter like that."

"They say her son's changed his name back to Barefoot."

"Yeah, that made Edie and me real happy. Lots of Barefoots in the county but I'm the only son of an only son and our line of Barefoots would've died out if Charlie had stayed a Johnson. What's particularly good is that Sarah didn't try to talk him out of it. I think she knows she made a mistake all those years ago when she let Malcolm Johnson have his way."

"Sounds like you don't care much for Malcolm," Dwight said mildly. "Wasn't he good to Charlie?"

"He didn't beat the boy or let him go hungry or naked," Nelson Barefoot said.

212

"All the same, Charlie's living with Edie and me now till he finishes school." He sat with his arms on his knees and watched the ash on his cigarette grow until it fell to the ground. "But you didn't come here to talk about Charlie or Malcolm either, did you?"

"No, sir. I was wondering what you could tell me about one of your workers. Jason Wentworth?"

"Wentworth?" Barefoot gave a scornful snort. "He doesn't work for *me*. I fired his ass a month ago. Lazy, shiftless, *and* a thief. Lucky for me, I'm bonded and insured for dishonest employees. I knew he'd been in a little trouble, but he shot me a line about wanting to stay on the straight and narrow, learn a good trade. You might not know it, but Jeff went through a stretch when he did some stupid things right after high school, but he straightened up once he and Sarah were married and the baby came along. I'm always willing to give boys like Wentworth a second chance, but if they need a third or fourth chance, they'll have to go find it with somebody else. Fool me twice? I don't think so. So what's he done now to get you asking questions about him?"

When Dwight told him, Nelson Barefoot shook his head grimly. "Well, I'm sorry to hear that. Maybe if I'd got him a little earlier . . . ? It didn't have to be like that, did it, Dwight?"

"I guess we all make choices, sir. Can you think why anyone would shoot him down?"

Barefoot frowned, stubbed out his cigarette, dug a shallow hole with the heel of his work boot, and carefully buried the butt. "Sorry, son, but I never get into the personal lives of my men unless I'm invited, and Jason Wentworth didn't send out any invitations. I didn't even know he had a brother. Least not a younger one."

Dwight thanked him and walked past the dismembered oak tree to his truck. As he reached for the door, he heard Diane Hobbs call to him above the noisy chainsaw. "Dwight! Wait a minute!"

She carried a clear plastic pint-sized box tied with silver ribbons. "Am I not right in thinking today or tomorrow's your anniversary?"

He nodded. "Today, actually."

The Hobbses had come to the dinner party Bo Poole had thrown for them last December and to the wedding as well.

She thrust the box into his hands. "These are some of my chocolate-covered fried pecans. I was going to say merry Christmas, but happy anniversary's even better. I hope

you're taking Deborah somewhere fancy tonight?"

"Tomorrow's our fancy night," he said.
"There's a dinner dance out at the country
club."

She beamed. "Y'all're going to that? We
are, too! Now you be sure and save a dance
for me."

Although it was now heading for lunchtime,
another quick call to Spivey's Plumbing
confirmed that Mr. Spivey was still working
on some busted water lines out at the
nursery where Dwight had bought twenty
crepe myrtles back last spring.

He spotted the plumber's truck parked
beside an empty greenhouse and pulled his
own truck up next to it. Inside, he found
two men repairing a network of thin black
plastic pipes that lay on the ground in an
inch or so of muddy water.

"My stupidity," Herman Forrest told
Dwight. "The main water supply comes in
here and then feeds to the other green-
houses. I've never insulated the pipes here
because I've never let the temperature drop
below fifty, but with the slowdown in the
building trade and fewer big landscaping
orders, I left these two houses empty and
never once thought about them freezing till

I noticed that the sprinklers and misters in the other houses weren't working."

Dwight commiserated with him, but before he could explain why he was there, the nurseryman said, "So. You here to start redeeming your gift certificate?"

"My what?"

Consternation flooded the man's face like the water on the dirt floor of this greenhouse. "Oh, Lord! Please, Major Bryant. Forget you heard me say that."

With a broad smile, Dwight said, "I'm getting a gift certificate for Christmas?"

"When I saw you drive up, I was sure that your wife gave it to you already and that you were here to pick out another tree or something."

Still smiling, Dwight shook his head.

"Look, promise you won't tell her I shot off my big mouth, please?"

"She'll never hear it from me."

"So how can I help you? I don't suppose you came to get *her* a gift certificate?"

"No, I want to talk to Mr. Spivey, but as long as I'm here, maybe I'll take a look around later and see what you've got blooming besides poinsettias."

"Sorry, Major. This time of year, it's all poinsettias."

■ ■ ■ ■

Although he had continued to work while Dwight and the nurseryman talked, the plumber, a short burly man of late middle age, had obviously been listening; and when Forrest walked away, he stood up and wiped his hands on a muddy rag. "Oren Spivey," he said. "I'd offer to shake hands but then you'd have to go wash yours."

"Major Bryant, Mr. Spivey. Sheriff's department. Sorry to interrupt your work."

" 'Sokay." He turned and gave his assistant some instructions, then led the way through the greenhouse and out into the sunshine. "You'd never know it was freezing last night, would you? This is what I love about North Carolina."

"You're not from here?" Dwight asked politely even though the man's accent had given him away as soon as he opened his mouth to speak.

"Michigan. Been here twelve years and I'm never going back." He gestured toward the mess of mud and pipes visible through the open door. "In there's a piece of cake compared to crawling under houses in minus-five-degree weather, using blow-torches to thaw a line that's buried a foot

217

deep in frozen mud. So how can I help you, Major?"

"I was wondering what you could tell me about one of your workers. Willie Faison?"

"Willie? He's been with me about a year now. Hard worker. Reliable. At least he was reliable till this morning. First time he's missed without calling in."

"Part of that's my fault," Dwight said and told him how Faison had discovered the bodies of the two Wentworths and then wound up drinking himself into oblivion. "See, the thing is, their stepmother thought they went hunting with Faison one day last week. You remember what day that was?"

Spivey frowned. Sunshine fell full of his broad square face and he squinted when he looked up at Dwight. "Sorry, Major Bryant. Somebody's got their times mixed up. Willie put in a full eight hours every day last week."

"You're sure?"

"Absolutely."

Dwight thanked him and walked slowly back to his truck, trying to reason it out. It would appear that Faison had told the truth when he said he did not go hunting with the Wentworths on Wednesday. Dwight had interviewed enough young men like Faison to have a pretty good sense of when they were lying. He was quite certain that something about that Wednesday deer hunt was a lie.

But what?

The deer stand?

Trespassing to hunt on posted land?

CHAPTER 18

"We'd a deal of work to finish up last night . . . and had to clear away this morning."
— *A Christmas Carol,* Charles Dickens

Court for me that Monday morning meant handling first appearances for those who had been arrested over the weekend. State law requires that they be brought before a district court judge within ninety-six hours. The jury box held today's first group of orange jumpsuits. All of them male. All charged with felonies.

I smiled at them pleasantly.

"Good morning, gentlemen," I said. "My name is Judge Knott. If this is your first time here, let me explain that this is not a trial court. You have the right to silence, and it's not in your interest to talk about the facts right now with the DA sitting there. If you go to trial, that's when you'll get a chance to be heard. This session is designed to review your bond, to tell you what you're charged with, and to inform you as to what your punishment can be. This does not mean that's the punishment you'll actually receive. That will be determined if you do wind up going to trial after talking to your attorney and if you are found guilty there. When your name is called, please step forward. I'll read the charges against you, tell you the maximum penalties, and ask if you're going to hire your own attorney or need the court to appoint one for you."

Most felons know to keep their mouths shut until they've spoken to an attorney, although someone will occasionally insist on trying to plead guilty then and there. I review their bonds and set a court date, usually about fifteen days out, depending on the arresting officer's next regularly scheduled court date. The whole transaction takes about three minutes.

When the felonies were disposed of, the jury box filled again with misdemeanors and minor charges and I went through my spiel once more, something I would do each time a new group was brought up from the jail below.

Repeat offenders know the drill, of course.

And for misdemeanors, they'll step right up and plead guilty without the benefit of an attorney, but first-timers are less confident about the outcome.

Like today.

I looked at the defendant who was next in line. White. Male. Twenty-nine. Brown hair. A good haircut now growing out, which would indicate that he was in the early downward slide toward losing his personal pride. Half defiant, half sheepish. The shuck I held in my hand — the envelope that held his record and that I would not look at until I'd reached the disposition stage — was so thin that this was probably his first offense.

"Mr. Anderson, you're here today charged with public intoxication," I said. "I see that you were arrested Friday night, but you appear to have sobered up now. Do you intend to plead guilty or not guilty?"

He hesitated. "Not guilty?"

In a whisper that was clearly audible to everyone in the courtroom, the young black man standing behind him said, "Fool! You wanna get out today? Say guilty."

He was right. The usual penalty for a minor charge like this is three days in jail plus court costs. If I give credit for time served, it saves taxpayer dollars and frees up space in the jail.

Anderson shrugged. "Guilty, ma'am."

"I sentence you to three days in jail," I said, "and give you credit for time."

During the morning break, I ran into superior court judge Ned O'Donnell at the drink machine.

"How's it going?" I asked. I knew he was presiding over a jury case, vehicular homicide by someone who had lost his license in a DWI case a few months before he smashed into another car and killed the mother of two small children. "You look harried," I told him.

"Thanks," he said dryly as he popped the tab on a Dr Pepper. "I have Ellen Hamilton sitting on the front row as close as she can get to the jury box. I've already had to warn her twice about huffing out loud every time Zack Young tries to make a point for the defense, but I can't stop her from rolling her eyes and making faces."

Young is one of the best attorneys in this part of the state and I'm sure Ellen is well aware of his win record in juried DWI cases.

"Better your court than mine," I said and returned to my own in a lighter mood, ready for the next group of prisoners.

With the holidays upon us, many were there because they had started celebrating a little too early and a little too well. Several had used their five-finger discount to go Christmas shopping, while others had cut, shot at, or punched out a fellow citizen, but most of them limited their words to "Guilty" or "Not guilty" when asked for a plea and to a simple "Yes" or "No" on the question of an attorney, and things moved along at a fast clip.

When I first announced that I was going to run for the bench, Daddy was so opposed that it added another row of bricks to the wall that had grown up between us since my mother died. He hadn't wanted me to study law in the first place. He thought there were too many unsavory characters wandering in and out of law offices, as he well knew, having wandered in and out of them many times himself back before I was born, when he was actively running a large bootlegging operation.

If he'd had his way, I would have stayed under his protective wing, teaching Sunday school or kindergarten, until he delivered me virginal and innocent into holy matrimony with someone who would be equally protective. It was bad enough that I was an attorney, representing clients who might or might not be innocent, but at least they

224

were men and women who could afford my services and who could technically claim to be upstanding pillars of the community. As far as he was concerned, district court handled the dregs of humanity, and he did not want his baby girl mucking around in a cesspool.

Eventually, we reconciled enough that I could tell him about the miscarriage of justice that motivated me to run, and he even wound up using a combination of influence and blackmail to help me onto the bench. He's still not happy about it, though; and I haven't been able to convince him that trying to give justice to people who may never have had their fair share is the most satisfying career I could imagine.

Which is why doing first appearances never bores me.

I read through the charges, asked my questions, set court dates, and made sure the paperwork was in order so that there would be no holdup on my part that would prevent any eligible prisoners from a chance to be back in their own clothes by Christmas morning.

When the last paper slipper had shuffled out of the courtroom and I had signed the last document, both hands of the clock over the rear door stood straight up on twelve.

I tapped my gavel. "Court is adjourned till one-thirty," I said and scooted out before anyone could grab the sleeve of my robe and hold me up.

Three minutes later, I was in my car, headed for the sprawling outlet center near the interstate just south of Dobbs.

The parking lot out there covers three or four acres and finding a space is not normally a problem. We're about halfway between New York and Miami, though, so the place was jammed today with out-of-state license plates attached to huge RVs. Christmas week is when the whole East Coast seems to play fruit basket, and this is a logical place to stop for lunch and grab some last-minute presents at discount prices.

A loudspeaker was booming out "Let It Snow, Let It Snow, Let It Snow," but here at midday, the air was so mild when I opened the door that I left my heavy coat in the car so it wouldn't slow me down and hurried over to the card shop, where I immediately picked out another roll of wrapping paper and a bag of stick-on bows. With everything else that was starting to pile up, I'm grateful that Santa Claus leaves all his presents unwrapped, but Dwight and I still needed to wrap the odds and ends that we're giving Cal.

My family is so large that everyone's name — children and adults alike — goes into a hat and we draw them out at Thanksgiving amid much secrecy. If you draw the name of someone in your own immediate family, you put it back or exchange with someone else.

I had drawn Will's name this year. For years, he's run his auction and antiques business by the seat of his pants, aided by nothing more than an eye for quality and some avaricious common sense, and yeah, okay, maybe a few cut corners. His shabby old building, a former tobacco warehouse, burned down last year. He used the insurance money to replace it with a slightly smaller, slightly nicer place, and he's become more interested in learning to identify what passes through his hands. Will is never going to go so upscale that other dealers quit coming around, hoping to find unexpected bargains, but his wife Amy told me that he'd actually started reading up on some of his finds. I called a bookstore in Raleigh and a clerk recommended an encyclopedia of silver manufacturers with detailed illustrations of hallmarks, reduced to $19.99.

I immediately gave her my credit card

number. Even with postage and tax, it was under the family's twenty-five dollar limit. *And* it arrived gift-wrapped.

Theoretically, we can't exceed that, and we are not supposed to gift anyone else, but of course there are always exceptions to any rule. Every year, Daddy sits with a pile of presents heaped up around his chair, and every year he says, "Now I *know* y'all didn't all draw my name."

And there's no way that Zach and Haywood aren't going to exchange little tokens with Adam and Herman. Twinship trumps ordinary siblings, but those are the only family-sanctioned exceptions.

Up until last year, though, I had no spouse and no child, so nothing was said when I gave my nieces and nephews funny Christmas cards with money tucked inside — a single bill whose value depended on their ages. Cal and Dwight's names had both gone into the hat last year, but I still sneaked and gave the kids their cards. Happily, my brothers and sisters-in-law were so accustomed to my ritual that only Barbara called me on it.

"If you must give them something, just give them the cards," she'd said, and then added somewhat sourly, "They get a bigger kick out of your cards than the money anyhow."

That was nice to hear, because I don't give one-size-fits-all cards. I aim for a funny zinger geared to each kid's personality or interest and then doctor them up. Reese, for instance. He found a wounded buck by the side of the road one year, someone else's trophy animal, and tried to hide it in the van of his truck. The buck revived and tore Reese and the interior of his truck to bloody shreds. I got him a card that featured an inebriated stag with an eight-point rack that read, "Buck up, deer! It's Christmas!" and glued a tiny strip of his tattered upholstery to one of the antlers.

I can waste as much time on picking out the perfect card as I would on picking out something more conventional. I still didn't have one to celebrate Annie Sue's new electrician's license or Jackson's athletic scholarship, but for Robert's grandson Bert, whose incisors hadn't grown back in yet, I lucked into a musical card that played "All I Want for Christmas Is My Two Front Teeth."

With forty minutes of my lunch recess gone, I spotted a card that featured an elaborately decorated Christmas tree. I pressed on a little bulge at the base of the tree and tiny LEDs began to twinkle. Perfect for Annie Sue.

Still nothing for Jackson, though. I finally gave up and bought a baseball-themed birthday card that had potential if nothing else presented itself in the next couple of days.

Precious time was eaten up waiting in line to pay and then more waiting in the sporting goods store, where I bought paper targets for Cal and a box of cartridges for Dwight. When I hiked back to my car, my watch read 1:18.

Lunch was a hasty forkful of my ham salad whenever I had to stop at a traffic light on my way back through town.

"Isn't eating a salad with a fork while you drive just as dangerous as texting on a cell phone?" asked my internal preacher.

"Give it a rest," said the pragmatist, who hates getting lectured. *"She's doing twenty-five miles an hour, not fifty-five or sixty."*

"All the same," said the preacher.

"Yeah, yeah, yeah."

I convened the afternoon session at exactly 1:33. Not too bad considering that I'd had to freshen my lipstick and got stopped in the hallway to accept congratulations from Judge Luther Parker for making it through a full year of marriage.

"You do know, don't you, that some people here were betting it wouldn't last that long?"

"So how much did you win?" I asked.

He grinned. "Lucky for me, betting's against my religion. I'd've lost big-time."

Between last-minute settlements and plea arrangements, I had finished everything on the day's calendar by four o'clock and was ready to call it a day when I was asked to sign a final document. After twenty-three years of marriage, Marian Louise Bledsoe-Jernigan and Frederick Spencer Bledsoe-Jernigan had decided to give each other a divorce for Christmas.

All the paperwork had been completed. The division of marital property had already taken place. No alimony was requested and their children were grown, so there was no question of child support.

"Your Honor," said Mrs. Bledsoe-Jernigan, "please note that I am asking to legally resume my maiden name."

I read through her application to change her name back to Marian Louise Bledsoe.

"Granted," I said.

"Hey!" said Mr. Bledsoe-Jernigan. "What

about *my* maiden name? I mean, my birth name?"

To his relief, I told him that he had the right to resume his former surname, too, and that I would incorporate the changes in the decree.

When I first came to the bench, the state did not provide for this circumstance. Until the General Assembly rewrote the law, a man was allowed only one legal name change per lifetime. In taking a hyphen, he would use up his one change. I still remember the bemused smile on the face of an ex-wife when her cheating husband realized that her name was legally linked to his in perpetuity, and that if the new wife-in-waiting wanted to take his name, it would have to be the hyphenated name.

I'm fairly sure that he was one of those who pushed for the change in Section 1 of G.S. 50-12.

Phyllis Raynor had clerked for me that afternoon. After we finished with the Bledsoe-Jernigan papers, we waited around for another half hour in case anyone else showed up needing a judge's signature.

"Y'all get many requests for name changes?" I asked her as we kicked back in our chairs.

Except in divorce cases, they are normally handled by the clerk of court's office and it's considerably more complicated. In addition to a hefty filing fee and filling out a two-page form, the petitioner has to submit a copy of his birth certificate, a valid photo ID, and a notarized criminal history record check for every county or state he's lived in within the past ten years. Changing one's name is not something to be entered into lightly.

"Several," Phyllis said. "My first was right after I started working for Mr. Glover. He had a weird Polish name — like eight consonants and only one vowel — and he was tired of nobody being able to spell or pronounce it. These last few years we've had a run by young men who want to change their names for religious reasons. Mr. Glover tries to talk them out of it because so many have come back and wanted to take up their original names again and he can't let them. And just this past spring, we had a young man who'd been adopted by his stepfather when he was a baby and he wanted to take back his birth name. Mrs. Brewer did the paperwork on it for him."

I nodded. "Charlie Barefoot."

"You know him?"

"Not really. Portland mentioned it to me

when we were talking about his sister — his half sister, that is. She's the girl who was killed in a car wreck last week."

"Really? Too bad right here at Christmas." She did not speak callously, merely as someone who had no personal connection. "What's his legal standing right now? I mean, if both parents suddenly dropped dead without a will?"

"His mother and his stepfather?"

"But it's not his stepfather, is it? Technically, I mean. Wasn't he legally adopted? Changing your name doesn't cancel out your adoption, does it?"

"No, of course not," I said. "You're right. And without a will, he would be legally entitled to everything a natural child would."

"And now he's the only child left," said Phyllis as she began to gather up her files and close down the computer. "Are they rich?"

"Certainly comfortable, I think. The father's a partner in Triple J Insurance."

"Well, yes, then," she said with a laugh. "I'd say that's pretty darn comfortable."

CHAPTER 19

"I don't know what they're doing out there. Playing some game or other, I suppose. I've always been so afraid, you know, that these young people would be bored by our Christmas here. But not at all, it's just the opposite."

— "The Adventure of the Christmas Pudding," Agatha Christie

Major Dwight Bryant — Monday afternoon, December 22

As long as he was almost in the neighborhood, Dwight decided that he might as well swing past the house and make himself another ham sandwich to replace the one he'd left back in the office. Besides, even warmed-over breakfast coffee would taste better than the weak dishwater he could get at any Cotton Grove fast-food joint.

Two white trucks were parked by his back door when he got there and Bandit was out of his crate, wagging his docked tail happily from the top step. Inside, he found Reese and Annie Sue at the kitchen table with half-eaten sandwiches on paper towels in lieu of plates. The decimated ham sat on the counter with bread, mayo, and lettuce they had pulled from the refrigerator.

"Oh, hey, Uncle Dwight!" Annie Sue said brightly when Dwight walked in on them. "Want me to make you a sandwich?"

"You sure there's enough left?" he asked. He noted that the coffeemaker was now empty, that the door of the microwave was ajar, and that two steaming mugs sat beside their paper plates.

"No problem," said Reese. He jumped up and flourished a sharp knife while Annie Sue slathered mayonnaise on the bread. "In fact, I think I'll have another one, too, if that's okay."

"Help yourself," Dwight said, amused. He should have known that the labor for upgrading their circuit breakers wouldn't come totally free and hoped Deborah didn't have plans for the leftover ham because there clearly weren't going to be any leftovers once Reese got through. He washed up at the kitchen sink and started a fresh pot of coffee.

"So how's it going?" he asked them when

they were all seated around the table and the smell of newly made coffee filled the kitchen.

"Fine," Annie Sue said. "We decided to install another box to accommodate the new breakers and give you some extra space if you ever want to wire another room or add a shed or something out back."

In retrospect, Dwight would realize that he should have been suspicious of her innocent-sounding remark, but it sounded logical, so he just said thanks and turned to Reese. "I hear you saw a big buck down in one of the back fields the other day?"

"I didn't actually see him. Just his tracks. The dewlaps left such a deep mark, though, that I'm sure it was a buck. If I get him, I'll bring y'all some of the meat."

"So," said Annie Sue with what he would later recall as studied casualness. "You working in the area today?"

"No, I'm on my way back to Dobbs. Just had some people in Cotton Grove I needed to talk to."

"Anything to do with the Wentworth brothers getting shot yesterday?" Reese asked.

"You heard about that?"

"Matt was in the same class as Ruth and Richard," Annie Sue said. "They were texting back and forth when we were over at Uncle Seth's just now, finishing up on his circuit breakers."

Dwight got up to pour himself more coffee. "They have anything to say about why he might've been shot?"

Reese, his mouth full of ham and lettuce, shook his head and held out his cup for a refill.

"What about the older boy? Jason? Y'all know him?"

He saw Reese glance at Annie Sue, who immediately turned brick red.

"Stop it, Reese!" she said. "It wasn't funny then and it's certainly not funny now that he's dead."

"What?" asked Dwight.

Reese grinned. "She thought he thought she was hot."

"I did not!" that sturdy young woman snapped.

As Dwight continued to look at her inquiringly, she gave a what-the-hell? shrug.

"Don't listen to Reese. See what happened was, you know the Huckabees? Live over on Forty-eight?"

Dwight nodded.

"Last summer they added on a couple of rooms so her mother could come live with them, and we got the job to wire it. Jason

Wentworth was one of the roofers, and yes, he did come on to me a little, but I'd heard about his reputation and I kept it light. He knew it wasn't going anywhere, but he still kept hanging around."

"And then a reel of copper wiring went missing," Reese said.

"We're not saying he took it," Annie Sue said, "but after that, we kept the truck boxes locked even though it was a pain in the neck to have to unlock them every time we needed something."

Dwight started to tell them how Nelson Barefoot had fired the older Wentworth boy for stealing, but at that moment the door from the garage opened and he saw the startled faces of Ruth and A.K., his brother-in-law Andrew's kids, with their cousins Richard and Jessica, two of Seth's. Haywood's sons, Stevie and John, were right behind them and they, too, seemed surprised that Dwight was there.

"We were passing by and saw the trucks," Steve said smoothly.

"We're thinking about taking in a movie in Garner," Jess said

Dwight didn't give their story a second thought. Dirt lanes spiderwebbed the farm and everyone used them as shortcuts. Besides, this gave him an opportunity to ask the kids still in high school about Matt Wentworth on an informal basis. Despite his Army years, he had gotten back home often enough that he had known all of these children from babyhood. The family resemblance between them — blue eyes, hair ranging from blond to light brown — was so strong that they could have been siblings as easily as cousins; and after he married their fathers' baby sister, they had segued smoothly from calling him Mr. Dwight to saying Uncle Dwight.

In answer to his questions, they told him that, yes, the shooting was a cause of much texting within the West Colleton student body, but none of the cousins had really known the dead boy beyond sharing one class or another with him this past fall.

"He was actually a little older than us," said Richard, "but he got left back in grade school and again last year."

"Any of y'all ever hear that he was hooked up with Mallory Johnson?"

They hooted at the idea.

"In the first place, Mallory didn't hook up with anybody," said A.K., a gangling eighteen-year-old with a perpetual appetite, as he spread a slice of bread with mayo and folded it around some lettuce leafs.

Fourteen-year-old Richard looked up

from nibbling at the shreds of ham left on the bone. "And even if she did, it wouldn't have been a loser like Matt Wentworth. Her dad would've had a fit."

Ruth, a freshman like Richard, nodded. "Emma said Mallory told the cheerleaders that she wasn't going to let herself get interested in anybody until she was off at Carolina where her dad wouldn't be hovering every minute. I don't think Mr. Johnson missed a single game that she ever cheered at."

"Yeah? Was he at Tuesday's game?"

"I guess. We didn't go," they told Dwight.

"Jess and I went," said A.K., "but I didn't notice."

Jessica shook her head. "Me either."

"Who were his friends?" he asked.

They shrugged and then came up with the names of a couple of kids who might have sat at the same table in the cafeteria. One of them was the name Mrs. Wentworth had mentioned, Nate Barbour. On the whole, though, they thought he was a loner, which pretty much squared with Dwight's impression.

"What about the alcohol that Mallory had in her system?" he asked. "What're people saying about that?"

More shrugs. "Nobody's saying anything.

Mallory didn't drink and she didn't take drugs. Not that anybody knew about anyhow. If someone slipped her something else at Kevin's party, it was probably Vicodin. Joy said none of hers were missing from her purse, but Kevin says someone took his mom's pills out of her medicine cabinet."

"Who's Joy and why is she on Vicodin?" Dwight asked.

"Joy Medlin. One of the cheerleaders," said Ruth.

"She was in that bad wreck right before Halloween," Jessica reminded him. "The one that killed Ted Burke and Stacy Loring. And Dana Owens is still in a coma. They say she's been flatlined from the beginning and her dad thinks it's time to pull the plug, but her mom's not ready for that yet."

A momentary pall settled over the cousins as the lingering effects of that tragedy hit them anew.

"And Joy Medlin's taking Vicodin?" asked Dwight.

Jessica nodded. "She's had a couple of operations on her ankle, but she's still on crutches and she's still in pain. She says she's going to wean herself off over the holidays even though there are times when it hurts too much."

"And she was at the party?"

242

"All the cheerleaders were except for Emma, and even she was there for a few minutes."

"Yeah, I heard about that," Dwight said with a grin for Annie Sue.

He filled a go-cup with coffee, told the kids to be sure and put Bandit in his crate before they left, and headed back to Dobbs. He did not see the purposeful looks they shared as the door closed behind him, nor did he hear Stevie say, "We brought extra shovels. Where're you planning to run the line?"

As he walked down the hall to his office a half hour later, Dwight met Raeford McLamb, who had spent the morning over in Chapel Hill. "Oh, hey, boss. I was just coming to report on the Wentworth autopsies." He held up a couple of neatly labeled plastic bags. "Thirty-twos, just like we thought. Two in the older boy, one in the younger one. No surprises except that the shooting took place earlier than we thought. A *lot* earlier. Richards tell you?"

Dwight shook his head.

"Friday morning."

"What?"

"Honest to god, Major. The kid had a time-stamped receipt from a breakfast place

243

on the edge of town. Nine forty-eight Friday morning. Blueberry pancake special with bacon and eggs. Eaten there, not take-out. The diener ran the gut and says he died about an hour later. Between ten-thirty and eleven-thirty at the very latest. Too bad he didn't take a little longer to eat breakfast, huh?"

"Or go to school like his stepmother thought he did," Dwight said grimly.

They walked on into the detective unit together, where they found Deputy Mayleen Richards working on the sheets of phone records Mallory Johnson's service provider had sent them. McLamb had called her an hour earlier from Chapel Hill and she had immediately passed that updated information along to officers who were out questioning Jason Wentworth's neighbors.

Brushing a strand of red hair from her eyes, she thumped the papers on her desk and said, "I tell you, Major, it's getting a little scary how much information these phone companies keep on you. I wonder if people would be so indiscreet if they knew their text messages were being saved?"

Technology was always a trade-off between convenience and privacy, thought Dwight, as he looked at the printouts of phone numbers that Richards was trying to put names to. Good when they needed to track someone's activities; bad to think yours could be tracked just as easily if someone wanted to attach spyware to your phone number.

Every time Mallory Johnson had used her cell phone in the last few months, there it was. Documented in date, time, minutes used, the numbers she had dialed, the numbers that had called her, even the general location of where she was when the call was made.

"My wife says this is why she doesn't leave her phone switched on," Dwight said.

My wife.

Even as he concentrated on what his deputy was saying, a small corner of his mind savored those words. They still awed him. After so many years of thinking she would never be his, here they were: ready to celebrate a full year of marriage.

"Any of these numbers connected to the Wentworth boy?" McLamb asked.

"Nope. Neither outgoing or incoming. At least not that we can tell. If he had one of those disposable phones with a prepaid card, there's no way to know. There's no land line at that trailer, just Jason Wentworth's cell phone, and when we found it this morning, it does show the 911 call that the Faison guy made. That number's not on the girl's records, though." She pointed to the last incoming number. "That's her dad's number right at ten-thirty. She didn't answer and it went into her voice mail."

Richards picked up the girl's phone and pressed some buttons and Dwight heard Malcolm Johnson's voice say, *"Mallory? I hope you're on your way home, honey. It's ten-thirty and tomorrow's still a school day."*

"What about her last outgoing?"

"It's her brother's number. The call lasted about three minutes, but Denning says her phone was switched on and the battery was drained."

Richards pointed to the time: 10:37. "The kids at the party say she left the Crowder house around ten-thirty. She must have talked to him right before she crashed."

She thumbed the stack of pages piled up on her desk. "Is there really any point to reading all these text messages?"

"Probably not." As much as he felt sorry for Sarah and Malcolm, their daughter's death was a lower priority than the Wentworth killings. "Why don't you start on the day of her death and skim back through a week or so? I don't expect anything to jump up about the Wentworths, but you never know. Let me have the brother's phone number, though. I'll see if she mentioned either of them to him."

As McLamb went on to his desk to write up his report, Dwight paused in the doorway. "What about calls to and from Wentworth?"

"Matt called him a little before nine Friday morning from his stepmother's house and there were several calls from Faison. One on Thursday evening, and after that, Faison's calls were sent right to voice mail, so I guess they were dead by then."

"Faison say anything useful?"

"Just that he wanted his gun and stuff. And he was pissed that Jason wasn't picking up the phone. Finally, on Sunday, he said that he was going to come over that night after he took his aunt to a movie." She smiled and added parenthetically, "Faison's lived with his aunt in Cotton Grove since he was twelve."

"Hello?"

"Charlie Barefoot?"

"Yeah. Who's this?"

"Major Dwight Bryant with the Colleton County Sheriff's Department. I was wondering if you could stop by my office this afternoon? I'd like to clear up a few things and — Hello? Mr. Barefoot?"

Dwight realized that he was talking to dead air and pushed the redial button. After five rings, Charlie Barefoot's voice said, *"Here comes the beep. You know what to do."*

"We seem to have been disconnected," Dwight said sternly. "Please call me." He carefully enunciated his number, then hung up and sat back in his seat.

Now wasn't that interesting?

Before he could decide what to make of the boy's action, Deputy Sam Dalton, CCSD's newest detective, rapped on the frame of his open door. Dalton had been put in charge of the patrol officers sent to canvass the Massengill Road area surrounding the Wentworth single-wide.

For a moment, Dwight was irresistibly reminded of Bandit when the terrier thought there was a big juicy bone in his immediate future. If Dalton had possessed a stubby little tail, it would be wagging in excitement.

"Sir," he said, "I believe we've got us a witness in the Wentworth shootings."

CHAPTER 20

An hour later, to the accompaniment of Bing's voice singing "I'll Be Home for Christmas," McMurtrie rang the doorbell of No. 3. The door was opened finally by a white-faced woman with burning black eyes and raven hair.

— "Silent Night," Baynard Kendrick

Major Dwight Bryant — Monday afternoon, December 22

Mrs. Alma Higgins had short white hair that feathered softly around a heart-shaped face, bright china blue eyes, and very fair complexion that was now finely wrinkled with age. At first glance, she looked like an old-fashioned pink-and-white porcelain doll that someone had slipped inside a green velvet pouch and then pulled the drawstrings up tight around her neck. A second glance showed that the green velvet tunic that she wore over matching green slacks had a stand-up ruffled neckband of the same material and that the drawstring was actually a thick gold necklace. Either the holiday outfit was a hand-me-down from a heavier woman or she had lost weight since she first acquired it.

Someone had rolled an armchair in from the conference room and seated her beside Mayleen Richards's desk. When Dwight joined them, he almost bumped into Rae-ford McLamb, who was on his way back from the break room with a cup of instant hot chocolate.

"Now isn't that so sweet of you!" the elderly woman exclaimed in a soft voice halfway between a girlish flutter and the cooing of doves.

"Mrs. Higgins," said Deputy Sam Dalton, "this is Major Bryant."

Her blue eyes widened as she looked up. "Oh, my goodness! You must be Calvin Bryant's son."

"Yes, ma'am," he said, trying to remember if he had ever met this woman before.

"Oh, honey," she cooed. "You're the spitting image of your daddy. He's been gone — How long is it now? Almost forty years? But it's like he just walked into the room. He and my second husband were in the Grange together, and I always notice the handsome men." Her laughter was a cascade of soft flute notes. "Not that Harold wasn't nice-looking, too, but nothing like your daddy. Or like my first husband either, for that matter. Or — oh, but you don't want to hear about them. You want me to talk about Friday morning, don't you?"

"If you would, ma'am." He pulled up a straight-backed chair and sat down. "Do you mind if Deputy Denning records this?"

"Not a bit." She watched with bright interest as that detective took up a position with his camera, and immediately began to fuss with her hair and to straighten her gold necklace. "I must look a sight." She turned to Mayleen Richards. "Do I still have any lipstick on?"

That young woman gave an encouraging smile. "You look just beautiful, Mrs. Higgins. Why don't you start by saying your name and where you live?"

Hesitantly at first, then with growing confidence, Mrs. Higgins repeated her full last name, which seemed to consist of several surnames, followed by an address out on Massengill Road. "After I divorced my second husband, I gave my daughter and her husband the farm and just kept an acre for myself in case I ever wanted to come back here to live."

She mentioned her daughter's name and it was vaguely familiar to Dwight. "Well, after James died — he was my fourth — I decided to move back up here from Florida to be near Mary and her children. We built me a little house on my acre even though Mary said there was plenty of room with her now that the children are grown, but I didn't want to be a bother."

She paused to lift the hot cocoa to her lips that were painted the same pale pink as her nails, and Dwight immediately said, "If you could tell us about yesterday morning, ma'am?"

"Oh, I *am* sorry. I do keep running on, don't I?" She laughed again, the tinkling laugh of a woman who has always known that most men were enchanted by both her laughter and her tendency to "run on."

Dwight glanced at Richards, expecting signs of impatience. Instead, Mayleen appeared to be fascinated by this preserved-in-amber example of pre-ERA femininity.

"You said you were on your way to get your hair done?" Dalton prompted.

"That's right. Every Friday morning, as soon as I hear the bells of the little Methodist church down the road begin to chime the half hour, I know it's time to leave for my standing appointment at eleven o'clock.

They're not real bells, of course, just a recording, and I don't know that I'd like to live right next door to them, but it sounds so pretty from a distance. Anyhow, I was driving down Massengill Road at about a quarter to eleven when a car came whipping out of a driveway on my right. The trees and bushes are so thick there that he probably couldn't see me, but I'm sure he never even slowed down to look. Just shot out and made a left-hand turn right in front of me. I was doing about fifty, and before I could put on my brakes I felt my car brush the rear end of his. Well, I immediately stopped, but he didn't. I got out and looked at my front bumper. You could see where it was scraped, but it wasn't enough to call it any real damage, and I must say I was relieved about that, because if he *had* stopped and we'd called the highway patrol to come out and take a look, I knew they would say it was my fault. After you pass seventy, they just assume your reflexes are poor and that any accident is always your fault. Down in Florida —"

Mayleen interrupted. "Excuse me, ma'am, but do you mind if I ask just how old you are?"

Mrs. Higgins cocked her head archly. "Oh now, honey, you know a lady never tells her age, but you lean your pretty little head a little closer and I'll whisper it in your ear."

The deputy did as she was instructed and her eyes widened in surprise at what she heard.

"So you see why I was just as happy not to have a trooper come out, although I do think that this was one time they would have taken the word of a somewhat older woman over some young man. I mean, I couldn't have scraped his car if he wasn't in my lane when I had the right-of-way, now could I?"

"No, ma'am. You say he was a young man? Black or white?"

"White, but I'm afraid that's all I can say. It all happened so fast that I really didn't have time to see him."

"But you think he was a young man?" Dwight persisted.

"That was my impression. Not white-headed, anyhow, or bald. I would have noticed that."

Dwight smiled, willing to accept that a woman who'd had four husbands would indeed have noticed. "What about the car itself, ma'am?"

"White," she said promptly. "And either a Honda or a Toyota. Fairly new, too. Mine's a silver Prius, and I looked at both makes very carefully when I was trying to decide which to buy last summer. My grandson thought the Prius would hold its value best, so that's what I got. You menfolks always know about cars."

"Two-door or four?"

"Four."

"Did you notice what the driver was wearing?"

"I'm so sorry, honey, but I didn't. Do you really think he's the one who shot those two young men?"

"We won't know until we find him," Dwight told her. "But it certainly sounds as if he was there at the right time."

They took her back over it again, and when it was clear that she could add nothing more, Percy Denning volunteered to drive her home and see if he could lift any paint samples from her bumper.

Dalton reported that someone on the other side of the woods from the Wentworth trailer told them that he'd heard four gunshots around ten-thirty or eleven, but he had not paid much attention. He assumed that Jason Wentworth was shooting at squirrels or rabbits again.

As Dalton swiveled around to his desk to begin writing up his report, Dwight paused and said, "So how old *is* Mrs. Higgins?"

Mayleen Richards grinned. "Would you

believe ninety-two?"

Shaking his head, Dwight returned to his own office and tried calling Charlie Barefoot again. Again, he was shunted into voice mail.

3:30. A half hour till his shift was technically over. With everything quiet for the moment, he decided that he would drive back to Cotton Grove and see if he could get up with that evasive young man before going home to shower and shave for dinner out with Deborah that night.

Accordingly, he arrived at the modest home of Nelson and Edie Barefoot a few minutes past four. He found Mrs. Barefoot outside, busily plugging in the Christmas lights that dripped from the eaves and adorned the bushes along the porch. She was pleased to see him, "But Charlie's not here right now, Dwight. He's gone over to see Sarah about something. Can I give him a message?"

"That's all right," he told her. "I'll catch up with him there."

Built at the crest of an acre lot that sloped off to the rear, the Johnson house was an imposing brick two-story with the multilevel roofline, peaks, and dormers that had come to dominate the landscape these past few years. Tasteful evergreen wreaths tied with red velvet bows adorned every window. A circular concrete drive led to a lower three-car garage and side door before continuing up the slope to the front. An older-model white Hyundai was parked by the garage. Charlie Barefoot's, Dwight assumed, and quite a contrast to the sporty red Miata that his sister had wrecked last week.

He slowed to a stop and, even though there was no reason to think that Charlie'd had anything to do with the Wentworth killings, he found himself automatically checking the left rear fender for a recent scrape. He did see a ding in the same approximate area as Mrs. Higgins had described, but even from several feet away, he realized that this one had a skin of rust that was too old to have formed since yesterday. He took his foot off the brake and continued on up the slope to the front door, where he got out and rang the bell.

No one immediately answered, so he rang again.

Just as he was reaching for the bell a third time, Sarah Johnson opened the door. She wore black slacks and a black V-neck sweater over a white cotton shirt with french cuffs. Her pretty face was ravaged and even thinner than when he'd seen her at the funeral home on Saturday. Her eyes were red-rimmed and she had a ball of tissues in her hand as if she had been crying, but she managed a watery smile as she invited Dwight in and ushered him past an enormous Christmas tree in the foyer into an informal sunroom at the back that overlooked a winterized swimming pool on a lower level and the woods beyond.

"Malcolm's not here right now, but do you have news for us?" she asked when they were seated and he had refused her offer of something to drink.

"News?"

"Who put the liquor in Mallory's drink," she reminded him. "Malcolm's convinced that she would still be alive if she'd had her normal reflexes."

"You don't?" he asked, hearing something different in her voice.

She leaned her head back against the couch with a tired sigh. "I don't know, Dwight. I've quit trying to understand any of this. It's not going to bring her back to know, so what difference does it make in the end? First Charlie and now Mallory. I've lost them both."

"Actually, it was Charlie I came to see,"

he told her. "Mrs. Barefoot said he was here."

She sat upright and her expressive eyes were suddenly frightened. "Why do you want him? What have you heard, Dwight?"

"Is there something I should have heard?" he asked gently.

"No, of course not! Everybody's upset. Nobody's making sense. Malcolm's raging around like a wild man and Charlie —"

She broke off and stood up. "He's downstairs getting some of his things. He's moved over to Jeff's parents' house, and I guess you've heard that he took back Jeff's name?"

Dwight nodded.

"Malcolm's been good to him, Dwight." She led the way to a carpeted staircase that curved down into a walk-out lower level. The railing was trimmed in cedar and ivy interlaced with red velvet ribbons. "There's no reason for Charlie to act like this. Yes, Malcolm spoiled Mallory, but that didn't mean he never loved Charlie. All daddies spoil their daughters, don't they? Mine did. I bet Deborah's did, too."

Her words sounded to Dwight like an argument she had made so many times that even she no longer believed it.

At the bottom of the stairs lay a pleasant space furnished like a casual den with several couches that faced a large flat-screen television recessed into one wall. A granite-topped wet bar was tucked under the stairs and wide french doors led out to the pool and terrace.

On the wall opposite the stairs were several closed doors.

"Charlie," Sarah called. "Honey?"

She crossed to one of the doors, gave a light knock, then opened it. "Charlie?"

Through the open doorway, Dwight could see a bedroom furnished in masculine colors and a full bath beyond that. The closet door stood wide and several drawers in the chest were half open. The lights were off, but another set of wide french doors let in enough December daylight to let them see that the rooms were empty.

Back in the den area, Dwight oriented himself and gestured to a door in the corner. "Does that go outside?"

Sarah nodded and Dwight quickly crossed to it. To the left lay the three-bay garage. To the right was the outer door he had noticed when he drove in. It was slightly ajar, and when he stepped outside, he was not surprised to see that the white Hyundai was gone.

CHAPTER 21

Well, I say, I do not see where we are going to get any beautiful gifts at this time of night, what with all the stores being closed, unless we dash into an all-night drug store and buy a few bottles of perfume and a bum toilet set as guys always do when they forget about their ever-loving wives until after store hours on Christmas Eve.
— "Dancing Dan's Christmas,"
Damon Runyon

I drove home in a pleasant state of anticipation that was further heightened when I hung my coat by the kitchen door and Dwight emerged from our bedroom in a fresh dark brown shirt, brown tweed slacks, and a crisply knotted tie in shades of gold and brown. His hair was neatly combed and even his cowlick was temporarily lying flat. He had shaved again and the smell of his aftershave lotion made me weak-kneed as our arms went around each other and our lips met.

He chuckled and looked down at me. "Nothing ol' married lady about *that* kiss."

"A year of practice makes perfect," I said, kicking off my shoes and unbuttoning my shirt. "Give me twenty minutes and I'll be ready to roll."

Tomorrow night would be more formal, but I wanted to look soft and alluring tonight. We had reservations at the Mexican restaurant that had led to Dwight's proposal. Back then, I had shoved the candle on our table aside because it had never crossed my mind that I might have a romantic relationship with this man I had known my whole lifetime. Candlelight would be welcome this time, though. I changed into a dark red blouse with a ruffled plunging neckline, and added dangly earrings that would sparkle in the flickering flame. My hair was loose, my skirt was tight, and my red patent leather heels were as high as I planned to be by the end of the evening.

I had just slipped the second one on when I heard Dwight say, "Yeah, okay. I'll call Sheriff Poole and we'll rendezvous there in thirty-five minutes."

A moment later: "Bo? Looks like we've got 'em! . . . Yeah, the truck and three of the crew, and they're heading in . . . Okay, I'll meet you at Tinker's Crossroads in fifteen minutes."

He had already hung his tie on the back of a chair, and when he saw me standing in the doorway, his face mirrored excitement and regret.

"I'm so damn sorry, Deb'rah, but I've got to go. The drug squad's finally located that panel truck and it's leading them right back to the area we suspected. If we catch these guys tonight, we can —" He groaned as he took in how I looked. "I wish I could wrap you in cellophane till I get back."

"Too bad, Major Bryant," I said, trying to keep it light. "Next time you see me, I'll be in flannel pajamas."

Disappointed though I was, I nevertheless reached for the shirt he was shucking off and hung it and his slacks back in his closet while he changed into jeans, pulled on a long-sleeved dark jersey, and fastened his Kevlar vest over that.

There was no point in pouting or stomping my foot. I knew what I was getting when I married him, and this was a case the narcotics squad had been trying to nail down for over a month. They had a tip that the dealers were using a panel truck as a mobile lab to cook up methamphetamine, but so far, the truck had roamed the area undetected.

"Tucker says they've been stealing license plates and magnetic signs off other truck doors every few weeks," Dwight said as he strapped on his gun. "No wonder we couldn't get a fix on them. Though how they can cook it up in a van and still be able to breathe and drive beats me."

He shook his head again as he looked at me. "I wish . . ."

"Yeah," I said softly, more than mollified by his regret. "Me, too."

"Don't wait up. God knows when I'll get home."

"Don't worry about me, darling. I'll fix myself a ham sandwich and —"

He was shaking his head with a rueful smile.

"What?"

"Good luck on that one. Reese and Annie Sue put a hurting on that ham at lunch, and some of the other kids showed up to polish it off. They did leave the bone if you want to make pea soup."

He grabbed the navy windbreaker with large white lettering that ID'd him as an officer of the Colleton County Sheriff's Department, gave me a long hard kiss, promised he'd be careful, and then he was gone.

Hey! Happy anniversary, Deborah!

Twenty-five minutes later, dressed now in jeans, a UNC sweatshirt, and ratty old house slippers, I was rummaging in the refrigerator, trying to decide what I was in the mood for, when Bandit yipped and trotted over to the door that led into the garage. A moment later, I heard voices inside the garage itself. None were deep enough to be Haywood's rumbling bass tones, but I half expected to open the door and see him there. Instead, I found myself looking into the surprised faces of Annie Sue, Reese, and several other nieces and nephews clustered around the fuse box. Or rather, around the fuse *boxes.* I hadn't noticed that we now had two boxes where before there had been only one. The second one was open.

"What's going on?" I asked.

"Aunt Deborah?" Annie Sue whirled on her cousin Stevie. "I thought you said you saw Uncle Dwight's truck go by."

"I did!" He gave me an accusing look. "He said y'all were going out to dinner tonight to celebrate your anniversary."

"He got called in to work at the last minute," I said. "So why are *y'all* here?"

265

They looked at Annie Sue, who said glibly, "We were on our way for pizza and I got them to stop by and help me test the new circuit breakers. I knew it would go faster if I could have someone flip the wall switches in each room."

With that, she briskly deployed the kids throughout the house and had them call out their locations to her as they switched the lights on and off while she kept watch on the fuse boxes. For some reason, they seemed to find the exercise highly amusing.

By the time she pronounced that everything was in order, they had talked me into going out for pizza with them even though I offered to order in.

"Why don't we stay here and watch *A Christmas Story?*" I said, something we'd been doing ever since enough of them were old enough to drive.

"We can do that after," Jessica said. "You don't want us spilling pepperoni or tomato sauce on your couch. C'mon, Aunt Deborah. It'll be fun."

I knew that the fun part would be getting me to pay for their pizza, but what the hell?

"I get to pick where we go, though," I told them and they didn't argue when I chose Big Ed's New York Slice, one of the new cafés that has opened up in the same nearby shopping center as the NutriGood grocery store. Big Ed's is a little more expensive than the pizza chains, but the taste is exponentially better. I might mourn for the farm that this shopping center has replaced, but when one of those incredible pizzas is set down on the table before me, it feels almost like an equal trade.

Heading for eight o'clock on a Monday night this close to Christmas, we had the place to ourselves except for a few people in and out to pick up orders to go. We pushed two tables together and were debating toppings when I realized that Annie Sue, Reese, and Stevie were missing. Counting Zach and Barbara's daughter Emma, who seemed to have heard about the impromptu party through osmosis, there were only eight of us.

"Oh, they said to start without them," said Seth and Minnie's son John. "Stevie's riding with Annie Sue and Reese and she wanted to drop off the new boxes at Uncle Zach's and Uncle Robert's. You know how he and Aunt Doris love to talk. They said if they don't get here in time, just to bring them one back."

The pizza maker on duty was a muscular middle-aged transplant from New Jersey — "Ed usually takes Monday nights off" —

267

who was willing to pile a full pie's worth of anchovies on the three slices that Jane Ann and I planned to split.

"Just make sure none of that rotten fish juice gets on our slices," said A.K.

For some reason, Jane Ann and I are the only ones in the whole family who like them. Even Dwight, who eats everything from raw oysters to calamari, thinks they're an abomination.

"Don't worry, I'll serve them separately," said the chef, who admitted he couldn't stand them either.

Ruth said she could tolerate their smell as long as she didn't have to eat any, and she took a chair on the other side of me. "I uploaded pictures of us making cookies Saturday, Aunt Deborah, and I sent you the link. Did you see them? There's a real cute one of you and Cal."

"I got the link," I told her, "but I haven't had a chance to look at the pictures yet."

Carols sung in Italian formed a seasonal backdrop to the happy chatter of my nieces and nephews as the ones who'd been away at college caught up with the kids still in high school. Suggestions were batted back and forth for get-togethers that would include girl- and boyfriends after Christmas, but for tonight they seemed to enjoy just being with each other, part of the close-knit clan we've all known since infancy. I know that some of them will eventually scatter to the four corners of the country, like Adam, Frank, Ben, and Jack, who come home so infrequently that their children are like strangers to us. Haywood and Isabel are mildly worried that Jane Ann seems interested in a classmate from Oregon, and who knows where Will and Amy's Jackson will wind up if he does make it to the major leagues after college?

My bittersweet musings were interrupted by an Italian version of "Jingle Bells" that made everyone laugh.

Our pizzas came, hot and crispy and fragrant with oregano and basil. I went ahead and ordered a final large pie to take home if the others didn't get there in time. At the rate the slices were disappearing, that would be in about fifteen minutes. A.K. sat on the other side of his sister and could almost eat a whole one by himself. Ruth had to snake a slice of the mushrooms and sausage he was working on before it was all gone. I paid with my credit card, and when my copy of the receipt arrived, she picked it up and said, "I wish whoever threw out that trash last week had paid with a credit card."

"What do you mean?" I asked, my mouth

full of hot melted mozzarella and salty anchovies.

"I told you about it. Remember? When the others were fixing the memorial where Mallory crashed? I picked up all the trash I saw along both sides of the road so it'd look nice. One of the things on the opposite shoulder of the road was a Bojangles' box, and a receipt had blown a little further down the road in the ditch. When we pick up the trash on our road, I always look to see if there's any way to tell who dumped it, don't you?"

I swallowed and nodded. It's amazing how many people will litter without realizing they might be tossing stuff with their names and addresses on it: credit card receipts, sales slips, old bills, junk mail. Our family has adopted the main road past the farm, and one or another of us is out there a couple of times a month to clean the shoulders and ditches. Haywood's occasionally taken garbage over to the address of the people who dumped it and politely asked them to quit littering on our road. Haywood's six feet tall and built like a Hummer, so most folks don't argue with him. Especially when he waves a soiled envelope with their name on it in their face.

Ruth took another bite of her pizza and

caught a mushroom that threatened to drop onto her shirt. "The thing is, it was from that Bojangles' at the edge of Cotton Grove and it was time-stamped ten-something the same night Mallory died. I was thinking that since Mallory crashed around ten-thirty, maybe they were driving past and saw something, but they paid cash, so there was no name on the receipt."

"Too bad you didn't save it," I said.

"I almost did. Along with all the other garbage. I stuck the bag in the trunk of Jess's car and then forgot about it till we were at your house Saturday morning. I guess I should have mentioned it to Uncle Dwight instead of just dumping it in y'all's garbage pail."

Which meant that it was gone, because Dwight always takes our garbage to the dump on Saturday mornings.

"Don't worry about it," I told Ruth as Jane Ann slid my half of the third pizza slice onto my plate. "The troopers probably would have picked it up if they'd thought it had any use."

When we got back to the house around nine-thirty, I saw flashlights bobbing around down by the pond.

"Who's that?" I asked, pausing on the

porch to squint out into the darkness.

"Just Reese and Stevie," said Annie Sue, who had come out on the porch when she heard all the cars pull up. "Bandit got out and we heard him barking down there so they went to see if it was a deer or something."

"I hope Reese didn't have his rifle with him," I said. "He knows better than to jacklight a deer."

"Oh, Aunt Deborah!" Ruth said. "You know Reese wouldn't do something like that."

The others laughed and I just shook my head at her innocence.

Bandit came bounding up, his paws wet and muddy. I grabbed his collar and reached for the old towel I keep hanging on a nail so that I could wipe him down before he tracked mud into the house.

"What was it?" I called when the two boys were within hearing distance.

"What was what?" asked Reese as he and Stevie came up on the porch.

"What Bandit was barking at," Annie Sue said quickly. "I told her y'all went to see if it was a deer that got him so excited."

"Oh." Reese switched off his flashlight. He carried a screwdriver in his other hand.

I laughed. "What were you going to do?

Stab it with that?"

"No telling what spooked him," Stevie said. "Is that pizza I smell? I'm starving."

We went inside and unboxed the food. In addition to a whole pizza, we had brought back several uneaten slices from our supper. Emma's brother Lee had turned up while we were gone and he dug in, too. Some of the kids played with Dwight's train while I made fresh coffee and brought out the jug of iced tea I keep in the refrigerator. A.K. and Lee asked to microwave some popcorn. When everyone had a beverage of choice and a bowl of popcorn within easy reach, I slid the DVD of Jean Shepherd's sweet tale of boyhood Christmas yearning into the player and we settled down to watch, some on the couches and chairs, others stretched out on the floor with cushions under their chins. We know all the best lines and a running obbligato echoed the soundtrack — "You'll shoot your eye out" and "You stay away from that turkey." It still cracks us up when Ralphie comes downstairs in those bunny pajamas.

At the final fade-out, there were yawns and stretches and a general movement toward the door with thanks for the pizza and hugs all around.

When the last car and truck had left the

yard, I whistled for Bandit and began stacking the dishwasher with the glasses and mugs.

Dwight came home as I sat at the coffee table with my laptop to download the pictures Ruth had posted on one of the photo sites. He noted the cushions all over the floor and sniffed the air. "Popcorn and pizza? The kids must've been over again."

"Hey, you should've been a detective," I teased.

"Hope you saved me a slice."

"Actually, there's one with pepperoni and meatballs and one with pepper and onions," I told him. "How it escaped A.K.'s notice is beyond me. That boy's got hollow legs. How'd it go tonight?"

"Six arrests, several grams of crank, and we confiscated some unregistered guns and a van that's got to be decontaminated. Guess how they sealed off the front seat from the fumes in the back of the van."

"Duct tape?" I asked.

He laughed. "How'd you guess?"

"Oh come on, Dwight! You know perfectly well that my brothers would have to give up farming if they ever quit making duct tape. That and baling wire's the only thing holding half their equipment together."

I set my laptop on the dining table, then

stuck the pizza in the toaster oven to reheat while he drew a glass of his homemade beer from the tap Daddy had given him last year so that he could keg his brew instead of bottling it.

"What's that you're looking at?" he asked, peering over my shoulder at the computer screen.

"Pictures that Ruth posted from Saturday. Awww. Look at Cal and Mary Pat!"

He pulled up a chair beside me to eat his supper and watched while I flipped through the thirty or so pictures from this year's cookie-baking session. Dwight wanted to linger on the one of Cal and me that Ruth had mentioned. She had snapped the shutter at the exact moment that Cal was cracking an egg while I watched in amusement.

"Get her to make me a copy of that one, okay?" he said.

As I moved the cursor up to click off the album, he stayed my hand. "What's that?"

"That?" I clicked to begin again in full-screen mode the slide show I had downloaded from Ruth's site. "This was the other morning when the cheerleader team and some of Mallory's friends went out to the crash site and put up their memorial to her."

Ruth had documented every aspect of the morning: the cars parked along the shoulder, the plastic flowers and little wooden cross being taken out of the car trunks, and the girls as they arranged it all on the ditchbank where Mallory's car had gouged out raw hunks of earth when it flipped. There was a picture of the short skid marks and then a long view of the whole scene from further back.

As everyone had commented, the road there was straight and level. Woods rose up on one side, the trees draped in dead kudzu vines. On the side where the car had flipped lay a fallow field.

"Why'd she take a picture of that stuff?" Dwight asked when we came to the one of some beer cans and a yellow Bojangles' box.

I explained Ruth's decision to clean up the litter and described how she had found a receipt that was time-stamped within a half hour or so of the wreck.

"Yeah? Too bad she didn't bring it to me," he said.

"That's what I told her. And she almost did. The bag was still in the trunk of Jess's car when they got here Saturday morning, but she threw it in one of our garbage cans."

I closed the file and turned off my laptop.

Dwight carried his plate and glass back to the sink and went on into the bedroom. I picked up the cushions and a few stray pieces of popcorn, then switched off the lights and followed.

When I got there, Dwight was already in bed and he propped himself up on one elbow to watch as I slipped off my jeans. "I'm really sorry about tonight, Deb'rah. I wanted this to be special. Make you think you were right to marry me."

"Oh, darling, do you really think a date on the calendar is going to make a difference in how I feel about you?"

"And I was too damn busy to stop in somewhere and get you a present."

I shook my head at him. "We agreed we weren't going to give each other anything, remember?"

"No," he said. "You agreed. I didn't. I guess you'll just have to make do with that."

He lifted my pillow and there sat a small flat velvet box.

"What's that?" I asked.

"Happy anniversary, Mrs. Bryant."

I lifted the lid. Nestled on a velvet bed was a narrow gold circlet etched in tiny leaves and flowers. As I lifted it out to slide it onto my wrist, I saw that it had been engraved inside with today's date and the words *One year, but who's counting?*

"Oh, Dwight, it's beautiful!" I threw myself down beside him so that I could hug

277

him properly.

"I thought it would go with the bracelet Miss Sue left you."

"It will," I agreed, lifting my arm in the air to admire the way it looked and imagining how it would look when paired with the blue forget-me-nots of that other bracelet. "I just wish I had something for you."

"Actually, you do." He grinned and tugged at the waistband of my Carolina sweatshirt. "But first we need to get rid of these flannel pajamas."

(Ping!)

CHAPTER 22

There was a startled stillness, and then
the colonel said slowly,
"Please say seriously what all this
means."
— "The Flying Stars," G. K. Chesterton

*Major Dwight Bryant — Tuesday morning,
December 23*

"Good job, everybody," Dwight said next morning as his briefing with the CCSD drug squad wound down.

While most drug users claimed they were hurting no one but themselves, meth labs with their volatile chemicals were serious health hazards to everyone living at the site, especially any children; and decontamination was a growing drain on EPA resources. Sometimes the only solution was complete demolition, which was the probable fate of the van they had seized last night.

"Wish we had some good news for you,

too, Major," Deputy Mayleen Richards said glumly when he asked for a progress report on the Wentworth shootings.

"It's like we've hit a brick wall on this case," Raeford McLamb said. "No leads. Just dead ends. We've talked to every name that's come up. Jason had pissed off the usual number of people for someone like him and so had the younger kid, but as for what motivated someone to gun them down?" He gave a frustrated display of empty hands. "He was drawing unemployment, but Employment Security Commission's pretty overwhelmed these days and all they could say is that his paperwork was in order. No help there."

"What about Mrs. Higgins's bumper?" he asked Denning.

"I brushed along the place where she made contact, but I don't know if there's enough there — one really tiny chip and some paint dust. We did get lucky in that the car's been in her garage since Friday. She doesn't drive in ice and her daughter took her to church on Sunday, but I don't know, boss. White on silver?"

"Did that Barbour kid the stepmother mentioned give you anything?"

"Nothing we didn't already know. He last saw Matt at school on Thursday, right after they announced that the Johnson girl had died. He says the same as everyone else — that if Matt claimed they were an item, he was lying, but he did say that Matt seemed pretty shaken up about her death. Nate Barbour made a smart-ass remark and Matt started cussing him. They mouthed off to each other some more in the parking lot, then Matt drove off alone. Our boy Nate's been caught with some pot. He's out on bail right now for shoplifting two cameras from Target, and I gather there was an assault charge that got dismissed. Turns out he worked part-time at the Welcome Home store last summer, but he denies all knowledge of how the store's stuff wound up in Jason's shed and was all innocent wide eyes when I asked him about it. I expect we'll be seeing more of him down the road."

"What about the grocery store where Matt worked?"

McLamb gave a sour laugh. "Nothing missing, if that's what you mean. And the manager had no complaints. In fact, he said Matt was pretty reliable. His hours were five till eight, nine if they were really busy or shorthanded, and he usually showed up on time. Did what was expected of him. Thursday night was the first time he'd missed without first calling."

"Anything from the bullets that killed them?" Dwight asked Denning.

That deputy shook his head. "Sorry, boss. All the slugs show the same characteristic marks, but until we get a gun to match them to, it's another dead end."

"What about the rifles you took from Faison's truck Sunday night? He's asking for them back."

"He can have 'em far as we're concerned. Both guns were dirty so it's hard to know when they were last fired. Faison's fingerprints were on both and the victims' on just one. Nobody else's. And, of course, they aren't the murder weapons." Almost as an afterthought, he said, "One odd thing. I found a piece of plastic wedged into the top of the rifle barrel that Jason borrowed."

"Plastic?"

"Yeah."

"What kind?"

Denning handed him a small baggie with a shard of clear rigid plastic inside. There was nothing distinctive about it, so far as he could see. Thinner than window glass. Flat. No discernible curvature.

"There were new scratches on the outside of the barrel tip. Like somebody'd smashed the rifle through a sheet of this plastic. Want me to send it to the SBI lab? See if they can ID it?"

"As backed up as they are? It'll be six months before they could get around to this."

"I saw bits of plastic like that on the floor of the trailer when Dalton and I were there yesterday morning," said Richards, glancing up from her paperwork. "Looked like something got broke and no one got up all the pieces. Want me to go back and get them?"

"No, I have Joy Medlin coming in this afternoon and I'd like you to sit in on the interview."

"I'll go," said Dalton. "It was there at the end of the couch, right, Mayleen?"

She nodded.

"Probably a waste of time," Dwight said, "but if we do eventually wind up sending it to Garner, might as well send them enough to work with."

Dwight stopped by the break room, refilled his coffee mug, and went on down to his own office to dig into some of the paperwork that had accumulated on his desk. This was his least favorite part of the job, but he learned long ago that if he did not keep up with the stuff as it came in, disposing of it would take even more time because he would have to go back and refresh his memory. Years ago, while still in the Army, he seemed to remember predictions that computers would eventually do away with paper. So much for predictions.

By 10:30, he was reaching for the last file when his desk phone rang and the duty officer at the front desk said, "Major Bryant? There's a Charlie Barefoot here to see you."

"Send him on back," Dwight said. He signed a final paper, put the file in his out-box, and walked over to the open door.

Watching his onetime teammate's son walk down the hall was almost like seeing Jeff Barefoot in the halls of their old high school. Same shambling, loose-knit walk, same shock of straw-colored hair, same narrow-set hazel eyes in a long face. Except for some minor updating, he could have been wearing the same uniform: jeans, sneakers, a dark blue Duke hoodie that was unzipped and the hood pushed back on this mild December day. There seemed to be nothing of Sarah in that face. The young man was all Jeff until he gave a sheepish smile and held out his hand, and then it was his mother's smile.

"Major Bryant? Charlie Barefoot. Sorry I hung up on you like that yesterday. I wasn't thinking clearly."

"No problem." Dwight gestured to the chair beside his desk. "You're here now." He sat down in his own chair and pulled a notepad toward him.

Barefoot sat with his elbows on the arms of the chair and tented his long fingers in front of him. "Mom says you and my real dad played ball together in high school."

Dwight nodded.

"So you knew all three of them back then?"

For a moment Dwight wondered who was interviewing whom here, then decided to go with the flow for a while. See where it led.

"I was a year ahead of them, but yes, I played with Jeff and Malcolm both. And your mother was a cheerleader. You play?"

"No. I'm as tall as my dad was, but I'm a klutz. What was he like?"

"I didn't really know him outside the gym. Back in those days, town and country didn't mix all that much. I was country. Rode the school bus. He and Malcolm were town. And he wasn't a starter till their senior year, after I graduated."

"He wasn't as good?"

Dwight shrugged.

"My granddad says he was better than Dad — Malcolm — my stepfather."

"He could have been," Dwight agreed.

"He just didn't want it as badly."

"And Malcolm always gets what he really wants." His voice was bitter.

"What he's willing to work for, Mr. Barefoot."

"Call me Charlie."

"Charlie, then. Look, son, I don't know what your problems are with your dad, but —"

"He's not my dad." He glared at Dwight across the desk. "He's only my stepdad."

Dwight shook his head. "He may not be your biological father, but he did become your legal parent when he adopted you, and changing your name doesn't change that."

"Maybe not legally, but as far as I'm concerned, we're done. I moved in with my grandparents a few weeks ago. I'm living in my real dad's old room now and I've learned more about him these last few weeks than I knew in my whole life."

No surprise there, Dwight thought. Remembering the rivalry between Jeff and Malcolm, he doubted if Sarah would have spoken much about her first husband to this boy, and certainly not in front of Malcolm, whereas there would be no brakes on Mrs. Barefoot's tongue now that she and her husband had him to themselves.

"I'm glad that's working out for you,"

Dwight said. "But I want to ask you about Tuesday night."

"What about it?"

"Your sister went to a party at Kevin Crowder's house. Were you there, too?"

The boy shook his head.

"According to your sister's phone records, she was talking to you when she crashed."

"No!" He almost strangled on the word and his Adam's apple bobbed up and down in his thin throat. He tried to meet Dwight's eyes but his own eyes were filling with tears and he dropped his head. "She called but I didn't pick up."

"Why?

"I don't know. I was driving back to my grandparents' house."

"Back from where?"

"Somewhere between Cotton Grove and Garner. I went to see a movie."

"Go with anyone?"

"No, I wanted to be alone."

"See anybody you knew?"

"No, I told you. I wanted to be alone."

"Did you know your sister was going to Kevin Crowder's party?"

"When we talked earlier that day, she said she might stop in at a party after the game, but she didn't say where. We didn't hang out together, if that's what you're asking. I don't know the guy, and even if I did, it would've been high school kids. Mostly jocks and their crowd."

"So you wouldn't know if she was seeing Matt Wentworth?"

"Who?

"Matt Wentworth. He was shot this weekend."

"Oh yeah, I heard about him and Jason. Mal with a Wentworth? No way!"

"You and Mallory didn't get along?"

"Look, if you're asking me if I loved my sister, yes, I did. If you're asking me if I thought she walked on water like everybody else did, then no, okay?"

"Is that why you didn't pick up when you saw her name on the screen?"

He shrugged and Dwight sat silently, letting the awkward pause stretch out until Charlie Barefoot blinked first.

"We had a fight when we talked that morning and I was still mad at her," he admitted, shame and sorrow in his downcast eyes.

"What about, Charlie?"

"N-nothing important. She thought I was being unfair to Da —" He caught himself. "To Malcolm. She didn't like some of the things I said. She didn't want me to change my name last spring and she didn't want me to move out. She said it was a slap in Mom's face, too. So we fought."

"Did she leave a message?"

He nodded.

"I'd like to hear it, if you don't mind."

He reached into the pocket of his jacket and pulled out a DVD in a cardboard sleeve. "I downloaded it from my voice mail to my computer so I could save it, and I made a copy."

Dwight reached for it, but Charlie seemed reluctant to let him have it.

"I didn't listen to it till I was driving to the hospital after Mom called and told me about the accident. I let her listen to it at the hospital while Malcolm was charging around making sure everybody in the emergency room knew who he was and what he expected of them, then I made them a copy the next day. Wednesday."

He laid the disc on the desktop and stood up. "I can't stand to listen to it again, so I'm going to go now. If you want to ask me anything else, call me. And leave my mother out of it, okay? She doesn't answer for me anymore."

"One final question, Charlie. Was your sister into drugs?"

"Because of what Malcolm's saying? No way, Major Bryant. As far as she was concerned, drugs — *all* drugs — were for losers. She wouldn't even try pot or alcohol. Not because she was so pure and righteous, but because they didn't fit her image."

Dwight gave a wry smile. "Too bad more of your generation doesn't feel that way."

"Our generation learned it from yours," the boy said.

When Charlie Barefoot had gone, Dwight took the disc into the detective squad room, explained what it was, and called for a player.

Richards pointed to one atop a file cabinet and as soon as Dwight inserted the disc and pushed PLAY, the room filled with the sound of a car engine, Christmas music from the radio, and the dead girl's voice.

"Charlie? Damn you, Charlie, why won't you pick up? You can't do this to us. To me. To Dad and Mom. Not here at Christmas. You don't — Omigod! Where did that — ? Dim your stupid — Get over! I can't see! I — oh, shit! No!"

There was a horrendous scream that seemed to go on forever above the music, interspersed by the thumps and bangs of the crash itself. For a moment or two all was quiet except for low whimpers and a half-whispered "Mommy?" that trailed off into silence.

Dwight started to push the eject button, but Richards said, "What was that?"

They listened to the ending again with the volume turned up to maximum.

"Is that a car engine starting up?" asked McLamb.

"And going away," said Dalton. "Not passing."

CHAPTER 23

"I wear the chain I forged in life . . . I made it link by link, and yard by yard."
— *A Christmas Carol,* Charles Dickens

Major Dwight Bryant — Tuesday afternoon, December 23

When Dalton returned well before lunch, he brought enough of those plastic pieces that they could fit it together like a jigsaw puzzle. Although most of the edges were missing, enough remained that they could tell it had begun as a six-by-six-inch square with rounded corners. Obviously it had fit onto or over something, but what?

Just as clearly, someone — Jason Wentworth? — had smashed it with the barrel of Willie Faison's rifle, which was how a shard got wedged inside.

"I went by where Faison was working and asked him if he knew anything about it since he was the one who took the rifle out of that trailer," said Dalton. "He looked a little freaked, but he didn't say anything."

"Well, damn!" As he suddenly recognized what this plastic had once covered, Dwight slapped the table so hard that the pieces slid apart. "Of course! Go haul Faison's sorry ass in here."

"Huh?"

In a few terse words, Dwight told Dalton why. "And get a search warrant for his truck."

Grinning, Dalton hurried off to do as he was told, and in less than two hours he was back with a very apprehensive Willie Faison. Dalton had also retrieved the broken flashlight Dwight had remembered seeing in Faison's truck box Sunday night and had bagged it up along with a few more shards of the rigid plastic lens, which he had found on the bottom of the box.

"It's yours, right?" Dwight asked him when they were seated in the interview room with the flashlight on the table between them.

"Yessir." The slender young man wore muddy jeans, scuffed leather high-tops, and a red plaid wool work shirt over a red tee. His dark eyes were wary as he searched the big deputy's face for a hint of what was coming.

"Part of the *stuff* you wanted back from Jason Wentworth?"

"And he went and broke it," Faison said indignantly. "You know how much them things cost?"

"I can imagine," Dwight said. "Halogen bulb? That's a real powerful light for crawling around under houses looking for busted water pipes. What was Jason going to use it for?"

Faison shrugged his thin shoulders. His hands were large and work-stained and already well callused. When he nervously brushed back a lank of dark hair from his forehead, Dwight saw skinned knuckles where the young man had evidently lost a struggle with a rusty pipe joint.

"There was no deer stand and no Wednesday morning deer hunt, was there, Willie? We know why Jason borrowed your gun and this flashlight. He was going to show his little brother how to hunt deer at night, wasn't he? Did you go along to hold the light?"

"No! I didn't go. I told you — I quit doing dumb stuff like that. He already lost his own gun for doing that and I told him if he wound up with the law taking mine, I was gonna take it out of his hide with a pipe wrench."

"So who did go on that hunt with them?"

"Guy named Jack McBane was supposed to go with Jase. It was just gonna be the two of them, but they had a falling-out, so he said the hell with it, he'd take his brother instead."

"What was the falling-out about?"

"Something to do with Jack's girlfriend. That's all I know. Honest."

"Jackson Dwayne McHenry, aka Henry Jackson, aka Dwayne Jackson," said McLamb, reading McBane's adult record off the computer screen. It was a record of escalating violence. He had punched out a store clerk at the age of sixteen, torn off part of someone's ear in a bar fight at eighteen, was arrested for shooting up a car at twenty.

As the list grew, they were beginning to think this could be their man, until McLamb uttered an involuntary expletive.

"He was tried in district court here last Friday. Found guilty of a misdemeanor DWI, Level One, and was immediately taken into custody. Damn! Talk about an ironclad alibi."

"McHenry's probably not the only violent guy Jason Wentworth ran with," Dwight said. "Maybe the flashlight got smashed in a fight. Keep digging."

Joy Medlin showed up at 1:30 right on schedule. To Dwight's surprise, however, she had been driven there not by her mother or father but by Jessica Knott, the seventeen-year-old daughter of Deborah's brother Seth.

Dressed in a dark blue warm-up suit, the injured cheerleader maneuvered into the interview room on crutches. The room was bare except for a metal table and four chairs. As Mayleen pulled out one of the chairs and reminded her that they had met before, Dwight shot an inquiring glance at his niece by marriage. Tall and sturdily built, with her grandfather's clear blue eyes, she wore black stretch pants and a red cardigan over a white turtleneck jersey. Her earrings were small gold bells that gave a tiny jingle when she moved her head.

Giving him a don't-blame-me shrug, she murmured, "Sorry, Uncle Dwight. She seems to think you won't be as rough on her if I'm here."

"And why would I be rough on her?" he asked.

She did not answer, but moved on into the room to take her friend's crutches and prop them in a corner.

He and Mayleen sat down at the table across from the two girls. When introductions had been made all around and the girls had asked to be called by their first names, Dwight said, "Joy, I'm told that you and Mallory Johnson were best friends since first grade?"

The girl nodded, her eyes wide and frightened.

Of what? Dwight wondered. Taking a second, harder look at her, he could see that she was basically a pretty young woman. Or had been. Today her face was gray and pinched. There were deep shadows, almost like bruises, under her eyes, and her jaw was tight, as if she were clenching her teeth.

Why?

And then he remembered that Jessica had told him at lunch yesterday that Joy planned to wean herself off all painkillers over the holidays.

"Are you sure you feel up to this?" he asked.

She nodded. "I'm fine."

"You're not trying to quit your pain medication cold turkey, are you?"

"No, sir. My doctor told me I could keep gradually increasing the time between doses. I'm due for another at three. I can make it." Her smile was probably a ghost of what it once was. "In fact, being here takes my mind off the clock."

"Did you know Matt Wentworth?"

"No, sir. I mean, I know he got killed this weekend, but he was a freshman and . . ." She hesitated. "Not to say something ugly about someone that just died, but he really wasn't anybody who . . ."

She looked to Jessica for help.

"He ran with a different crowd," Jessica said smoothly.

"Yes."

"What about Mallory? Did she ever go out with him?"

"You're kidding, right?"

"No. He told his stepmother that she was his girlfriend and that he gave her a necklace for her birthday last weekend and took her to a movie."

"*Mallory?* Not in a million years, Major Bryant. She wouldn't be seen dead with —"

Her eyes filled with tears as she realized what she had said. She brushed them away impatiently. "Besides, her birthday's in June, not December."

"How old are you, Joy?" Dwight asked abruptly.

"Eighteen. Why?"

"Legally you're an adult now, but before I go further, I need to tell you that you have the right to counsel."

"A lawyer?" Her eyes widened even more. "Do I need one?"

"I don't know and I can't advise you on that."

"Anything I say can and will be used against me?" In a wry voice, she said, "Isn't that what they say on all the cop shows?"

He did not return the smile. "That part's accurate."

"Uncle Dwight!" Jessica protested.

"I'm sorry, Jess, but this may be a murder investigation and she has to be warned."

"Murder?" said Jessica. "It was an accident. She swerved off the road and wrecked her car. How could that be murder?"

"Jess, honey, I think you ought to wait outside."

"No, please, let her stay," said Joy.

Until then, Mayleen Richards had been silent. Now she placed a calming hand on the girl, who was becoming increasingly distraught. "He's right, Joy."

"But shouldn't I be here as her witness or something?" Jessica asked, reluctant to abandon her friend.

"Not unless you've suddenly acquired a law degree, Jess. There's a bench out there in the hall. Go sit on it, please, and close the door when you leave."

Half angry, half scared, Jessica did as she was told.

Once the door was closed, Dwight again reminded Joy that she was entitled to an attorney.

"I don't want a lawyer," Joy said. "I want to get this over with."

"As you wish. Do you see that camera over the door?"

She nodded.

"We're going to record your statement. Richards?"

In a quiet voice, the deputy recited the date and time, the people present, then gave the girl a formal reading of her rights. "Do you understand that, Miss Medlin?"

"Yes."

"And you waive your right to an attorney of your own free will?"

"I do."

"Do you wish to make a statement at this time?" Dwight asked.

"Yes, please." She took a deep breath. "I want to confess to causing Mallory's death."

"How did you do that?"

"I put a Vicodin tablet and some vodka in a Coke and switched cans with her when she wasn't looking."

"When was that?"

"About ten or fifteen minutes before she left the party."

"Was it your pill or Mrs. Crowder's?"

"I'm not sure. I think it was mine, but I lost count when they got mixed up."

"So you were the one who stole Mrs. Crowder's pills?"

Joy nodded. "Everybody knows I've been taking Vicodin for my ankle and Kevin said his mother was taking them, too, and that they seemed to be pretty strong and she was trying to do without them. I figured that meant they would be in her medicine cabinet. Our friends were all over the house, so I used the master bathroom and found them in the medicine cabinet."

"Why?" asked Dwight.

"Because I was hurting and my doctor wouldn't give me anything stronger. I still had five days to go before I could get a refill and I was down to just three days. So I poured Mrs. Crowder's pills into my prescription bottle. Only I didn't realize that hers were twice as strong as mine till after I got home and looked at them more closely."

"And that's what you gave Mallory?"

"I thought it was mine, but it must have been Mrs. Crowder's. Why else would she run off the road like that?" Tears rolled down her cheeks and she fumbled in her purse for tissues so that she could blow her nose. "I mean, I heard afterwards that she was taking Benadryl for her cold, but even with that and the vodka, one of my regular pills shouldn't have made her so groggy that she would crash. I didn't mean for her to die, Major Bryant," she sobbed. "Honest. I thought maybe she might sideswipe a mailbox or go in the ditch. Like being drunk or something. So that for once everyone wouldn't think she was perfect — that she could mess up, too."

"Is that why you're taking yourself off the Vicodin?"

She nodded, shamefaced. "I don't care how much it hurts anymore. At least I can still hurt and Mallory can't. And it's all my fault."

"Were you jealous of her, Joy?"

"I hated her!" the girl said vehemently.

That surprised both officers. "I thought she was your best friend."

"No. That's what she said. That I was *her* best friend."

Dwight glanced at Mayleen for help.

"Why did you hate her, honey?" the deputy asked.

"Stacy and Ted are dead because of her. Dana might as well be dead, and I'm going to limp the rest of my life. All because she wanted to mess up what Stacy and I had."

"What do you mean?"

"She'd been putting the moves on him for over a week, pretending like it was all in fun, that coming on to him was just playing. I told him that, too, but he was, like, flattered. She was so pretty and so hot, he didn't care if it was a game with her or not. I told her to quit it, but she wouldn't. She kept texting him sexy messages. He thought she was going to put out for him when she'd never done it with anybody. That night — okay, I know he'd had a couple of beers too many and maybe he wasn't thinking clearly, but all the same . . ."

She shook her head angrily. "See, she suddenly quit texting him. That was part of her game. Go after them till they respond and then quit cold like she was going to drop them. Bang! She wouldn't answer her phone if they called and she wouldn't text them back. It drove guys crazy. It drove Stacy crazy. He kept checking his phone even though I was sitting right there beside him. Then finally, while we were driving home after a game, she texted him. Told him that if he dropped me off early, he could call her when he was alone and they could have phone sex. Oh, that's not what she wrote, but that's what she meant, and he got so excited, he just stomped on the gas. Two minutes later, he was dead and my ankle was shattered in a million pieces."

She pulled more tissues from her purse and blew her nose and wiped her eyes, but the tears kept coming.

"So, yes, I hated her for that, but I swear I never meant to kill her. I *didn't!*"

At that, she turned to Mayleen.

"What's going to happen to me? Will I have to go to prison? Oh, God! Mama and Daddy! This is going to wreck their lives."

"I don't know," Dwight told her honestly. "It will be up to the district attorney. We still don't have all the details of that night." He pushed a legal pad over to her side of the desk. "For now, though, I want you to write out what you just told us about taking Mrs. Crowder's pills and how you put a pill and some vodka in a Coke and gave it to Mallory. Then sign and date it."

"And then I can go home?"

"And then you can go home. Just promise me you won't do something stupid."

"Like kill myself?" She gave a bitter laugh. "I thought about it. I felt so bad, I almost took all of Mrs. Crowder's pills. But then I knew I couldn't do that to my parents. Seeing how torn up Mallory's folks are?" She shook her head. "This is going to hurt them

304

when they find out what I've done, but not like it would if I killed myself."

CHAPTER 24

The southern colonies, largely rural and unhampered by Quaker and Puritan dissenters . . . cultivated Christmases of a very different sort.
> — *Christmas in America,*
> Penne L. Restad

With Christmas bearing down upon us, I could understand why the DA's office wanted to reduce the backlog of cases that had built up under Chester Nance's poor management, but when ADA Julie Walsh handed me yet another batch of miscellaneous add-ons that various attorneys had pushed to be heard that Tuesday afternoon, I guess I let my exasperation show.

Although it goes against my grain to bad-mouth a Democrat, in my heart of hearts, I really wish Nance's moderate and extremely efficient Republican opponent had won.

"Sorry, Your Honor," Walsh apologized.

"I'm pretty sure these are the last of the day."

Julie Walsh looks like a sweet little school-teacher with her sandy blond hair in a loose braid, sensible pumps, and a businesslike tweed jacket over a black turtleneck and black slacks, but she has the persistence of a dog worrying a bone when she's pushing for a conviction, so I listened to the plea bargains she had worked out with the ac-cused and their attorneys and agreed with most of them, although I did increase a couple of the penalties and lowered some of the others depending on the aggravating or mitigating circumstances of each case.

Not everything was serious that afternoon and a certain holiday lightheartedness permeated the proceedings once a twelve-year-old child took the witness stand to testify that yes, indeed, she certainly did see the defendant pick up a two-by-four and smack her uncle on the head. With the face of an angel, blond curls, bright blue eyes, and a ruffled white blouse, she could have stepped off a Christmas card. She placed her small hand on the Bible and swore to tell the truth, the whole truth, and nothing but the truth.

Because of her age, I leaned forward and said, "Do you understand what you just said, Taylor?"

Taylor nodded her curly blond head. "Yes, ma'am."

"And do you know what will happen if you don't tell the truth?"

"Oh, yes, ma'am," she said earnestly. "I'll go to hell and the devil's fiery furnace."

Suppressing a smile, I told Ms. Walsh she could proceed. I thought it was safe to assume that we'd hear nothing but truthful answers to her questions.

In the late afternoon, I looked up and saw my niece Jessica enter the courtroom. There was a lull in the proceedings as Walsh conferred with an attorney who wanted to change his client's plea, and I motioned Jess forward.

"What's up?" I asked in a low voice, seeing the unhappiness on her face.

"Uncle Dwight wanted to talk to Joy — Joy Medlin — and she asked me to come with her. But now he won't let me stay in the room. She said she didn't want a lawyer, but I'm afraid she's going to say something she'll wish she hadn't and shouldn't she have somebody in there with her? Somebody on her side?"

"How old is she, honey?"

"Eighteen. And yes, I do know that means she's an adult and can speak for herself, but she's hurting so bad, she can't be thinking clearly."

"Did you call her parents?"

"No. She didn't want them to know where we were going." Her eyes were troubled as she confessed, "They think we're Christmas shopping."

Joy Medlin had been at that party, so if she was now spilling her soul to Dwight, it wasn't much of a stretch to wonder if she was responsible for the alcohol in Mallory's bloodstream.

"I'm sorry she didn't wait and get an attorney," I told Jess, "but your Uncle Dwight's not going to put thumbscrews on her. He'll go by the book."

"But —"

"Don't worry, Jess. For what it's worth, if she tells him anything that's self-incriminating — *if* — I imagine an attorney will find a way to get it tossed out."

It was Job's comfort, but the best I could offer under the circumstances, and she accepted it glumly.

"Now I've really got to get back to work. Are you still sitting with Cal tonight?"

She nodded and I watched her leave as unhappy as when she came. I couldn't fathom why Joy would spike her best friend's Coke, if indeed that's what she'd done, but I've had enough teens in my courtroom — hell! I've watched enough of my own teenage nieces and nephews mess up — to know that they can do stupid and impulsive things without considering the consequences.

Like Frederick Arnold Hallman, seventeen, white, brand-new short haircut, and dressed in a gray suit he had outgrown. He rose to plead guilty to setting off a string of firecrackers inside a local movie house. An elderly black man had thought a triggerhappy gunman was firing randomly and promptly had a heart attack. The man had recovered and the boy had been so genuinely remorseful that he had mowed the man's grass all summer and they had become friends. With the older man there to speak on his behalf, I gave an appropriate fine, added some community service, and put the boy on unsupervised probation for six months.

My last case for the day was a middle-aged black man who had violated his probation so that he was not only on the hook now for his original suspended sentence, but was about to get an additional three months' prison time.

This was not the first time he'd faced lockup, and his attorney had come prepared.

"Your Honor, my client hopes that in view of the season, you'll let his two sentences run concurrently rather than consecutively."

Her client was nodding vigorously and I fixed the man with a stern look. "And why should I do that, Mr. Adams?"

" 'Cause of all my hardships, ma'am. See, I've got a lot of people depending on me. My mama's got the sugar, my wife's real poorly, and now my daughter's got the smiling mighty Jesus."

"The what?" I asked.

"The smiling mighty Jesus," he repeated.

I looked at his attorney, who with a perfectly straight face said, "I believe his daughter has spinal meningitis, Your Honor."

"In the spirit of the season, hmm?" I said, matching her deadpan face. "Very well, then, Mr. Adams. Both sentences to run concurrently. And I hope your daughter recovers soon."

Bridesmaids are always being told that those long Cinderella-type gowns they're required to buy can be worn again to cocktail parties and formal occasions.

Not true.

And the three short dresses I've walked down various aisles in? One was a sickly shade of brown for an autumn wedding, one was stiff satin in Pepto-Bismol pink for Valentine's Day, and the third had a lime green bodice, a wide coral waistband, and a turquoise flared skirt. (I believe that wedding was supposed to evoke the beach.)

So when I picked out my wedding dress, I really did plan to wear it again. The strapless silk brocade sheath had a side slit to make dancing easier and was the color of pale champagne. A matching fitted jacket had kept it ladylike for the wedding, but tonight I substituted a silky soft stole woven in subtle stripes that merged from pale beige to deep gold. I had put my hair up in a modified french twist, and added gold earrings, my new gold bracelet, and a necklace that lay like a flat gold collar. When I emerged from our bedroom, the look on Dwight's face was worth all the trouble I had taken with my makeup.

"Oh, wow, Aunt Deborah!" said Jess.

Cal beamed at us. "You and Dad look really nice."

I curtsied and Dwight, who looked more than nice in his dark suit, gave a formal half bow, then held my coat for me. As he opened the door and I was giving last-minute instructions, car lights swept across the yard.

"Emma and Ruth and some of the others are coming over, if that's okay," Jessica said. "We want to work on our party piece. We're doing something special this year."

Every year, we gather at Daddy's for a big communal Christmas dinner in the potato house where we held our reception last year. After the food is cleared away and gifts have been opened, everyone's encouraged to step up to the front and perform — to play or sing, recite a funny poem, act out an original skit, or collaborate on something amusing. Mother started the tradition the year she married Daddy as a way to help her young stepsons develop self-confidence. From the conspiratorial grins Jess shared with Cal, this year's performance might top last year's. That one had a heavenly choir that swooshed around overhead on swings hung from the rafters while Richard flew down from the back on a cable slide, waving sparklers that almost set the tree on fire.

"No sparklers inside," Dwight said sternly as the kids trooped past.

"Don't worry, Uncle Dwight," Stevie said with a laugh. "It's warm enough tonight that we can set up on the porch."

"Set what up?" Dwight asked suspiciously.

"Ask us no questions, we'll tell you no lies," chanted Jess, who seemed to have bounced back from the heavy load she was carrying earlier. "Just remember that you promised to call when you're leaving Dobbs, so we can get all our props cleared away before you get home."

"*And* give us time to put out all the fires and sweep up the glass," Richard added with a mischievous glance at the others.

Delighted to be included in the merriment, Cal straddled the back of the leather couch as if he were riding a horse and called to us that he'd keep an eye on everybody.

They saw us off in high glee.

Dwight and I had both gotten home late and this was the first quiet moment we'd had together. At the end of the drive, before he turned onto the hardtop, Dwight looked over at me and smiled. "Hey," he said.

"Hey, yourself," I said and leaned in for a kiss.

"How 'bout we just skip the dance and go check in at the Dik-a-Doo Motel?"

I drew myself up in indignation. "Why, Major Bryant. Just what sort of woman do you think I am?"

"Not think, Judge Knott. *Know.*"

The moon, now in its last quarter, would not rise until well after midnight, but zillions of stars were crisp sharp points of silver and the air was so clean and clear that the Milky Way swirled with more brilliance than I had noticed in months.

As we drove, I asked him about his interview with Joy Medlin. "Did she admit that she was the one who put booze in Mallory's Coke?"

"Where on earth did Jess find time to tell you that?"

"She didn't. She did come up to my courtroom after you kicked her out of your interview with Joy, though. She was worried because Joy was talking to you without an attorney present."

"Joy Medlin was reminded of her rights," Dwight said. "More than once."

"I'm sure she was, darling. I'm not accusing you of anything wrong. But if she was on edge because of taking herself off painkillers, I can just imagine someone like Zack Young arguing about the admissibility of whatever she told you."

"I've been in the burn box before," he reminded me.

Between Jess, Dwight, and needing to satisfy my own curiosity, I realized I'd have to recuse myself if Joy were charged with a crime and came up before me, so I went ahead and said, "But she did spike Mallory's drink, right?"

"With more than vodka," he said grimly.

315

"She threw in a Vicodin for good measure."

"But why?"

"Remember what Mama told you about how Mallory liked to flirt with other girls' boyfriends?"

I nodded.

"She was pulling the same thing with the Loring boy. Joy says Mallory texted him just before he wrecked the car and offered to give him good phone sex once he was alone."

"Oh," I said.

"Joy blamed Mallory for the wreck and she's probably right. Mayleen's going to get the phone company to pull that message. If it's as raw as Joy says it was, there's no question it would have excited a horny teenage boy who'd had too much to drink and was hot to dump his passengers and get home."

"Oh, Lord." I sighed.

"Yeah." He pulled a DVD from his jacket pocket. "Look, I don't want to spoil the whole evening, but would you mind if I play a disc that Charlie Barefoot made of Mallory's last voice mail? She was leaving him a message when she crashed. It's pretty hard to take, but we've all listened to it several times and we can't quite agree."

"Agree about what?"

"Listen to it first. I don't want to influence your interpretation."

I took the disc and slipped it into the player. A moment later, I heard Christmas music and Mallory's voice scolding her brother for not picking up and for wrecking the holidays for her and their parents. There was an annoyed injunction to an oncoming car to dim its lights, then the sound of the crash. Her moans and her call for her mother broke my heart and I wondered if Sarah and Malcolm had heard it. When all was silent, I reached out to replay it, but Dwight turned up the volume and said, "No. Listen."

Very faintly as if from a distance, I heard a motor catch and then fade away.

He gave a nod that I could turn it off and said, "So what's your take?"

"I need to hear it again," I said and pressed the play button.

Once again the Christmas music, Mallory's voice, the crash, and another car engine.

"You hear it?"

"I did," I told him. "Did you ask Charlie about it?"

He looked puzzled. "Ask him about that other car?"

Now it was my turn to look puzzled. "No, about what he cut out of the message."

"Huh?"

"Isn't that what you meant?"

"What are you talking about?"

"I'll play it again. This time, try not to listen to Mallory's voice. Listen to the music."

I pressed PLAY again and a syrupy sweet version of "Silent Night" performed on bells could be heard beneath the dead girl's voice. This time, because he was listening for it, Dwight could clearly hear that the music skipped a few bars. Had there been singing, it would have been the equivalent of several words missing between "holy infant" and "sleep in heavenly peace."

"Well, damn!" said Dwight.

CHAPTER 25

It is a fair, even-handed, even noble adjustment of things, that while there is infection in disease and sorrow, there is nothing in the world so irresistibly contagious as laughter and good-humour.
— *A Christmas Carol,* Charles Dickens

"Have Sarah and Malcolm heard this?" I asked, when Dwight had listened to the disc twice more.

Each playing took away some of the horror and heartbreak for me, but I imagined it would be progressively worse for Mallory's parents.

"Yeah. Charlie said he let Sarah hear it at the hospital and then he made copies so she could listen to it with Malcolm the next day. I don't get it, though. Why the hell would he cut it?"

Dwight likes to think that he can compartmentalize and keep his official life strictly separate from the personal, but he's really not much better at it than I am. Given his druthers, I was pretty sure he'd ditch our dinner dance, drop me back at the house, and go make Charlie Barefoot shake loose an unedited version of the message Mallory had left on his voice mail.

"Look at it logically," I said as we neared the country club. "If the deletion had anything at all to do with the wreck itself, other people on the road, a big dog or a deer, wouldn't he leave that in?"

"I guess."

"So I'll bet she was probably yelling at him for something he's either ashamed of or doesn't want you or Malcolm to know about."

He dimmed his lights against a steady stream of oncoming vehicles. "How do you make that assumption?"

"What you just said. He let Sarah listen to it at the hospital, so that means she heard an unedited version on his cell phone. He wouldn't have had time to make a copy yet. I'm willing to bet that what Malcolm heard the next day was the same as this copy here. Maybe he was doing drugs or something that he knew Malcolm would hit the roof over, but that Sarah might let slide. Or maybe he said something ugly to Mallory that he didn't want Malcolm to know about now that she's dead. For all we know, he could've accused her of sleeping around or breaking up relationships like Joy said and the deletion was about that. Maybe he'd heard a rumor that she was partly to blame for Stacy Loring's wreck and killing two kids. He'd feel pretty awful if she died upset about something like that, wouldn't he?"

"I guess," Dwight conceded.

"I'll make you a deal," I said. "If you'll put this out of your head for tonight and just enjoy the evening, I'll break our separation of powers agreement this one time so you don't have to drive all the way into Dobbs tomorrow to find another judge."

"You'll sign me a search warrant?"

"Well, it does sound as if he's concealing evidence in an official investigation. If any other officer gave me this much cause, I wouldn't think twice about it. Deal?"

He grinned. "And all it's going to cost me is wining and dining and dancing with you for a few hours?"

"That's all."

"You drive a hard bargain, Your Honor."

An enormous live Christmas tree, decorated in gold ornaments and tiny yellow lights, cast a golden glow over the vaulted entrance hall. Because the country club had been built in the mid-seventies, when new money from the Research Triangle began overflowing from Wake into Colleton County, no corners had been cut. Floor-to-ceiling windows at the rear of the hall overlooked the eighteen-hole golf course, and there were the usual tennis courts, the obligatory outdoor swimming pool, and a small gym with exercise machines.

When I was single, in private practice, and living in Dobbs with Aunt Zell and Uncle Ash, I had joined because it was a good place to entertain clients and Uncle Ash was on the membership committee. Once I became a judge, however, I let my membership drop and have had no reason to regret it. Neither Dwight nor I play golf or tennis, we can swim in the pond in warm weather, and we get plenty of exercise working around our yard.

But it's always fun to come in for special occasions like tonight, and we were greeted by so many old friends and professional acquaintances that it took us over twenty minutes to get to the main ballroom and locate Portland and Avery. Dwight had been slightly self-conscious about not owning a tux, and he was relieved to see that dark suits like his far outnumbered the more formal ones. Uncle Ash looked elegant in his tux, though, and Aunt Zell was beautiful in a rose-colored sleeveless gown with a matching rose-colored lace jacket.

Her hair had turned silver while she was still in her forties and her soft curls brushed my cheek when she greeted me with a kiss. Except for their hair, she and Mother had borne only a fleeting resemblance to each other, and it pained me to realize that Mother would be nearing eighty had she lived.

I showed her the bracelet that Dwight had given me and her smile widened. "I saw it before you did, honey."

"You did?"

"Dwight came by the house and took lunch with us one day. Before he went and had it engraved, he wanted to know if I thought it'd go with Sue's bracelet."

I hugged her again. "I'm glad you said yes."

"Now y'all be sure to save us both a dance," said Uncle Ash as he took Aunt Zell's hand and tucked it on his arm. "I'm gonna want a turn around the floor with the second-prettiest gal here."

She laughed and patted Dwight's arm. "And I'll lower my standards for you, honey."

We stopped at the reception table to hand in our tickets and get the drink tickets that came with our reservations, then went on into the ballroom that had all the partitions rolled back to create the largest space possible. Avery was on his way back from the bar with two full glasses and he offered to show me our table while Dwight went to fetch our own drinks — bourbon and cola for me, with branch water for him.

"I'd give you a hug," Avery said, "if I thought I wouldn't spill my wife's daiquiri down your back."

"I'll consider myself hugged," I told him, thinking once again how lucky it was that Portland and I genuinely liked each other's mates. Avery's an attorney from Wilmington, and when he and Por first hooked up, I'd been afraid it would affect our friendship, but he's as easygoing as Dwight and has a great sense of humor. Back whenever I was between men and needed a last-minute escort, Avery had never shown any snobbery if I drafted Dwight to make up a foursome, nor had he ever acted as if there was a difference between his law degree and the way Dwight had earned his commission as an officer in the Army. In fact, Por told me later that Avery had early on asked her if I was ever going to wake up to the fact that Dwight was not my brother.

Despite saying that she would get the club manager to pull up two extra chairs to a table for two, Portland seemed to have snagged a table for four. Space between the tables was tight, but there are times when I don't mind being jammed and squeezed and this was one of those times. The more people, the more festive, and I was smiling happily when I slid into a chair across from my childhood friend.

She just shook her head at me. "I keep forgetting that you love last-minute Christmas shopping, too. Great stole, by the way."

There was nothing much she could do with dark hair that was so thick and curly except to keep it clipped short, but her crystal earrings flashed sparks of fire and the plunging neckline of her black halter-topped dress showed off a figure she had worked hard to return to its pre-baby slenderness.

"Big difference from last year this time," I said.

"Oh, honey! Last year this time I was bearing down and cussing Avery and trying to tell my obstetrician I'd changed my mind about having a baby."

Avery made a big show of looking at his watch and said, "Actually, last year at this precise time, our daughter was already twelve hours old and you were cussing me because I wouldn't bring you a burger with double cheese and onions and a margarita on the side."

"And hadn't I damn well earned them?"

"Right. You'd have given the baby colic right away."

Their affectionate bickering ended when Dwight joined us, but before he could put our drinks down, Diane Hobbs and her husband Randy appeared at his side. Randy, a recently retired magistrate, was resplendent in a tux with a red paisley cummerbund, and Diane, who works for our dentist, wore a strapless red silk gown that showed off toned upper arms that would have put Michelle Obama to shame.

I thanked her for the chocolate-covered fried pecans she had sent by Dwight. "My nieces and nephews eat anything they can get their hands on, but I think I hid them where they won't find them. They're too good to be devoured by kids with underdeveloped taste buds."

She laughed and announced that she was there to claim a dance with Dwight.

The median age of the people here tonight looked to be about sixty-five and the band had probably been instructed not to play any music written after the fifties unless it was slow versions of the Beatles. That was okay with me. There's a time and a place for everything and I was totally in the mood for the romantic music of that era.

Randy Hobbs is a dear and he never once stepped on my toes, but I was ready to change partners when "Moonlight in Vermont" came to an end and the band segued into "Moon River."

For a man of his size and build, Dwight is surprisingly good on the dance floor. He's not a flashy dancer, no Fred Astaire or Gene Kelly moves, but he gives the impression that he could if he wanted to, which makes it fun to follow his lead.

We found Aunt Zell and Uncle Ash, and after dancing to "Moonlight Becomes You" — "I'm sensing a theme here," Uncle Ash said dryly — we took a turn around the floor with Luther and Louise Parker to the tune of "Blue Moon." He's the district's first black judge and he was resplendent tonight in a tux with a red-and-gold cummerbund that matched Louise's long gown.

We returned to our table a moment before Avery and Portland got back, too. Even though the ice had melted in our drinks, they still tasted good after the dancing.

The waiters began to bring out our plates

and the band took a break while we ate. I chose the poached salmon and Dwight took the stuffed chicken breast so that we could eat off each other's plate if one entrée proved less tasty than the other. Por and Avery did the same and Avery insisted on treating us to a bottle of Riesling so that they could toast our anniversary and we could toast the birthday of their daughter, who was home being spoiled by Por's parents.

With mischief dancing in her dark eyes, Por looked up from buttering her roll and said, "I hear you got a Christmas present this morning."

I paused with a forkful of dill-dressed salmon in midair, unsure what she meant. "I did?"

"Didn't Dwight tell you?"

"Tell her what?" he asked.

"Don't you get a morning report of everyone who's been arrested overnight?"

"We get it, but I don't always read it when we're as busy as we've been these last two days," said Dwight.

"So neither of you know that Zack Young has a new client?"

"Don't gloat, honey," Avery said, cutting into his breast of chicken.

"Who?" we both asked her.

"Philip Hamilton."

"Who?"

"Ellen Englert Hamilton's seventeen-year-old son. He got pulled last night for a DWI. Blew a point-twelve's what Gwen told me."

Gwen Utley's a magistrate who keeps a jaundiced eye on everything that happens in the courthouse.

"You're kidding," I said.

Portland shook her head. "Gwen never kids. She says that the first thing Ellen did when she came down to bail him out early this morning was call Zack Young. The second thing she did was resign from being president of the Colleton County MADD chapter. When it comes to throwing the book at a DWI, it would appear that being a mom trumps everything else."

Okay, it was mean of us. It was petty and uncharitable and totally callous. Nevertheless, Portland and I high-fived each other right there in the Dobbs country club and Avery had to catch the wine bottle we almost knocked over.

"We must be getting old," I said as we drove home that night. "There was a time when I'd've been embarrassed to leave a dance before midnight."

Portland had started yawning at nine-thirty, and when they decided to pack it in at ten, Dwight and I realized we were ready to head on home, too.

As promised, I called Jess to let her know we were on our way.

"Any progress in the Wentworth murders?" I asked once we had cleared town and were back in the country. I had been shocked to hear that those two bodies had lain exposed to the freezing rain and sleet for almost three days and he had amused me by describing Mrs. Alma Higgins of the four husbands.

Now I listened while Dwight described how they seemed to have hit a dead end after he realized that the brothers had probably been jacklighting deer again and that Faison confirmed it. "Faison did give us the name of a guy who had potential as our killer."

"But?"

"But he was in your court Friday morning and you gave him jail time."

"Oh. Sorry about that."

"Me, too. But you know all that equipment that was missing from the Welcome Home store? I forgot to tell you. We found it in a shed back of Jason Wentworth's trailer. And it turns out that Matt Wentworth's friend Nate Barbour used to work at the store."

"He say what they did with the concrete Jesus?" I asked.

"No. But then he claims not to know anything about the shed or the thefts."

That reminded me of the defendant who wanted his jail terms to run concurrently because his daughter had the smiling mighty Jesus.

Dwight laughed out loud at that and we were in a good mood as we drove into the yard to find some eight or ten vehicles, not just the kids' but some of their parents.

"What's happened?" he asked.

I started to panic when I saw Seth, who's five brothers up from me, come around the corner of the house alone. He was hatless as usual, and before he could meet us at the porch steps, I smelled smoke on his denim jacket.

"What's wrong?" I called.

And Dwight said, "Where's Cal?"

Seth heard the urgency in our voices and made a calming motion with his hands. "Everything's fine. We've got a little bonfire going down by the pond. The children want to give you the Christmas present they've all chipped in for, but first you've got to get out of those fancy dancing clothes, though I have to say, you do look mighty pretty, honey." He paused a couple of beats and grinned widely. "You look mighty pretty, too, Dwight."

Both of us would trust Seth with our lives, and since he was clearly enjoying the moment, we didn't argue, just hurried inside and changed into jeans and sweatshirts.

When we came back out, dressed for anything, Seth led us down the slope behind the house to the long pond and I saw Annie Sue's truck parked next to Reese's.

Several of my brothers who live locally had come with their wives, even Barbara and Zach. Herman, Annie Sue's dad, is pretty much confined to a wheelchair these days, but he sat beside Haywood in the golf cart Isabel uses to run around the farm on.

Cal and several of the cousins were lounging on heavy canvas tarps. They had fetched lawn chairs from the garage and I saw Daddy seated on the far side of the bonfire with Ladybell, his redbone hound, at his feet.

As Dwight, Seth, and I drew near, everyone yelled, "Surprise!" and at that instant, Annie Sue must have thrown a switch because the deck and two nearby willows sprang into colorful light. The kids had run Christmas tree lights on hooks along the base of our long narrow pier, all down the railing, and up into the trees. The lights reflected in the pond so brightly that I clapped my hands in delight.

"Do you like it?" asked Annie Sue. "Are you surprised?"

"Oh yes," said Dwight, answering for both of us. "So this is what y'all've been doing when you were supposed to be installing circuit breakers?"

"She done that too, ol' son," Haywood called.

"Come on," said Reese, grabbing me by the hand, while Jane Ann and A.K. pulled Dwight along, too.

"To get the full effect, you need to go all the way out to the end of the pier and take a look from there."

We didn't argue. Once we were at the end and looked back, it really was magical — the colored lights, the bonfire, the happy faces of our family. Cal came running and squeezed in between us to grab our hands.

"Let 'er rip!" Reese called, and suddenly we became aware of light and sound behind us. We turned and there about twenty feet off the end of the pier, a jet of water shot up a good six or seven feet into the air.

"Oh — my — God!" said Dwight, as the bubbling geyser changed from blue to green to red to yellow from submerged floodlights. "My idea," Reese said proudly.

CHAPTER 26

And being, from the emotions he had undergone, or the fatigues of the day . . . much in need of repose, went straight to bed without undressing, and fell asleep upon the instant.

— *A Christmas Carol,* Charles Dickens

"See now, Dwight, what you gotta do next summer," said Haywood when we were all sitting around the bonfire later, "is get the wood and some shingles and a roll of window screen and we'll build you and Deborah a pond house here. Waist-high walls, the rest screens."

"I'll wire it," said Annie Sue.

"Make the west wall solid and I've got some neon beer signs that would look real good hanging on it," Reese said.

Getting into the swing of things, Will remembered that he had picked up a few himself at a going-out-of-business sale last month. "I can let you have 'em real cheap."

Barbara rolled her eyes and Dwight tried to look stern. "I'd appreciate it if y'all would quit encouraging her."

The whole family knows I've been crazy for neon ever since I was a child. There used to be a corner café on Dawson Street, on the way out of Raleigh. With windows on two sides and walls that were thickly hung with neon signs, that café was as colorful as a Christmas tree, and whoever was behind the wheel would always circle the block for me so I could look my fill. When I was sixteen and newly driving, I stole a blue guitar beer sign from a convenience store in Makely and had to spend the summer working off my crime to Daddy when he found out about it. The store owner let me keep it, though, and it's still in my old room back at the homeplace — along with a multicolored OPEN TILL MIDNIGHT sign I came home with after a New Year's party when I was living with Aunt Zell. I still don't know where or how I acquired that one. I keep thinking they'd look great on the wall of our back porch, but Dwight says they'd look tacky.

"Two are tacky," I agreed. "Eight or ten would be a collection."

"A tacky collection," he told me.

"I think those signs would be cool," said Cal, who was sitting between us.

I put my arm around him and gave him a quick squeeze. "Two votes for neon over here!"

It was almost midnight, but Cal was on a sugar high from toasted marshmallows, and yes, that was probably why Haywood, Herman, and Robert were still awake, too. Between them, they'd emptied a whole bag.

The kids dumped more fallen limbs on the fire, and Dwight and I listened while they interrupted each other in their eagerness to tell how they had decided to gift us with the fountain: how close they came to being discovered when Dwight came home unexpectedly for lunch yesterday, and how they were sure I'd realize that they were there last night to finish connecting a line they had buried from the new breaker box to the outlets they had installed on the pier.

"Who was brave enough to get into that cold water to set up the floodlights and pump?" I asked.

Stevie raised one hand and pointed to Reese with the other. "A friend of mine lent us some wet suits and skin diving equipment so we could finish setting everything in place today while y'all were at work. And yeah, it was really cold."

They showed us the switch for the recirculating pump that powered the geyser and the one for the submerged spotlights.

"And we went ahead and ran some extra wire in case you want a ceiling fan in your pond house," said Annie Sue.

The kids seemed to take it for granted that we were going to build one so we could sit there on a summer evening and admire the fountain without being eaten by mosquitoes. In fact, they had already decided they could rig an outdoor shower and that an open-air pond house would make a cool place for summer parties. Most farm ponds, including the other five or six small ones on our land, are for irrigation and not at all pleasant to swim in — too shallow and too weedy; but this one covers about four acres and stretches across a long natural depression that was always too swampy to farm. One hot droughty summer when all the waterholes were drying up, Daddy had bulldozers come in and scoop it out so deeply all around that when they got to the center, they hit some underground springs and almost lost one of the dozers.

The pier was another cooperative effort by my nieces and nephews and extends far enough out that we can swim without coming into contact with mud or weeds.

The colored lights that shimmered on the surface of the water must have revived ancient memory, because when there was a lull in conversation, Daddy said, "I ever tell y'all about the first Christmas after my daddy passed? The tangerines?"

There was a chorus of nos from his grandchildren and calls of "Tell us" from Will, Zach, and me. Robert, being older, smiled as if he knew the story and already anticipated our reaction.

"Well," said Daddy, "the way it was is that I was still three months shy of turning fifteen when my daddy died and left me the man of the family. There was Mammy, and Sister and Rachel and the twins . . ."

His voice always trails off whenever he mentions his younger twin brothers, Jacob and Jedidiah. Jacob had drowned in Possum Creek when the two were sixteen, and Jed immediately ran away, lied about his age, and joined the Army. He was killed in a training exercise at Fort Bragg before he ever got out of the state.

"Anyhow, it was getting on for Christmas and we was poor as Adam's housecat. Mammy'd already told the little ones that Santa Claus probably won't gonna be able to find our house, but they didn't believe her and just kept talking about what they was gonna find in their stockings. Mammy'd made a rag doll for Rachel outten a flour sack she'd bleached white and did its hair and pigtails with tobacco string. Sister'd used pokeberries to dye a sack purple and stitched up a little doll dress and bonnet. I whittled out new slingshots and whistles for the boys and Mammy'd sent me over to the store to trade some eggs for a little poke of Christmas candy, but all the same, it was looking like a mighty thin Christmas."

Tenderhearted Ruth, who was seated on the tarp nearest him, squeezed his wrinkled hand and said, "Oh, Granddaddy, you must've felt just awful."

Cal was solemn-faced, as if trying to get his mind around a Christmas with nothing plastic or electronic under the tree.

"Now right before Christmas, there come a rain like I ain't seen in no December before nor since. Was like a hurricane only not no wind, just a hard, hard rain coming straight down like water outten the pump in our kitchen sink. Possum Creek flooded something awful. Getting on toward nightfall the next day, a truck drove into the yard and it was a man up from Florida looking to buy a couple of jars of whiskey from my daddy. Said he had two more deliveries to make over in Cotton Grove and he needed something to keep him warm on his trip back home, 'cause he was freezing to death up here."

Daddy paused and gave a foxy grin. "He must've finished off a jar of something a little earlier, though, 'cause it struck me that he was well on his way to being right warm already.

"Well, he left when we told him Daddy was gone, but it won't thirty minutes till here he come again, walking this time. His truck'd got stuck trying to cross the creek and he wanted me to help him get it out. See, the road won't paved back then and the bridge was down almost level with the water, so mud was up to his axles before he ever got to the bridge. He said he'd give me fifty cents if I'd help him. Back then, fifty cents was like five dollars now, so I went right out to the lot and hitched up ol' Maude."

"Who was ol' Maude, Granddaddy?" Cal asked.

My heart lifted at his unconscious use of that name because it surely meant that he felt himself a part of my family.

"Best mule we ever had," Daddy explained. "Strong as a Cub tractor and biddable as a dog."

High praise indeed.

"When we got down to the creek, we unloaded the back of the truck to lighten it some and I seen he was carrying a pile of Florida fruit. Wood crates of oranges, tangerines, and some big yellow things I ain't never seen before. First time I ever laid my eyes on grapefruit.

"We stacked them boxes up on the creek bank and I tied a rope from Maude's traces to the back of the truck, then that man heaved on one side and I heaved on the other and little by little we could feel it start to pull loose.

"The thing was though that Maude was a-straining so hard that just as the truck come free, she let loose with a load of her own and the man stepped right in it. Well, sir, he jumped back, and when he did, his feet slid out from under him and he flailed back into that pile of crates. 'Fore you could say Jack Robinson, two crates of them tangerines tipped over and went tumbling down the creek bank, where they busted open on the rocks and the high water just carried 'em right away.

"That man was cussing Maude and cussing me and even though I helped him load the truck back up, when I asked him for my fifty cents, he told me I oughta be a-paying *him* fifty cents for them tangerines and he just drove off without a thank-you or a kiss-my —"

At this point, Daddy broke off and lit a cigarette to cover his chagrin at nearly using a crude expression in mixed company.

"So what'd you do, Granddaddy?" asked Annie Sue.

"Won't but one thing I could do," he told her. "I took Maude back to the mule lot and got my dip net and a gunnysack and went down to the fish trap I had rigged up a little further down the creek. Sure enough, when I got to it, there was all them shiny orange tangerines bobbling around in amongst the brush that'd got backed up from my trap. Took me almost an hour to fish them all out and lug that gunnysack back up to the barn. I give Mammy enough so everybody's stocking got tangerines, even mine and hers. Then I lugged the rest of 'em to Cotton Grove and traded for some store-boughten stuff Mammy'd been needing. Thanks to ol' Maude, it was a real fine Christmas."

My brothers began to recall some childhood Christmases and my nieces and nephews chimed in with their own memories. How long we would have sat out there talking and laughing, I don't know, but the wind shifted and the temperature started to drop. Cal's eyelids were at half mast and Herman told Will he was about ready to get on back to Dobbs if he and Amy were ready to go, too.

Seth and Richard gathered up the tarps, Reese turned off the fountain, and Daddy gave the fire a final poke that shot glowing sparks up into the starry sky.

We trudged reluctantly back up to the house. There were good-night hugs all around and "See y'all on Christmas Day," then Cal went to bed and we were alone except for Jess and Ruth, who stayed to help clean up.

"Looks like I'll need to make a garbage run tomorrow afternoon," Dwight said as the girls carried another bag of dirty paper plates and napkins out to the garage. "If I wait till Saturday, all the barrels will be overflowing."

I don't know if it was his remark or because Ruth was standing there, but the combination triggered my memory.

"Hey, wait a minute, Dwight!" I said. "Saturday? Annie Sue and the little ones were here before you left for the dump, but Ruth and Jess didn't come till after you got back."

"So?"

"So whatever Ruth threw in the barrel Saturday morning should still be there!"

"Huh?" said Ruth.

"Come on," I told her, hurrying out to the garage, where the five barrels were neatly lined along the wall: one for glass, one for aluminum, one for plastic, and two for general household trash. "You said you picked up trash when y'all were doing that memorial for Mallory Johnson, remember?"

She nodded.

"Where did you toss it?"

She pointed to the barrel nearest the outer door.

By now Dwight realized what this meant and he said, "Wait a minute, Deb'rah. Let Ruth find it. No coaching. Stand over here, Jess, honey, so you can see. This probably won't come to anything, but if it does result in somebody going to trial, y'all might be called as witnesses."

Both girls were wide-eyed as Ruth lifted out the bags that had been brought out from the kitchen waste container since Saturday. There on the bottom was a blue plastic bag from one of the local drugstores.

"That's the one," Ruth said.

She fished it out, unknotted the handles she had tied together, and held it open so we could peer inside.

I saw crumpled napkins, greasy papers, a yellow box, three beer cans, a stained drink cup, and a dirty beer bottle.

"What about that receipt?" I asked.

She started to reach inside, but Dwight stopped her.

"Whoever dumped this probably didn't see a thing worth knowing. All the same, there's no point in adding more prints before I can get my crime scene deputy to take a look."

He carefully reknotted the bag and herded the girls back inside, where he found a clean sheet of paper, smeared some graphite on Ruth's fingertips, and rolled her prints to her awed astonishment.

Jess tried to insist that she would have spent the evening there anyhow, but a deal's a deal. I made her take the money we owed her for watching Cal and sent them home.

"Don't worry about the rest of the mess. We'll take care of it," I said, even though I knew it was all going to have to wait till the next day, tired as we both suddenly were. While I hung up the finery we'd tossed on the bed when Seth made us change clothes, Dwight printed out a search warrant form that would let him seize Charlie Barefoot's phone and computer.

I signed it, and twenty minutes after the girls left, we were both sound asleep.

CHAPTER 27

"There are many things that are
   unbelievable," said Poirot.
"Especially before breakfast, is it not?"
         — "The Adventure of the Christmas
                  Pudding," Agatha Christie

Major Dwight Bryant — Wednesday morning,
December 24
7:25 in the morning and Nelson Barefoot's
truck was still in the driveway when Dwight
parked his truck in front of the Barefoot
home. Charlie Barefoot's white Hyundai
was there, too.

With the search warrant Deborah had
signed for him the night before tucked in
the inner breast pocket of his khaki windbreaker, he walked up to the front door and
rang the bell.

He and his detectives had come to a
temporary dead end on the Wentworth
murders, but while Deputy Raeford

McLamb tried to dig up some more leads, Dwight hoped to wrap up their investigation of Mallory Johnson's death and get it out of their way, clear the decks for an all-out push to find the Wentworth shooter.

At first glance, Joy Medlin's confession would seem to explain the wreck, but Mallory's voice had not sounded slurred or disjointed to him. If a low-dose pill and a shot of vodka had been slipped into a soda ten or fifteen minutes before she left the party, as Joy claimed, it was possible that there had not been enough time for the concoction to take effect, even with the Benadryl.

Instead, maybe it was the fault of an oncoming vehicle, although with such a long straight stretch of highway, wouldn't there have been longer skid marks? And where was the other vehicle's skid marks?

Mallory's fleeting "Dim your stupid —" shriek to an oncoming vehicle sounded as if someone had suddenly blinded her by flicking on their high beams. That "Get over!" would imply that the vehicle was in her lane, more than enough reason for her to brake and swerve.

Although the other driver might have stopped, he (or she?) had not rushed to help. Instead, he had calmly restarted his engine and driven away. Not a hit-and-run, but just as culpable in the eyes of the law.

Until he heard Mallory's complete message, though, Dwight knew he was only second-guessing himself.

The inner door opened and Mrs. Barefoot immediately smiled in recognition, then pushed open the glass storm door to invite him in.

Easy to see where Jeff and now Charlie had gotten their height, Dwight thought. Tall and thin like them, she had iron gray hair tied back with a red ribbon. Her green sweatshirt, worn over black stretch pants, was imprinted with a colorful Christmas design of bells and balls and Rudolph with a wreath around his neck.

"Dwight? My goodness! You're up and out mighty early."

"Sorry," he apologized, but before he could ask for her grandson, Mrs. Barefoot immediately ushered him past the formal living and dining rooms, back to the heart of the house: a large family room with a kitchen at one end, a dining table and six chairs in the middle, and a den at the other end with couches, recliners, and a large flat-screen television in a built-in niche over the fireplace. A tall thin artificial fir tree stood in the corner and presents were heaped around the bottom. Its lights were off but rays from the rising December sun caught the tinsel and sparkled on the shiny glass ornaments.

His nose was assailed by the mingled odors of a full country breakfast — country-cured ham, red-eye gravy, hot black coffee, and made-from-scratch biscuits. A carton of eggs rested on the counter beside the stove ready to be scrambled. A jar of homemade fig preserves was already on the table.

"I was just taking my biscuits out of the oven when I heard the bell," she said, beaming at him. "Now you sit right down at that table and let me get you some coffee. This early, I bet you haven't had a bite of breakfast."

"Actually, I did," he said as she handed him a mug of steaming coffee. Deborah wasn't due in court until 9:30, so she and Cal were still asleep when he left, but he wasn't going to admit that his breakfast had been a bowl of cornflakes.

"All the same, I bet you could find room for a ham biscuit," she said cheerfully, brushing a smear of flour off Rudolph's red nose.

"I thought I heard voices," said Nelson Barefoot from the doorway. "You caught me sleeping in, son."

351

He poured himself coffee and joined Dwight at the table. "Everything going okay?"

"Yes, sir, and I don't mean to interrupt y'all's breakfast, but I need to speak to Charlie a minute."

The older man looked at him expectantly, but when Dwight didn't elaborate, he said, "Well, he ought to be out in a minute. I heard him stirring around when I came down the hall."

Dwight stood to finish his coffee. "If he's up, maybe I could go on back? That'll let me get out of your way quicker."

Husband and wife exchanged glances, and although her eyes were troubled, she said, "Certainly, Dwight. It's right down the hall."

She led the way and tapped on a door. "Charlie? You decent?"

"Ma'am?" He opened the door, barefooted, unshaven, his hair looking like a bird's nest, but dressed in jeans and an open-collar rugby shirt. He was clearly startled to see the big deputy behind his grandmother.

"Major Bryant's here to see you, honey. Don't y'all talk too long now or the biscuits will get cold."

Charlie was clearly unhappy to see him,

but he moved aside so that the deputy could come in. The room was basically tidy. The covers had been pulled up on the bed and books were piled haphazardly up on the desk, which also held a lamp and a laptop, but there were no piles of clothes or dirty dishes.

"I'll keep it short, Charlie," Dwight said, reaching into his breast pocket. "This is a search warrant that allows me to take your cell phone and your computer in for examination."

"*What?* Why?"

"I think you know why, Charlie. Did you really think we wouldn't notice that you had cut out part of the message your sister left on your voice mail?"

"I — I don't know what you're talking about." His eyes dropped and he glanced uneasily at his computer.

Dwight held out his hand. "Your cell phone, please."

The youth gestured to his bedside table.

"Is her message still on this?"

Charlie nodded. "Look, if something got left off when I was trying to transfer it to my computer . . . I mean, I'm no geek. I don't always know how to do things. I told you. I listened to it once, and after that, I only heard enough to know it was the disc.

I couldn't stand to keep hearing her die over and over."

"I can understand that, son. All the same, if we're going to get to the bottom of what happened to her, we have to know all the facts."

"What's to know?" His voice was suddenly angry. "Somebody spiked her Coke and she crashed. Is knowing anything else going to bring her back?"

Dwight knew there was no answer to that. He flipped open the cell phone, located Charlie's voice mail, and flipped through the entries till he came to 16 December 10:37 p.m., keyed PLAY, and held it to his ear.

Charlie abruptly turned and walked over to the window to stare out into the backyard where cardinals and blue jays swooped in and out to the feeders and small finches jostled for their leavings.

This message was longer than the one Dwight had heard before.

"Charlie? Damn you, Charlie, why won't you pick up? You can't do this to us. To me. To Dad and Mom. Not here at Christmas. You don't have one shred of proof. Gallie What's-his-face said he dropped him off at six and his mother was mad at him for getting home so late? So what? That doesn't prove a damn

thing. Who remembers stuff like that anyhow? Besides — Omigod! Where did that — ? Dim your stupid — Get over! I can't see! I — oh, shit! No!"

When it ended, he turned it off and said, "Who's Gallie?"

"I don't know," Charlie said, still staring, watching the birds outside his window. "That part didn't make sense to me."

"He go to her school?"

"If he does, I never heard her say."

He looked at the boy's rigid back and said quietly, "We *will* find out, Charlie."

The boy turned to face him and it was Jeff's face. Jeff's eyes. A muscle twitched in his jaw. "I hope you do."

Dwight put the cell phone in the pocket of his jacket.

"You still going to take my computer? I need it for school."

Dwight hesitated. He now had Mallory's complete last message on the phone. If he took the laptop in, Mayleen Richards could probably find evidence that Charlie had deliberately cut out a few words, but so what?

"I guess not," he said.

"When can I get my phone back?"

Dwight scribbled his number on a notepad. "Call me around noon. Is anything on here password-protected?"

The boy nodded. Half reluctantly, half defiantly, he said, "It's Avenger. With a capital A."

"Avenger?"

Charlie shrugged. "They tell you to pick an unlikely word, and that one just popped into my head."

After leaving the Barefoot home, a little after eight, Dwight stopped to fill up his gas tank. Mrs. Barefoot had insisted that he take with him a ham biscuit as big as his fist, lightly moistened with red-eye gravy, and it was testing all his willpower not to unwrap that fragrant napkin sitting on the dashboard instead of waiting for his drive over to Dobbs. He closed the door on temptation and stood beside the truck. While the gas pumped, he dialed the Johnson number and was relieved that Sarah was the one to answer. He was even more relieved to hear that Malcolm had already left for work and that, yes, he could come over.

One of the garage doors was open when he got there and Sarah waited for him with a large cardboard box that was filled with beautifully wrapped gifts. He instantly realized that these were presents meant for Mallory.

"I'm glad you came, Dwight. Isn't there a gift barrel for needy people at the courthouse?"

He nodded.

"Would you mind taking these in for me? I didn't want to do it in front of Malcolm. I've put a sticky-note on each one to say what it is. Most of them are clothes. They say when you stop believing in Santa Claus, that's when you start getting clothes for Christmas. She did love pretty things."

Her voice wobbled a little and her eyes grew brighter but she quickly gained control of herself and walked over to his truck. "Is there room on your front seat or do you want to put them in back? I can tape the top down if you think I ought to."

"No, they'll fit." He lifted the box and Sarah opened the truck door for him. It was a tight squeeze, but he managed to wedge it in.

She was dressed today in red slacks and a heavy black shawl sweater that seemed to envelop her slender frame. "Amazing how warm it is today after all that ice, isn't it? Y'all lose any trees? Malcolm had the yard service here most of yesterday picking up all the broken limbs."

Dwight realized that she was chattering to delay whatever it was he wanted to say to her and that she was clearly not going to invite him inside. That was fine with him.

"Charlie tells me that you and Malcolm heard Mallory's last message."

She flinched, then nodded.

"Or rather that you heard all of it, while Malcolm got an edited version."

"What are you talking about, Dwight?"

"The version he gave Malcolm left out what she said about the Gallie kid."

"Gallie kid?"

"Who is he, Sarah, and why didn't Charlie want Malcolm to know what Mallory said?"

"I don't know what you're talking about and I don't know any Gallie."

Dwight pulled out Charlie's phone. "Want me to play it for you again, Sarah? Refresh your memory?"

"No!" She pushed the phone away. "No." Her voice trembled. "Please, no."

"Then I'll have to ask Malcolm," he said implacably.

"*No!* Haven't we been through enough? You don't know what you're messing with, Dwight. Do you want to wreck my whole life? Do you know how bad Charlie feels that he and Mallory were fighting when she died? Leave it alone, Dwight. *Please.* It's none of your business!"

And with that she whirled and ran into the garage, pushing the automatic switch as she passed. A moment later the garage door closed smoothly and silently.

When Dwight walked into the squad room shortly after nine, there was an open box of Krispy Kreme doughnuts sitting atop one of the file cabinets and Mayleen was delicately licking sugar from her fingertips, but he shook his head when she pointed to the box. Mrs. Barefoot's ham biscuit had been delicious and filling, but so salty that all he wanted at the moment was a big glass of water.

He set the phone on Mayleen's desk and told her Charlie's password while she looked for a napkin to clean her fingers. "He claims that the editing was accidental, but I'm beginning to think that it doesn't matter, so don't waste much time on it."

"Why not, Major?" Dalton asked.

"I know we were all hoping that whatever he cut out of Mallory Johnson's message would throw more light on her wreck, but I'm afraid it doesn't. Not that I can tell. See what y'all think."

He turned on the cell phone's speaker and pulled up the relevant voice mail. Once again they heard "Silent Night" and Mallory Johnson's voice.

He played it through a second time, but switched it off before they had to listen to Mallory's dying moans.

"Who's Gallie?" asked Dalton and McLamb together.

"Who knows? I called my mother on the way over here, but if he was ever a student at West Colleton, she's not familiar with the name. She's going to call some of the other principals. See if they have a kid named Gallie. I'm pretty sure Charlie and his mother know who this Gallie is, but they don't want to discuss it. Mrs. Johnson says it's none of our business, and unless you can suggest how it has any bearing on the wreck, I don't think we should pursue it. Just make us a complete copy of Mallory's message, Richards, and see if there's anything else from that night that might be relevant. I told Charlie he could have his phone back at noon."

"You say Avenger's his password?" Richards asked.

"Yeah." He turned to Denning and handed him the bag of trash. "This might not be relevant either, but my niece picked it up around the site early Friday morning. It's trash from the Cotton Grove Bojangles' and she says there's a receipt taped to the box that's time-stamped about thirty or forty minutes before Mallory crashed."

Denning opened the bag, saw all the greasy papers, and beamed as if it were a stocking full of goodies. "I should be able to get some fine prints off this."

He carried it into his makeshift lab, pulled on a pair of latex gloves, and carefully itemized each item:

3 aluminum beer cans (Budweiser)
1 Bojangles' box
4 greasy napkins
1 receipt for an 8-piece chicken box — time-stamped 9:45 p.m. December 16
1 muddy beer bottle (Pabst)
1 crumpled form letter notifying the recipient of a sale on tires
1 foam Hardee's drink cup with plastic lid and straw
1 empty cigarette package (Marlboro)
2 red plastic straws
1 sheet of rain stained notebook paper covered with third grade math problems

Humming to himself, Denning took the paper with the fingerprints of Major Bryant's niece and set to work.

A large map of the county covered half of a

wall in the squad room, and after quickly making an electronic copy of Mallory's message, Mayleen Richards eyed the distance from the Bojangles' at the edge of Cotton Grove to the site of Mallory Johnson's crash where the trash had been found. "That's no more than a thirty-minute drive, Major. It could well have been tossed by the person whose headlights blinded her. If you're eating chicken and littering at the same time, you might forget to dim your lights and you might swerve across the center line."

"Let's don't get ahead of ourselves, Richards," he cautioned. "*Might* and *did* aren't even kissing cousins. That trash could have been thrown out anytime between ten-something Tuesday night and six-thirty Friday morning when my niece picked it up."

Mayleen Richards tossed her red head and reached for a folder. "I beg to differ with you, sir. Here're the pictures the trooper took that night and the next morning."

The pictures were in black and white. One of the night pictures, taken from the front of Mallory's car and looking back, showed faint blurs of white on the far shoulder. An almost identical shot the next morning showed trash in the same location. Again, though, even if they blew it up, the distance was probably too great to be able to say for certain that it was a Bojangles' box.

"Any good attorney would call it wishful thinking."

She grinned. "Well, it *is* Christmas and we've all been good, haven't we?"

He laughed and went on into his office, but Mayleen noticed that he took the disc and the player with him.

She sat down at her desk, opened Charlie Barefoot's cell phone, and when prompted for a password, typed in "Avenger."

CHAPTER 28

The more he thought,
the more perplexed he was.
— *A Christmas Carol,* Charles Dickens

Next day was Christmas Eve and I almost overslept. Cal wasn't all that eager to get up either. By the time we left the house, we were both cranky with each other.

"Try to take a nap today, if you can," I told him, wishing I could crawl in for one myself. "We'll be up again late tonight and a full day tomorrow."

He yawned and nodded, although I knew that once he was with Mary Pat and Jake, the excitement and anticipation would kick in.

When I dropped him off at Kate's, Erin Gladstone, the live-in nanny, told me that Kate had already planned some downtime for the children that afternoon. Erin planned to head out after lunch to spend Christmas with some friends in Durham, so I handed her a small gift and a fairly large check and wished her lots of merriment.

Although we didn't get started much before 9:30, court was due to recess for the holiday at noon. Happily, I had heard everything on my docket by 11:17, so when Dwight sent word for me to stop by his office when I was finished, I wished everyone a merry Christmas, slung my robe over my arm, and headed downstairs.

With the search warrant I had signed for him that morning, he had picked up Charlie Barefoot's phone and Mayleen Richards had transferred the uncensored message to a DVD disc.

Dwight was disappointed with it, though, and when we were in his office with the door closed, he said, "It doesn't give us any more information about the wreck itself, but she was sure as hell upset about something, and that, combined with the other stuff in her system, probably had her too distracted to pay attention to the road. You picked up on something we missed the first time around, let's see if you can make more sense out of this than I can."

A DVD player from the squad room now sat on his desk and he mashed a button and once again I was listening to Mallory Johnson's angry young voice over the bells of "Silent Night."

I had to take several deep breaths after listening to Mallory die again. "Who's Gallie What's-his-face?" I asked.

He shook his head.

"Didn't you ask Charlie?"

"Of course I did. He says he never met the kid, and yet I get the feeling there's something there that's important."

He told me how he had gone by the Johnson house, how Sarah had given him all of Mallory's presents to donate to the clerk of court's gift drive, and how she, too, had first denied knowing any Gallie and then told him it was none of his business.

"Mallory said this Gallie's mother was mad at him for being late," I mused. "Why would a kid getting home late ruin Christmas for everybody? Does he go to West Colleton?"

"I spoke to Mama and she said she'd ask around, but she's never heard of a student called Gallie at her school."

"I guess you don't want to ask Malcolm yet?"

"Not after Sarah's reaction. She doesn't want him to know and the poor guy's hurting bad enough without adding to it. Whatever's going on in that family, I guess she's right. If it doesn't have any bearing on the wreck, then it really isn't any of our business, is it?"

"Every family has its secrets," I said lightly, hoping he would never learn all the facts behind my first appointment to the bench. "I don't suppose you want to have lunch?"

"No, I'll grab a bowl of chili across the street. You off to pick up Cal now?"

"After I run a couple of errands. Don't forget that Kate and Rob are expecting us at six."

He gave me an absentminded kiss good-bye and I went out to the parking lot, with Mallory's words running through my head. Calling him "Gallie What's-his-face" made it sound as if she didn't know him. A kid from another high school? On the other hand, something about his mother being mad at him because he didn't come straight home was ringing a distant bell. Unfortunately, the bell was so distant that it faded from my mind as I tossed my robe in the car and ran through the mental list of things that still needed doing before tomorrow.

Most of Dwight's family would gather at Kate and Rob's tonight for dinner and to exchange gifts. Tomorrow was when my family would get together.

Kate and Rob are very dear. I've come to love them almost like blood siblings. They are thoughtful and kind and Dwight and I are eternally grateful that Cal can go there after school rather than day care. The evening would be warm and loving and in perfect Christmas-card taste.

And the get-together with my rowdy bunch?

Not so much.

I was smiling as I drove out of the parking lot, but when I got to the intersection where I should have turned left to go home, I spotted Reid Stephenson, my cousin and former law partner, taking the steps to our old office two at a time. Now why did I look at Reid and think *Gallie?*

The light changed from red to green. Instead of turning left, I drove through the intersection and parked in front of Lee and Stephenson, Attorneys at Law. Maybe Reid would like to buy me lunch.

CHAPTER 29

"Do they really catch deer that way?
How vile."
— "The Running of the Deer,"
Reginald Hall

*Major Dwight Bryant — Wednesday afternoon,
December 24*

Deputy Mayleen Richards tapped on Dwight's open door shortly after one and said, "Charlie Barefoot's here for his phone. Okay if we give it back to him?"

"Find anything else relevant to our investigation?"

"No, sir."

"Then let me have it." He took the cell phone and walked down to the front desk where the boy waited. As persuasively as he could, he said, "I told you, son, that your dad and I played ball together. Are you sure there's not something more you can tell me about your sister's death?"

369

Charlie met his gaze without blinking. "You played ball with Malcolm, too," he said bitterly; and without waiting for Dwight to reply, he took the phone and left.

Puzzled, Dwight went back to his office. Was Charlie somehow implying that Malcolm was involved with Mallory's death? When everyone said he idolized his daughter? Would have lain down in a mud puddle so that she could walk across without dirtying her shoes?

It didn't make sense.

The squad room was semi-deserted by now. Everyone expendable had taken off for the holiday. Richards had straightened her desk and already had her jacket on. He knew that she would be spending tomorrow with Mike Diaz's extended family because her own family members were still hostile to their relationship.

"Okay if I leave now?" she asked.

"Denning gone yet?"

"I don't think so. I know he wanted to run some fingerprints through IAFIS —"

Before she could finish the sentence, Percy Denning hurried in, excitement and triumph gleaming in his eyes. "Guess what, ya'll? I ran the prints off the beer cans and the chicken box and got a hit. Jason Wentworth! So then I checked our own records

370

and the other multiple prints are his brother Matt's! So that bright light the Johnson girl was screaming about?"

"Faison's halogen flashlight!" Mayleen exclaimed. "Of course! They were sitting there next to the woods with their lights off, getting ready to jacklight the field for deer."

"And when a car came zipping along, they probably thought it'd be a hoot to jacklight the driver."

They could all picture it in their minds. The seemingly deserted road, the girl talking on her cell phone, angry at her brother, oblivious to any dark truck parked next to dark trees. Then suddenly a blinding light, that seemed to come from out of nowhere and at such an odd angle that she must have thought it was in her lane. No wonder Matt had been so shaken up when word came that Mallory had died. No wonder he'd skipped school Friday and gone out to talk with Jason.

"So the Wentworths killed Mallory, but then who killed the Wentworths?" said Dwight.

Even as he said it, he had a sinking suspicion that he knew. "Sorry, Richards," he said, "but I need you to check the gun records. See if Malcolm Johnson ever applied for a permit for a thirty-two. And find out what kind of car he's driving these days. Denning, hop upstairs and see if there's a judge still around to sign us a search warrant. I don't know how the hell he knew the Wentworths were there, but —"

"I know," said a voice behind him.

Dwight turned and saw Deborah standing there, white-faced.

CHAPTER 30

"— I dreamed me and Rosita was married instead of her and him; and we was living in a house, and I could see her smiling at me, and — oh! h — I, Mex, he got her; and I'll get him — yes, sir, on Christmas Eve he got her, and that's when I'll get him."
— "A Chaparral Christmas Gift," O. Henry

Lunch with Reid was as informative as I had hoped. I had a name now to go with a conversation I'd had back in June, but I still didn't know what it could mean until I remembered Saturday morning and how irate Isabel had been when she realized that Jane Ann's college friends had dropped her off at my house to bake cookies rather than taking her straight home.

Once again, Isabel was my go-to person, only this time, by the time we finished talking, she realized what I was asking. "Oh,

Lord, honey. You gonna tell Dwight?"

"I think I have to, Isabel. Don't you?"

Now I stood in the doorway of the detective squad room. I had heard enough to realize that the Wentworth boys had blinded Mallory with that flashlight and that Dwight and his deputies now suspected Malcolm of gunning them down on Friday morning.

I heard Dwight say, "I don't know how the hell he knew the Wentworths were there, but —"

"I know," I said quietly.

"Deb'rah?"

"Jessica said she'd heard that Malcolm was so torn up and half mad with grief that he was out walking that road the next morning, trying to figure out why Mallory swerved. He was probably looking for a dead dog or something. Instead he found fresh chicken bones and probably a piece of junk mail with Jason Wentworth's name on it. I can't swear he was in my courtroom the day I confiscated Wentworth's rifle and hunting license for jacklighting deer, but I can't swear he wasn't. Doesn't matter, though. The *Clarion* ran his name when they did that article about illegal hunting practices last fall, remember? Malcolm would have jumped to the same conclusions y'all did in a heartbeat."

I turned to Deputy Denning. "If you can't find another judge upstairs, I'll sign a search warrant for that bastard's house."

Dwight frowned at me.

"Sorry," I said, realizing a little late that I probably ought not to go blabbing the rest of my suspicions to the world. "All the same, I *will* sign one if all the others have left for the holiday."

I let Dwight lead me into his office and close the door.

"What's all this about, Deb'rah?"

"Charlie Barefoot thinks Malcolm killed Jeff. I do, too."

"What?"

"And right now, Isabel probably does, too."

"Isabel? How did the hell did Isabel get into this?"

"Last summer," I said. "Wrightsville Beach. Our summer conference?"

He smiled, remembering the Jacuzzi in my hotel room. "Yeah?"

"I told you that the trial lawyers were having their conference, too. Remember? I had a drink with Reid and some of his colleagues that first night before I found one of my colleagues floating in the river?"

"So?"

"There was an attorney at the table that they called Gallie. Not a high school student, Dwight. Someone out of Malcolm's past. I had lunch with Reid just now and he says the guy's real name is Paul Gallagher. He married a girl from Asheville and has been in practice out there ever since he graduated from law school. He's originally from Fuquay, though, and when he heard that I was from outside Cotton Grove, he asked me if I knew various people. Malcolm Johnson was one of several he mentioned. He said he and Malcolm used to room next door to each other at Carolina and hadn't seen each other in years till he ran into Malcolm and his son in Raleigh last spring. He said the son wanted to hear all about what Malcolm was like when they were in college."

Dwight still didn't get it. "What's that got to do with Jeff Barefoot? Or Isabel, for that matter."

"Gallagher said he was poor as Job's turkey back then. Didn't have a car and Malcolm often gave him a ride home since Fuquay's right on the way to Cotton Grove. Maybe I'm jumping to conclusions without a net," I said, "but I think you ought to look up the records, see if there was much of an investigation when Jeff Barefoot fell off his roof that night and supposedly hit his head on a rock. See if that's the same day the kids would be getting home from Carolina. Fuquay's only twenty minutes from Cotton Grove. If he says Malcolm dropped him off around six, why did it take Malcolm two hours to get home?"

Exasperated, Dwight said, "Now how the hell do you know it took him two hours?"

"I called Isabel. That woman doesn't forget a thing."

When my sister-in-law answered the phone an hour earlier, I had asked her if she remembered telling me how Malcolm and Sarah had married.

"Oh, honey, yes," she'd said. "I can't stop grieving for them. Especially poor Sarah, losing her daughter right here at Christmas just like she lost her first husband. It was a blessing for her to have another fine man wanting her, but it sure did hurt Jeff's mama. I told you about that."

"Yes. That she was bitter because Malcolm got Jeff's wife and Jeff's son and Jeff's life." Hesitantly, I had asked Isabel, "I don't suppose anybody asked where Malcolm was when Jeff fell off the roof?"

"Now, you know something? That's exactly what Jeff's mama wanted to know

377

when Sarah was fixing to get married again. She just couldn't believe that Jeff would fall off his own roof when he'd been up and down so many roofs his whole life."

"She thought Mal had something to do with it?"

"No, not really. That was the grief talking. Like I said, Jeff and Mal stayed real good friends. Only time they had a cross word was when Jeff and Sarah eloped to South Carolina. He thought Jeff should've told him so he could be the best man."

"So where *was* he, Isabel?"

"Driving home from Chapel Hill for Christmas. I heard he hadn't been in the house a half hour till somebody called him about Jeff's fall. His mother was so provoked. She'd made a dinner party 'specially so Malcolm could meet the daughter of some fancy-pants businessman in Raleigh. They were supposed to eat at seven-thirty, but he didn't get home till almost eight, and even then, soon as he got that phone call, he left and went right over to Jeff's house. He was so tore up about it, he even finished stringing up the lights and threw the rock into the gully out back of the house so Sarah wouldn't have to see it."

"Now wasn't that real thoughtful of him?" I had said.

At that point, Isabel had caught her breath. "When you say it like that, honey . . . you don't really think — ? Do you?"

"And then he married her eight months later."

"Oh, Lord, honey," she had said. "You gonna tell Dwight?"

When I finished repeating that conversation to Dwight, I said, "Don't you think Jeff's mother might have hinted at something like that to Charlie when he and Malcolm started having problems? Then Charlie met Gallagher last spring and right after that he changed his name. You don't think the two events are related?"

"That's an awfully big jump, shug," Dwight said. "You don't know that Jeff died the same evening this Gallagher person hitched a ride. Or that it was even the same Christmas."

Even while he was throwing up reasonable objections, I could see his mind working.

"Malcolm always did go after whatever he wanted, but this? I don't know, Deb'rah."

Denning and Richards returned almost together. Denning had caught Judge Longmire on his way out the door. He agreed to hang around a few minutes longer if it turned out that Malcolm Johnson really did own a .32.

"He does," said Richards. "Bought it eight years ago. What you want to bet that he's the one that smashed Faison's flashlight?"

"Get me a warrant form," Dwight told her.

He turned to me with a what-can-I-tell-you look on his face.

I fixed him with a stern eye. "It's not even two o'clock yet. If y'all can't find that gun and book him in three hours, you're not much of a detective. Besides, it's your family. Six o'clock, mister."

CHAPTER 31

> . . . but he knew what path lay straight
> before him, and he took it.
> — *A Christmas Carol,* Charles Dickens

*Major Dwight Bryant — Wednesday afternoon,
December 24*

"Hope you know what you're doing, Bryant," said chief district court judge F. Roger Longmire when he signed the search warrant fifteen minutes later. "His daddy's got a lot of influence up in that end of the county."

"I know," Dwight said. In addition to Richards and Denning, he had pulled McLamb off his search for more Wentworth enemies and radioed a couple of patrol cars to rendezvous with them a mile from the Johnson home.

"Maybe I'll ride along with you," said Sheriff Poole when Dwight briefed him on the situation. "If it goes down like you think,

I'll bring him back to Dobbs, see he gets his lawyer, and you can just go on home to Deborah and your boy."

Bo almost never talked about his late wife, but something in his voice told Dwight that he still missed Marnie pretty badly and that Christmas was making it worse.

"Why don't you come have Christmas with us at Mr. Kezzie's tomorrow?" he said as they neared Cotton Grove. "You know there's always room for another pair of legs under his table."

"Aw now, I couldn't do that," Bo said. "Could I?"

"Sure you can. You just have to promise not to ask what the fruitcake's been aged in."

The sheriff chuckled. "Well, if you're sure . . . ?"

"I'm sure. Bring along your banjo, though. With the Knotts, you have to sing for your supper."

When the small cavalcade of official vehicles pulled into the circular drive, Malcolm Johnson was outside on this mild winter day with a pair of branch loppers, cutting out some broken limbs from the dogwoods scattered across the front. Twigs and branches were piled in his garden cart. The middle garage door was up and they could see a white late-model Toyota inside.

"What's happening, Dwight?" he called when his old teammate stepped down from his truck and Denning moved toward the garage with his video camera. Upon seeing the smaller man who emerged from the other side of the truck, he frowned. "Sheriff Poole?"

Although he and Dwight were the same age, Johnson's hair had a little more gray and his Carolina sweatshirt and black chinos hung loosely on his tall frame as if he had recently lost weight.

"Sorry to do this, Malcolm," Dwight said, "but we have a warrant to search your premises for a handgun. Also to impound your car if it has a dent on the left rear fender."

"My gun?"

"The thirty-two you bought eight years ago."

"Malcolm?" Sarah Johnson had appeared in the front doorway and looked out at them with troubled eyes.

"It's okay, honey. Stay there."

But she stepped out onto the porch. "Dwight? What's going on?"

"Sarah, please," Malcolm said, his voice anguished.

"Is it about Mallory? Did you find out who spiked her Coke?"

"I'm sorry," Dwight said again. "We're not here about that, Sarah. We're here to get Malcolm's gun."

"His gun? But why?" She turned to her husband. "Malcolm, why do they want your gun?"

He held out his arm to her, but when she kept her distance, he dropped it as if in surrender.

"They think I shot the guys that killed Mallory. That is why y'all're here, right, Dwight? You want to see if the bullets you found in those bastards came from my gun? Well, so what? They got what they deserved and —"

"Now hold on here a minute," said the sheriff, stepping forward and waving his hand to silence Malcolm Johnson. "We've not asked you any questions and you might want to stop right there, son, and think if you want your lawyer here before you say anything else."

"Yeah, you're right, Sheriff. Sarah, honey, go call Pete Taylor and tell him —" He glanced at Dwight and Bo. "I guess I ought to tell him to meet us at the jail?"

Bo nodded.

"Better call my dad, too."

"For God's sake, Malcolm! What have you done?"

"Don't worry about it, Sarah. Everything's going to be all right. Just go call Pete and Dad, okay?"

Pale-faced, she went inside to do as he'd asked.

When she was gone, Johnson turned to them with urgency. "Please. This is going to be rough on her, coming on top of Mallory and all this mess with Charlie. Try not to upset her any more than you have to, okay? There's no need to tear our house apart. The gun's upstairs in our bedroom, in the nightstand on the left side of the bed."

Dwight nodded to Richards, and as she entered the house, Denning walked up the drive from the garage. "There's a scrape mark in the right place, Major, and it looks like the Higgins car left a little silver paint on that fender."

Malcolm Johnson heard those words as if it were nothing to do with him. Well, the man did sell insurance, thought Dwight. He must have calculated the odds already. A father temporarily deranged by grief? Who guns down the men who probably were responsible for his daughter's death? With all the evidence they had — and they would no doubt find more before it came to trial

— a jury would have to find him guilty, but his attorney would have argued their incompetent DA down to the lowest possible charges. Malcolm might get a little prison time, but by the time his case wound through the courts, he stood a good chance of winding up on probation with a suspended sentence. And few people in his circle would shun him for his act or think less of him.

On the other hand, if he'd murdered for another man's wife as Deborah and Isabel and Charlie Barefoot thought? The Barefoots might be blue-collar, but they were as well respected in Cotton Grove as Shelton Johnson and his two sons. Probably better liked, too. To learn that Malcolm had killed Jeff to get Sarah? No, that was not something people would easily overlook. Nor Sarah either, he suspected.

"We know about your friend Gallie," he told Malcolm. "Or should I say Gallagher?"

It was a direct hit. The blood drained from Malcolm's face. "What the hell are you talking about?"

"You don't remember the guy who hitched a ride home with you the Christmas that Jeff died?"

Malcolm's eyes darted toward the front door. "You're not going to say anything like that to her, are you?"

"Why not?" said Bo, stepping in to get a closer look at the fear on Malcolm's face. "If she's involved, she's gonna need a lawyer, too, won't she?"

"*Involved?* You think Sarah — ? For the love of God, Dwight! You used to be my friend. We trusted each other out there on the court. Please, man, don't say anything to her about Gallie. I couldn't bear it if she — Listen, I'll confess to the shooting. I'll make a statement right now. Is it a deal?"

"No deals," Dwight said. "But we don't have to say anything about that other matter now."

Malcolm let out the breath he'd been holding. "Thank you."

Richards came down the front steps with the handgun inside a plastic bag. "Smells like it was recently fired, Major."

She was followed by Sarah Johnson, whose dark eyes seemed to have sunk even deeper into her skull. "Your dad's on his way over. Pete said he'd meet you in Dobbs."

"Thanks, darling. Everything's going to be all right. I promise you. I'll be home as soon as Pete can sort this out." He gave a rueful laugh and looked at Bo. "Am I under arrest yet, Sheriff? Or can I change clothes and wash up?"

"No need to change," Bo said mildly.

"I'm coming with you," said Sarah.

He smiled down at her and drew her thin body close to his. "Thanks, honey. Just let me wash up and get my wallet, Sheriff."

Dwight glanced at Bo, who shrugged. While it was most unlikely that Malcolm Johnson would try to run, the house did back up on thick woods and probably had several rear exits. Better to forestall that possibility than risk having to stage a manhunt, thought Dwight, and he signaled for McLamb to follow their suspect into the house.

Bo patted his chief deputy on the shoulder and shook his head in wonderment at Mayleen Richards, who was standing there, too. "Well, Dwight, I said I wanted the Wentworth killings wrapped up by Christmas and damned if you didn't do it. Sure didn't expect it to come out like this, though."

"Me either, Bo."

"You got any hard evidence in that other matter?"

"Nope. And after all this time, I doubt there is any. His mother's dead and Shelton Johnson's sure as hell not gonna remember anything about a dinner party that would cast suspicion on his son. We can question this Gallagher man, see just how much he actually did tell Charlie. As for Charlie, it'll depend on which he wants more: revenge for his real father's death or to spare his mother any more hurt."

"Don't forget his password," Mayleen Richards said.

Bo Poole looked puzzled. "His password?"

"For his phone," she told him. "Avenger."

Bo gave a sour laugh, then rocked back on his heels. "Mayleen and me, we can take it from here, Dwight. You might as well go on home and enjoy your Christmas."

"You sure?"

"You know good as me that this is just the opening round. Shelton Johnson will post his boy's bond and he'll be back home before dark."

"You've got my cell number if anything comes up," Dwight said, then, wishing them all a merry Christmas, he got in his truck and headed for the farm. Not even four o'clock yet, and because he would be practically passing it on his way through town, he swung by the Wentworth house.

As he reached the door, Mrs. Wentworth opened it and was even more startled than he to see someone standing there.

"Major Bryant!" she exclaimed. "I didn't hear the bell."

He smiled and shook his head. "Sorry. I

didn't get a chance to ring it yet."

"I was just coming out to turn on my lights," she said and reached down to plug a tangle of cords into the multi-outlet socket beside the door. Immediately the near bushes twinkled with colorful lights. "Was there something I can do for you?"

"No, ma'am. I just stopped by to say that we've arrested the man who shot your stepsons. I can't give you any names or details yet, but I thought you'd like to know that."

"Did he say why he did it?"

"I'm sorry, ma'am. It'll come out, but I can't talk about it right now."

"Well, I guess that's something anyhow. Thank you, Major."

Dwight had started to turn away when she said, "Did you see it?"

"See what, ma'am?"

"I went ahead and opened the present Matt put under the tree for me. But it wasn't just from him. Jason signed the card, too."

She pointed to a small grotto she had constructed between two of the foundation bushes. The grotto was framed with several strands of clear lights and there in the center stood the small concrete Jesus that had been stolen from the Welcome Home store, his hand raised in blessing.

Mrs. Wentworth looked at him with a sad smile. "I guess Jason finally realized that I loved him, too."

Although the Johnson house and grounds looked imposing from outside, inside the house felt like a real home, spacious and soundly constructed. No expenses spared, thought Raeford McLamb as he trailed the couple upstairs, keeping a discreet distance. No hollow-core doors here. They were thick solid wood, the ceilings were at least nine feet high with crown molding, and he detected not the slightest wobble in the curved banister.

When they reached the master bedroom, which was carpeted in a thick moss green that echoed the custom-made quilted spread on the king-size bed, he hung back in the doorway to give husband and wife a semblance of privacy. French doors opened onto a wide balcony with wrought iron railings that mimicked vines and leaves. Tall oaks and maples would shade the balcony in summer, but winter's late afternoon sunlight filtered through their leafless branches now.

At the near end of the large room sat an overstuffed couch and a comfortable-looking lounge chair. Low bookcases held framed family photographs and McLamb immediately spotted a picture of Mallory in her homecoming queen gown and tiara. In another, she and her mother sat on a white wicker loveseat while her father and brother stood behind.

Despite the sheriff's telling him he needn't change, Malcolm Johnson took off his Carolina sweatshirt and pulled a dark blue crewneck sweater over his head.

"You married, Deputy?" he asked, as his head emerged from the sweater.

"Yessir."

"Children?"

"Two. A boy and a girl."

"They all excited about Santa Claus?"

McLamb nodded. "We don't have a fireplace and they keep trying to figure out where's the best place to hang their stockings. I think they're gonna make me put up hooks beside the tree."

Johnson paused in the doorway of the bathroom. "How long you been married?"

"Eight years now."

The older man glanced at his wife, who was folding up the discarded blue sweatshirt. "Going on twenty for us." He caught her hand. "And except for this week, it hasn't been a bad twenty, has it, honey?"

She smiled and he squeezed her shoulder, then walked into the bathroom.

"Leave the door open," said McLamb and moved over to the doorway, where he could keep the man in full view.

The bathroom was as lavish as everything else he had seen in this house: marble slabs on the floor and counter, a large walk-in shower with the toilet hidden in an alcove at the rear. A frosted glass window probably opened onto the balcony, but there did not seem to be any other exits. Nevertheless, he watched as Johnson squirted toothpaste on the brush and turned on the water.

The years of being a gracious hostess seemed to kick in as Sarah Johnson smoothed the wrinkles from the quilted spread. "How old are your children? Do you have pictures?"

"Yes, ma'am," he said, and with one eye on Johnson's back, he pulled out his wallet to show her the photo taken last week of both his children seated on Santa's broad lap. "This one's Rosy and that little guy is Jordo."

"Such a sweet age," she said. "I hope you're enjoying them."

He put his wallet back in his pocket. "We do, ma'am."

"They grow up so fast. They'll be gone in

393

a blink of the eye."

At that her own eyes filled and McLamb glanced to the bathroom. Johnson had filled the basin with water and was bending over to wash his face when suddenly the sink and counter and tiled floor was splashed with red and Johnson slumped to the floor, a razor blade in his hand. Blood pumped from a deep gash on the side of his neck.

"Oh, shit!" McLamb cried and darted into the bathroom, grabbed a towel, and tried to apply pressure to the base of Johnson's neck.

Sarah Johnson was screaming and she crouched beside her husband as his blood soaked her hands and shirt.

With eyes wide open, he tried to reach for her. "Sorry," he whispered. "I loved you so much . . . so . . ."

The blood stopped spurting and a moment later he was gone.

CHAPTER 32

The stockings were hung by the chimney
    with care,
In hopes that St. Nicholas soon would be
    there.
> — "A Visit from St. Nicholas,"
> Clement Clarke Moore

To my complete and utter surprise, Dwight drove into the yard around four-thirty as Cal, Bandit, and I were coming back from the woods with a basket of holly, cedar, and pine so that I could make a fresh centerpiece for the dining table.

Cal gave his dad a wave and went on into the house to take a shower.

Instead of getting out of the truck immediately, Dwight gave me a wait-a-minute gesture and opened the door, with the phone still to his ear. When he finally did emerge, his face was grim.

"What's wrong?" I asked.

"That was Bo. Malcolm Johnson's killed himself."

"Oh, Dwight." Even though I was sure he had killed at least three young men, the news was still shocking. "How? Why?"

"We went out to arrest him just now. When I left, he was on his way in to wash up and get his wallet. Bo thinks he palmed a razor blade when he opened the bathroom cabinet to get his toothpaste, and even though McLamb and Sarah were standing right there by the open door, he cut his jugular before they realized what he was doing. He practically begged us not to mention Gallagher in front of Sarah. I guess he couldn't stand to see her learn that he'd killed Jeff."

"Poor Sarah." I sighed. "Do you have to go back?"

"No, Bo says he'll take care of it."

"You want me to call Kate and say we can't come?"

"No." He took a deep breath as if to shake it off and reached for my hand. "Let's walk down to the pond and take another look at that damn fountain."

We walked and talked for a good forty minutes, and yes, that silly fountain finally did make us smile again when we turned it on.

We agreed that we wouldn't mention the murders or Malcolm's death at the party tonight. No need to cast a pall for the others. And once we had loaded our presents for Dwight's family in the trunk of the car and headed out into the cool evening, Cal's excitement and high good spirits kept us from dwelling on it.

Kate's first husband, Jake Honeycutt, had inherited a house that had been in his family for well over a hundred years. Initially built as a four-over-four wooden farmhouse, the passage of time and the family's increasing prosperity had brought extensive remodels and renovations that added porches and ells and a long single-floor addition on the back until it was difficult to see the original lines of the house.

Inside, all was warmth, red velvet ribbons, glowing candles, and traditional decorations that would have made Scrooge's nephew feel right at home. A wide central hall ran the length of the original house and the staircase that curved up to the second-floor landing had a thick evergreen garland twined in and out of the railings. ("Fake cedar," Dwight murmured in my ear, although it looked so real, he had to touch it to be certain. "Don't be a snob," I murmured back.)

Both the front and back parlors had pocket doors that could be opened to form a large space. The front parlor was the living room with two large couches and several lounge chairs. After Jake's death, Kate had turned the back parlor into a formal dining room.

We were the last to arrive and barely had time to drink a festive cup of nonalcoholic eggnog before Bessie Stewart, Miss Emily's housekeeper who helps out in the kitchen on occasions like this, called us to the table.

Not counting R.W., who sat at a corner in his high chair, fourteen of us sat down to an early dinner. Kate had put all the leaves in the table so that the children wouldn't have to be shunted off to the kitchen.

Dwight's sister Beth and her family had gone to spend the holidays with his people down in South Carolina, but Nancy Faye and her husband James and their three stair steps who range in age from six to ten were there, as was Miss Emily.

When we first arrived, I did not immediately recognize the elderly woman who now sat between Rob and little Jake until Kate said, "You remember Mrs. Lattimore, don't you, Deborah? Jake's great-aunt?"

"Of course," I said, taking her thin hand

in mine. "How nice to see you again."

"You're Susan Stephenson's daughter, are you not?"

"Yes, ma'am," I said, instantly reverting to my childhood when I had been slightly afraid of this tall, autocratic woman.

"You're the judge?"

I nodded.

Widowed when she was in her early forties, Jane Lattimore had never remarried, but lived on alone in a huge Queen Anne house near the center of Cotton Grove. Built when houses of that size occupied half a block, it had a wrought iron fence all around the property and a life-size iron deer stood on the side where her grandchildren, who were all slightly older than me, used to play croquet and badminton when they came to visit her. I think she had three or four children, who scattered to the far reaches of the country soon after finishing school, but she continued to live alone in that big house except for a housekeeper and a widowed cousin. Her youngest child was Anne Harald, a Pulitzer Prize–winning photojournalist, who lived in New York and occasionally had shows of her photographs at a gallery in Raleigh.

Last year, when I was trying to sort it all out, Kate had patiently sat me down with a family tree she had drawn up for Mary Pat. Kate's cousin Philip, a wealthy venture capitalist, had married Jake's cousin Patricia, who was much younger, and both had died before Mary Pat was three.

She then showed me that Jake's grandfather and Mrs. Lattimore had been brother and sister, which made Mrs. Lattimore his great-aunt and her children his cousins. I'm pretty good with family trees, but my head was spinning when she finished. Nevertheless, it did help me understand how Kate wound up with a rather valuable painting. Before his death, Jake had been fairly close to Mrs. Lattimore's granddaughter, a homicide detective with the NYPD until she inherited a fortune from the artist Oscar Nauman, who had been her lover when he died. She had given Kate one of his works when little Jake was born and it hung in the front parlor. The painting didn't really go with the antique furniture, but the colors were nice.

Mrs. Lattimore has always been a very large fish in small-pond Cotton Grove. She's sat on just about every board the town has, but her abiding love is for the school system, and it was thanks to her efforts that shabby old Zachary Taylor High was torn down and replaced with modern West Colleton. Even though Jake is dead and Kate is no blood kin, Kate still keeps a watchful eye on his great-aunt and often invites her to dinner. This was the first time I had laid eyes on her in over six months and I was shocked to see how fragile she now seemed. Once or twice during dinner, I saw Kate's lively face look with concern at her son's great-great-aunt; and when we moved back into the front parlor after dinner, I pulled Kate aside to ask if Mrs. Lattimore was ill.

"I'm afraid so, but she won't admit it. She's ninety-one and she says she's not going to spend her last few months in chemo with a bald head. Worse, she's made me promise not to say anything to Anne or Sigrid, but I don't know, Deborah. Maybe when you —" She clapped her hand over her mouth like a guilty child.

"Maybe when I what?" I said.

She grinned. "Never mind. You'll soon find out." Then raising her voice, she said, "Okay, everybody. Who's ready to open presents?"

"Me," cried Nancy Faye's daughter Jean.

"Me, too!" Cal and Mary Pat sang out at the same time, which made them dissolve in giggles.

Soon the living room floor was awash in torn Christmas paper and discarded ribbons and bows.

There were the usual sweaters and scarves for the adults and toys and books for the children, but what blew me away was the gift that Kate and Rob gave us.

Elaborately wrapped in a small gold box was what looked like two brass house keys.

Puzzled, I said, "What do they unlock?"

"My New York apartment," said Kate with a happy smile. "You guys never got a honeymoon and you've never been to New York together. The apartment's going to be empty for most of January because my tenant's going to Italy then, so I asked if you could housesit for part of the time."

"Really?" I looked at Dwight. "Can we do this?"

"Well," he said as a slow smile spread over his face, "I've got a lot of vacation time coming and you haven't taken off much this year."

"Here," said Miss Emily, handing Dwight an envelope. "This goes with it."

Inside were tickets to a Broadway show that was getting good reviews. I hadn't spent much time in New York since shortly after Mother died when I ran away from home and did some stupid things. Suddenly my head was filled with images of the city: the crowded streets, the delicious-smelling delis, the small funky clubs, the graffiti, the library where I first met — Well. Never mind *that* particular image.

"Oh, golly, Kate!" I jumped up to give her a hug. "And all we got you was a sweater."

"Which I love," she assured me.

By nine o'clock, all the presents had been opened and the little ones were yawning. As Dwight and Cal were taking some of the gifts we'd received out to the car, Mrs. Lattimore pulled me aside and thrust into my hands a small heavy package wrapped in brown paper and tied with string. "I've been so worried about what to do about this," she said. "When Kate told me she was going to lend you and Dwight her apartment, I knew this was the answer. I can't trust it to the mails and Dwight *is* a police officer, isn't he?"

"Excuse me?" I said, bewildered by both the package and her words.

With a hint of her old imperiousness, she lifted her chin and fixed me with her crystalline gray eyes. "Please take this to my daughter Anne in New York. She'll know what to do with it."

Before I could protest, she turned back into the room and called for her coat.

"I'm ready to go now," she said, and Rob,

who was to drive her home, immediately escorted her down the steps.

There was nothing else to do but to slide the package into a shopping bag with some of Cal's toys and grab my own coat.

Once home, Cal announced that he was going straight to bed so that Christmas morning would come sooner. With a self-conscious grin, he hung his stocking on a hook over the fireplace and went and got into his pajamas. Dwight and I tucked him in and Dwight said, "Sleep tight, buddy. Sure hope Santa leaves you something besides switches and coal."

"Not funny, Dad," he said with a big yawn.

Because we had to wait till he was asleep to help Santa come, I went and put on my own pajamas.

When I came back out, Dwight was sitting on the floor watching his train circle the tree, its small headlight shining and an occasional low *tooot-tooot* of its whistle.

I sat down on the floor beside him. "That's a pretty amazing gift from Kate and Rob."

"It is, isn't it?"

"You do want to go, don't you?"

"A week in New York? With you? Of course I do. It's such a great city."

I was surprised. "You sound like you know

it pretty well. I didn't realize."

"Guess I never talked much about it. After Jonna and I split up and she left D.C. to move back to Virginia, I used to take the train up to New York two or three times a month. Hey, why don't we do that, too?"

"Do what?"

"Take the train instead of flying."

"I've never been on a train," I said.

Now it was his turn to be surprised. "In that case, then, maybe we should splurge and get a compartment." He gave me an exaggerated leer. "Get an early start on our honeymoon."

I leered right back at him. "You saying there are even more things I don't know about you?"

He laughed, then we both lapsed into silence until he sighed and blew the whistle.

I touched his hand. "There's something so sad and mournful about that sound, isn't there?"

"Yeah," he said and I knew he was thinking about this past week, too. The Wentworth boys lying dead while ice rained down on them. Sarah and Malcolm standing beside Mallory's coffin. Malcolm's suicide.

But life, of course, does move on. Dwight stood up and pulled me to my feet. "Guess we'd better get started," he said and went down the hall to make sure Cal was asleep before we began bringing in his gifts.

When Dwight came back a few minutes later, he was smiling.

"Asleep?" I asked.

He nodded. "But it's the damnedest thing."

"What is?"

"There's like a bunch of little shiny things right over his head."

"What?"

He nodded solemnly. "I don't know, Deb'rah. Maybe I'm wrong, but they look just like dancing sugarplums."

ACKNOWLEDGMENTS

My heartfelt thanks to retired district court judge Shelley Desvousges and to Karen Scott for setting me straight on certain legal technicalities; to Dana Mochel for a funny incident; to Brynn Bonner Witchger for excellent suggestions; to Luci Hansson Zahray, the mystery world's "Poison Lady"; and, as always, to Rebecca Blackmore, Shelly Holt, and John Smith, who have given indispensable help almost from the very beginning of Deborah Knott's career. I truly could not have written these books without them.

And finally, my long-overdue thanks to Les Pockell and Celia Johnson, who have done as much as any two editors possibly could to fill the void left by Sara Ann Freed.

ABOUT THE AUTHOR

Margaret Maron grew up on a farm near Raleigh, North Carolina, but for many years lived in Brooklyn, New York. When she returned to her North Carolina roots with her artist-husband, Joe, she began thinking about a series based on her own background and went on to write the first Deborah Knott novel, *Bootlegger's Daughter*, a *Washington Post* bestseller and winner of the major mystery awards for 1993. *Up Jumps the Devil* won the Agatha for Best Novel of 1996. *Christmas Mourning* is her sixteenth Deborah Knott mystery.